A Stranger's Promise

Betsy Lowery

WESTBOW
P R E S S®
A DIVISION OF THOMAS NELSON
& ZONDERVAN

Scripture quotations marked NIV are taken from The Holy Bible, New
International Version®, NIV® Copyright © 1973, 1978, 1984, 2011 by
Biblica, Inc.® Used by permission. All rights reserved worldwide.

Scripture quotations marked NKJV are taken from the New King James Version®.
Copyright © 1982 by Thomas Nelson. Used by permission. All rights reserved.

Scripture quotations marked HCSB are taken from the Holman Christian
Standard Bible®, Copyright © 1999, 2000, 2002, 2003, 2009 by Holman Bible
Publishers. Used by permission. Holman Christian Standard Bible®, Holman CSB®,
and HCSB® are federally registered trademarks of Holman Bible Publishers.

WestBow Press books may be ordered through booksellers or by contacting:

WestBow Press
A Division of Thomas Nelson & Zondervan
1663 Liberty Drive
Bloomington, IN 47403
www.westbowpress.com
1 (866) 928-1240

ISBN: 978-1-9736-4821-5 (sc)
ISBN: 978-1-9736-4820-8 (e)

Library of Congress Control Number: 2018914575

Print information available on the last page.

WestBow Press rev. date: 11/06/2019

No one has greater love than this,
that someone would lay down his life for his friends.

John 15:13, Holman Christian Standard Bible

Acknowledgments

In addition to my indulgent, supportive family and a host of friends and colleagues who are constantly encouraging me to keep writing and who have read early drafts of this novel, I wish to thank the following persons who spent time answering my questions: Peggy McCleskey, Duluth, Georgia; Dawn Lowery, M.S, R.D., L.D., UAB Medical Center, Birmingham, Alabama; Kay Wilburn, attorney, Dominick Feld Hyde, P.C., Birmingham, Alabama; Sergeant Robert Owens, Vestavia Hills Police Department, Vestavia Hills, Alabama; Cheryl Allmon, East Tennessee Children's Hospital, Knoxville, Tennessee; Kathy V. Sealy; and Darrel Holcombe, Sanctuary Book Store, Alabaster, Alabama, for ready publication advice wrapped in wise spiritual counsel.

Credit is given to a film documentary, Southern Highlanders, produced by the Ford Motor Company in 1947, for content adapted into the memoirs of "Mildred Cantrell." Lyrics from *The Kentucky Waltz* (1946) quoted in chapter 5 are the work of Bill Monroe.

Points of interest in "Crook Mountain, Tennessee"

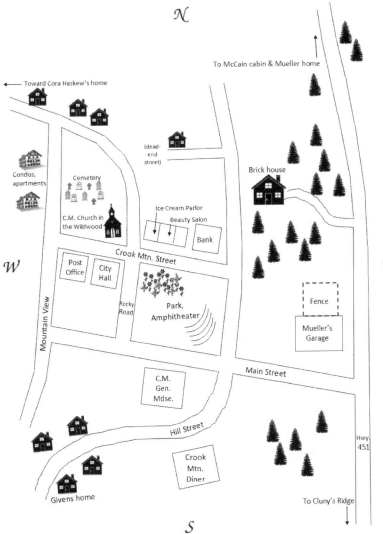

N

Toward Cora Haskew's home

To McCain cabin & Mueller home

(dead-end street)

Condos, apartments

Cemetery

C.M. Church in the Wildwood

Ice Cream Parlor

Beauty Salon

Bank

Brick house

Crook Mtn. Street

W

E

Post Office

City Hall

Rocky Road

Park, Amphitheater

Fence

Mueller's Garage

Mountain View

Main Street

C.M. Gen. Mdse.

Hill Street

Hwy 451

Givens home

Crook Mtn. Diner

To Cluny's Ridge

S

Chapter 1

"Corpus Christi. That wouldn't be code for some curvy young thing spelled K-R-I-S-T-Y, would it?" Joan teased her husband, leaning down and pressing herself gently against his back. Her joke only served to remind her how thankful she was for their thirty-plus years together and for his faithfulness to her, to his work, and to their children. Joan kissed the back of his smooth neck. Some work-from-home guys might let little things like grooming neatness slide during the week, but not this guy. She bothered him a few seconds longer, running her fingers over the masculine roughness of short, neat beard on both sides of his face.

Lee kept on typing his response to a work e-mail in the office nook in their second-floor bedroom. Finally, he hit *Send,* sat back, and swiveled the generous, leather desk chair around. "Believe me, if this bridge project spares our crew much time for thinking about curvy young things, you're the only one of those I'd want by my side."

"If you consider fifty-seven young." Joan's fingers involuntarily reached up to touch that pesky region of little wrinkles around her mouth. *Oops. Fresh lipstick there. Don't touch!* Obviously, she'd gotten distracted after applying it. She reached for the lipstick tube and tossed it into her pink and orange travel cosmetic bag. It lay on the king-sized bed alongside her other luggage, hastily packed and almost ready to go. "But thanks for the thought, anyway. And for the 'curvy'." She wiggled and leaned a fraction toward him.

Lee's eyes flew to some of the curves in question and he grunted something that made Joan send him a come-hither look in return, though such thoughts were probably best deferred in view of her immediate plans. And his, too. Work was bound to be utmost in his mind in spite of this short break for banter. "Well, I'll know the real story of your work trip if I see videos popping up on Instagram of you and a bunch of guys in a corner booth singing *Vive la Compagnie*."

Lee answered with one of his classic dry chuckles, a shade more communicative than his characteristic grunt. "Hoisting a few to a French drinking song? I can't quite picture that. Anyhow, it seems to me you're the one who's constantly showing off a knowledge of other languages."

Joan smiled. It was always nice to have one's range of talents noticed. "Oh, that's just become second nature, trying to make a point with those in this family who still think all I learned in college was how to play volleyball."

"And that all I was was a Rambling Wreck from Georgia Tech?" Lee was still in the conversation but was also monitoring his computer, constantly having to see if new stuff had come in. One day, maybe, he'd get to the point of being as semi-retired as she was. Of course, a semi-retired civil engineer did contribute a tad more to the family bank account than a semi-retired dietitian did. She'd best get her things down to the garage and let him work undisturbed.

"Exactly." *Whatever that really means.* Almost simultaneously she considered Googling "rambling wreck," reminded herself to check with their neighbor Mary one more time about housesitting while both she and Lee were gone, and kept the conversation going. "I suppose the full picture of parents' earlier lives will always be shrouded from their children. *C'est la vie.*"

Lee stood up, stretched, and reached toward one of Joan's suitcases, not yet zipped, on the bed. "This one all ready?" Joan frowned, then nodded. Maybe it wasn't ready, but the wise response was to be appreciative of her busy better half's desire to be helpful. "Well, get along with you, then." He zipped the bag shut. "And mind you don't drive all the way to this Crooked Mountain, or wherever Melinda has convinced you to go in her place, plagued by such deep thoughts as why kids can't picture their parents as kids. This is supposed to be a few days of unexpected R&R after your last teaching gig, remember?"

Joan nodded. This last course, science of food for college freshmen and sophomores, had taken more from her than she'd expected. It had finished before the Christmas break, but here it was almost April and she was still "resting up" from it. Maybe she wasn't still feeling as young as all that.

A sudden stab of guilt reminded Joan that other people had greater reason than she did for needing to rest up. Melinda had rented the mountain cabin for herself but had had to vacate after only a couple of days so she could go help her brother, whose wife was so weak and sick. Joan shook her head in sympathy. *Cancer treatments.* If it would make her generous friend feel better, Joan would do her best to enjoy the rent-paid cabin. Not only that, but to make the trip benefit Melinda as well as herself. Somehow.

Mr. Engineer was now condensing loose items on the bed into a smaller, neater grouping. Joan ribbed him about being a compulsive organizer. "It takes one to know one," he shot back.

"You're not trying to boot me out the door as soon as possible, are you? It's only about a four-hour drive including stops." That might not cover the extra seven miles due north to Crook Mountain from Cluny's Ridge. Come to think of it, she might hit the larger tourist town first, before its shops began to close for the day. "I'll get there well before dark."

"Ah, but if I know you, you'll detour straight to Cluny's Ridge and hit the artisan soap and candle shops and whatnot. You said this secluded cabin is near there, right? We don't need any more hand-carved flutes or whistles, do we?"

Well, there you go. He'd nailed her. Joan rolled her eyes at herself and quirked her mouth over a certain impulse purchase made during one of the several family vacations they'd taken to Cluny's Ridge. "I don't take the entire blame for that. Sam goaded me into it by claiming to be the only viable musician in the family. And I did make a good stab at learning to play that flute." She squared her tall frame to lend force to her defense. "Besides, it *is* a beautiful piece of workmanship." The handsome instrument in lighter and darker grains of cedar now lived in a lighted mahogany cabinet in the living room, approximately just under where she and Lee stood sparring. There, it perfectly offset the emerald green Fabergé egg replica on the shelf above it and the Beth Evans mini canvas of a red cardinal on the shelf below it.

Shoes. Joan's mind flew ahead. Melinda had said the cabin's driveway was gravel. *Food.* Was there enough in the house for Lee until his day of departure, which apparently was yet to be determined? Enough for her to grab some things out of the pantry to take with *her*?

She asked him to halt on closing the largest of her three matching cases. After inspecting its contents one last time, she zipped it shut herself and let him move it from the bed to the floor. "Speaking of flutes and music, isn't there a song just perfect for this impromptu trip I'm taking?" She grinned as the hand motions came to mind from many years ago. "In a cabin in a wood," she sang, making the tent shape of a roof with eight fingers. "Little man by the window stood." Through pretend binoculars she peered at a handsome man whose short, neat beard had a few flecks of gray in it. A man who didn't appear thrilled at the prospect of spending the next half minute listening to her finish such a silly song. So, she left the part about the "frightened as could be" rabbit unsung.

She took her phone and her keys from the bed in one grab. Pushing the keys into a front pocket of her tan stretch jeans with one hand, she started a quick text to Mary with the other about what the betta fish would need. This nest was empty of children, and, since Wally had died, of pets. Except for the fish, which was really almost more of a household decoration. It didn't even have a name. Keeping the fish at arm's length by not naming it was a defense mechanism after losing their beloved Great Dane. But hadn't Lee been dropping little hints lately that it might soon be time for another dog? She wasn't quite ready.

"Off on another thinkfest?"

"Not at all." Okay, that was a fib. "I'm emptying my head and heading to the Smokies for R and R and R."

Lee frowned. "Rest and relaxation and...?"

"Writing. Silent *w*. I want to get started on this healthy eating presentation for senior adults."

"And so much for emptying your head. That gig is for September, right?"

Joan nodded. She got his meaning, loud and clear. She did have almost six months before leading the mini-workshop. Still, she mustn't let her brain fall too idle. This speaking engagement would go toward keeping her Registered Dietitian credentials valid.

"Well, send me your pictures of rhododendron and morning skies and such." Lee helped Joan load the camera bag onto one of her shoulders. "I can't promise how much time I'll have to appreciate and respond to them, but that's never slowed you down before."

Joan grinned with a saucy smirk. Lee knew her well. "You've just reminded me I need to pick up some extra double-A batteries. Okay, all ready." They moved toward the stairs, sharing the load of her luggage, which wasn't light. She was taking enough comforts of home to make the most of this unplanned opportunity.

"That's another R. *Ready.*"

"Clever. See, I love you for your mind, and not just for your terrific body. And, by the way, let's plan on a nice reunion after I get home from my triple R and you return from your bridge. I can think on the dinner aspect while in Tennessee, and you can think on the rest." She bent and let go of the handles of everything she'd been carrying and pressed her face against Lee's firm chest, reaching under his untucked golf shirt while her baggage in his arms had him helpless to stop her. He'd pulled that maneuver on her plenty of times when her hands were full of grocery bags or folded laundry she wasn't willing to drop. They'd be apart for a while, after all. They needed a good farewell embrace. Still, Joan's agile mind raced on to yet another new task she'd given herself: what gourmet dish to fix for said reunion dinner. *Food. Calories and fat. Exercise.* "If I get in some good walking, which I'm bound to do, maybe I can get this *gluteus* a little less *maximus.*" She gave a wry groan and dropped her arms from where they'd been, to pat the area in question.

"I don't see any problem there."

"Sweet." She kissed him on the cheek. "But I'll try to work on it, anyway, in the hope that you'll keep on looking!"

Joan maneuvered her Honda CRV toward I-85, grateful that the sun was already warming the vehicle enough to offset the cool of the early spring day. "Call Melinda," she commanded her phone without taking her eyes off the road. The call was answered promptly, and the women chatted about the logistics of their pre-planned meeting for a quick snack and the handoff of the keys to the cabin.

"If train A leaves Tennessee at 10:00 traveling seventy miles an hour, and train B leaves Georgia at eleven, doing ninety…just kidding!" Melinda laughed into her phone.

Joan begged for mercy, gliding into the passing lane to overtake a sluggish work truck. "Please, no! Lee or Sam might like to solve that math problem the old-fashioned way—like father, like son—but I'll take the smart way out. Let's each put Zaxby's in as an intermediate destination and see which location gives us roughly the same arrival time."

Cornelia, Georgia, turned out to be the location. Melinda's "train" had left earlier and had been cruising about five miles per hour over the speed limit.

At the counter, Joan looked at the menu board, almost tasting the thick garlic toast. *Think of your hips. Look at that buttery crust with disdain and be strong. Nothing tastes as good as skinny feels! There will be a time; just not today.* She cocked her head toward Melinda. "If I say 'no' to the toast, I can order the boneless sweet and spicy wings with some dietary self-respect intact."

Melinda laughed, then ordered the Cobb "Zalad" with grilled chicken, gracefully accepting the cashier's compliment on her hair. That seemed to happen more often than not when the two met "halfway" for lunch as they occasionally did within the larger Atlanta perimeter. Joan got her share of admiring glances, too, but middle-aged, tall blondes with their girlish figures reasonably preserved were not especially remarkable next to a younger woman with a similar physique and shiny, shoulder-length curls of striking auburn.

Soon after they sat, Joan inquired after Melinda's sister-in-law.

"Catherine doesn't complain much, but the fatigue and nausea get her down. She's frustrated not to have the strength to help the kids with homework and just interact with them more. Michael has stepped up admirably." Melinda frowned. "That didn't come out quite right. I just mean that they all, including the kids, are doing what they have to do, a day at a time." She flipped a strand of hair off her neck and turned up one corner of her mouth in what wasn't a smile. "Just like all of us, I guess."

"True." Joan bit robustly into a fork-pierced round of glazed, breaded chicken, uttered some "yums" in hope of lightening the mood, and tried to ignore a twinge of guilt over having had— now hypocritically—nagged Lee very recently about ordering fries and sweet tea twice in one day. "I loved all those random movie quotes you were texting me from the cabin hideaway, FYI. Keep it up." They liked a lot of the same entertainment and literature in spite of their age difference. Maybe Melinda would get a little time at her brother's to go on joking with Joan by text, but that seemed unlikely. This selfless friend had chosen to exchange great escape for great sacrifice.

In the parking lot, the uneven breeze was stimulating and the sun was still out in full force, but both women shivered. Joan clutched at the sleeves of her tan denim jacket as a rush of uncertainty made her more uncomfortable than the chilly air was doing. "Look. I'm beginning to feel very selfish here. And Lee's already been needling me about diverting to Cluny's Ridge for early Christmas shopping." She salved her conscience immediately on that score, however. Gift-giving for Christmas and birthdays had come to mean, more often than not, unique pieces of hand-thrown pottery with a practical purpose like cooking or lighting, or consumables like local preserves and honey. The Ryans tried hard to avoid burdening family members and colleagues with run-of-the-mill decorative items that amounted to household clutter, or with jewelry or clothing they might not like enough to wear. Still, that agenda—noble and globally responsible though it was—paled in comparison to what Melinda was doing. Joan offered to abandon the whole cabin thing and follow her friend to her brother's if she could be of help.

Melinda declined. It was a time for family, she said. And she had a point. The presence of a complete stranger must be an intrusion under such trying circumstances. "Besides, if I know you, you'll find some useful purpose where you're going. More than *I* did, being such a slug, sticking to the cabin, snacking and watching movies I've seen a hundred times." Joan countered that rest was just as vital to life as adventure was, then complimented her friend on the pictures she had taken and shared of redbud trees and rhododendron around the cabin.

Melinda waved that off, sheepish about having been too afraid to venture farther away in case she might stumble onto one of the black bears sometimes sighted in the area. Then she explained the cabin's security system and handed Joan the door key. The women hugged.

Settling into her front seat, Joan pulled sunglasses down from the top of her head and glanced into the rear-view mirror, fingering the fine bangs of her short hair back into place. From the next parking space, Melinda tapped her horn and threw a hasty wave with one hand as she started to back out. Joan waved back. "Call me," she mouthed with a pantomime of a phone held at the side of her face.

<hr />

The miles were passing smoothly. Friday was notoriously a heavy travel day most everywhere, but traffic was light nonetheless. But any traffic *anywhere* was going to be better than Atlanta traffic! Joan smiled. *Crook Mountain, Tennessee.* She had never heard of the place until Melinda had chosen to vacation there. As Melinda herself had admitted, she'd done little besides loaf around in the cabin and walk short distances to take pictures. *I'll certainly do more exploring than that.* It was a shame single-mom Melinda hadn't been able to stay in her cabin, seeking her own brand of R and R to address her own stress and exertion. But it was just like her to rejoice in the knowledge that someone else, in her place, would be there to enjoy doing whatever. Exercise. Explore. Shop. Take pictures. Talk to new people.

Watch out. It would be easy to forget recent mentions of rest and to stay right in step with her usual pace, packing each day with a full agenda. Some people were just naturally Type A. *C'est la guerre.* Tonight, though, she might take a cue from her friend and sprawl out on one of the beds for another chapter or two of *One Block Over: Things I Discovered Not Far Off the Beaten Track.* She'd grabbed the book practically at random off an end cap during her last browse through the public library. Its author, Lloyd Conway, was telling stories of Americana he'd found by diverting "one block over" from the roads most trip-planning apps directed drivers to travel. "Too many people miss too much by being in too big a hurry to get to point B as quickly as possible," the dust jacket asserted slightly redundantly. Chapters were about this restaurant, that view, that park, this homeowner or that rose garden the photojournalist had discovered simply by planning time for intentional detours. The next pages of Conway's chronicles might turn out to be the most interesting part of this trip. Who knew?

After a quick stop to stretch, find a restroom, and gather a few extra snacks including trail mix, a couple of Gala apples, and some pecan divinity she ultimately returned to the shelf knowing the candy kitchens in Cluny's Ridge would offer better, Joan buckled up one last time and studied the remainder of her driving directions. Within the hour, her navigation app announced the last major change of highways, and billboards for the attractions of Cluny's Ridge soon began popping up: cable car ride, offbeat museums, gem dealers, artisan district, pancake house, aquarium. Joan smiled. Good trips, those they'd made to Cluny's Ridge as a family when Sam and April were younger. Sam's vocal excitement over fudge and candied popcorn had given way, gradually, to less-vocal excitement over girl-watching. April's interests had evolved from thrill rides to the thrills of shopping, eating, and having her nails done. These family memories of Cluny's Ridge would do for right now; Joan had already decided to put off her shopping detour to another day, if only to be able to tell Lee later that he'd been wrong about her going there right off the bat.

The billboards seemed to disappear with a single cut-off, and the territory changed quickly into the totally unfamiliar. Joan paid more attention to the upcoming turns, expecting around the next bend, or the next, an attractive little village called Crook Mountain. Or, the mysterious destination might be a one-traffic-light crossroads. Common sense had told her to spend time packing instead of looking at satellite pictures of the town's streets and businesses. She'd only found out early this very morning that she'd be traveling at all.

The road curved sharply left, then right, then left. It was curtained by dense spring foliage. "In two miles, turn right," her app said. A sign indicated a left turn leading to Crook Mountain, but evidently the cabin wasn't in that direction. A couple of residential mailboxes at the foot of a heavily-wooded incline on the right were overgrown with weeds. Taking these hairpin turns at under thirty miles per hour afforded a pretty good look. Letters spelling "M-u-" were visible on the black mailbox, but any other letters once there were worn away. No surprise at that, given the mailbox's state. Its rusty lid hung by one bolt. Its wooden post was splintered and crooked.

Joan tried mimicking the Australian accent in the voice that had just told her again to be planning to turn right very soon. "Tuhn roit." She tried it again and laughed at her effort. *Not exactly. Maybe if I'd majored in drama instead of nutrition...* Her Siri guide, male (who had to be ruggedly handsome and muscular), sometimes was called upon to direct her to even the most familiar destinations around Duluth, like her mainstay market and dry cleaners, if she happened to be in the mood to hear his voice. As Melinda would say, "I'd let that guy give me directions from the kitchen sink to the pantry!" Just now, the voice spoke again and startled Joan a little. In making the indicated right turn, she left the firm, level pavement of the highway and felt her tires start crunching over large pieces of gravel.

The tailored grounds she'd been imagining, with flower-lined sidewalks for casual foot travel, did not appear. Not after the first bend, and not after the second. This road, that presumably led to the cabin, appeared to steepen dramatically just ahead, and an immediate concern for safe *car* travel drove away thoughts of easy *foot* travel. Joan instinctively gripped the steering wheel harder and bit her lower lip, inhaling sharply a second later as her tires skidded. How would coming back *down* this incline be? She shifted into second gear. Melinda hadn't mentioned the steepness of this rocky drive. Joan grimaced, and almost immediately her Australian guide said, "Arrived at destination." *Listen to him! So calm, so indifferent. Can't he see these white knuckles here?* She let out a hefty sigh of relief and unbuckled her seatbelt, at last able to lift her eyes from the gravel and survey the exterior of her new, temporary home.

Chapter 2

Joan eased from behind the wheel into the breezy quiet of the sunny day, rotating her arms and doing several half-squats to limber up. The landscaping immediately around the house was in marked contrast to the rough gravel and general overgrowth of the driveway. A happy difference, starting with the high-quality pea stone that now cradled her four tires. Perky pink and purple blossoms said "welcome" from an assortment of free-standing pots of geraniums and petunias. A rustic-looking wheelbarrow, set in a bordered flower bed along the front of the cabin, held more of the same. Stepping stones divided a small, neat lawn into equal portions and led to the front porch steps of an attractive, one-level structure. With a feeling of good fortune, Joan reached into the car for various items of her baggage and dug the house key from her pocket.

The interior design, the amount of sunlight admitted, the two bedrooms, and the modern kitchen and bath all pleased at first glance. The cabin appeared to be no older than four or five years based on the colors and styles of flooring, walls, fixtures and appliances. It wasn't meant to mimic the rustic digs of frontier settlers. Not at all. "Nice." Joan quickly decided on the front bedroom and placed her things accordingly. Snapping a "selfie" with her phone, including as much of the attractive house as possible in the background, she texted the picture to Lee so he'd know she had arrived safely and to show him she was in a good place.

In the kitchen, the meaning of a couple of Melinda's cryptic messages became apparent—hints about provisions left there because Melinda couldn't easily travel with them or because she simply wanted Joan to have them. The refrigerator sparkled of cleanliness, which made its few and fresh contents the more appealing. Pesto spread, labeled with the recommendation it be paired with the Melba toast crackers in one of the cabinets. A Vermont cheese with cranberries in it, Greek yogurt in a couple of flavors including Toasted Coconut & Vanilla, and low-fat milk and "lite" sour cream—grouped and labeled—for a no-cook banana pudding, the rest of the ingredients being nearby on the countertop along with a corresponding note and the recipe. Sweet Melinda. In spite of her disappointed plans, she had gone to some effort to welcome the substitute guest.

The dresser drawers looked clean and smelled fresh. In fact, the whole cabin seemed to be under excellent care. No sense living even partially out of her suitcases from Friday to Wednesday. Humming bars from the last music that had been playing in the car, she placed sleepwear and underclothes in the dresser. Sneakers, flats, and sandals went on the closet floor; several outfits on hangers, on the bar above. Most of those were pants. She'd decided this morning, without taking any time to actually research the matter, that her few days' stay in the little mountain burg wouldn't likely require skirts of any nature.

In the living area, a guest book with a bright red cover lay open to the page where the most recent tenants had left their names and comments. Printed or written in flamboyant cursive were locations around the southeast (Florida, Georgia, Alabama) and points beyond (Missouri, Pennsylvania). The Waters family from Gainesville had found the weather good for skiing in

January and had had a great time except for a costly transmission repair they hadn't counted on. The Perkinses from Birmingham had loved the secluded locale and the food at the Crook Mountain Diner, but also noted they'd had to have a flat tire fixed during their stay. Joan's brow wrinkled. Two mentions of car trouble there. Hopefully, that wasn't the going trend. Involuntarily she glanced out the window at her pretty CRV.

The cabin as stocked between Melinda's efforts and her own would cover a few meals, but that mention in the guest book of a local diner had piqued Joan's curiosity. And what besides that eatery did the town of Crook Mountain, population unknown, have to offer? Quaint shops and antique barns? Surprising architecture, prize rose gardens, trickling brooks, scenic views? Joan grabbed purse, keys, and camera bag and headed for the door in order to find out. Whatever was to be discovered once she was safely back down the steep gravel drive would be entirely a surprise. Excellent!

⋙◆⋘

The *first* surprise was that more people didn't lose control of their vehicles on these steep grades—if this driveway were typical, and it probably was. Or, maybe they did lose control. Maybe that's why small mountain towns stayed small! Two or three skids and at least one prayer later, Joan was safely down. Her foot stayed on the brake. This far away from Atlanta traffic was found the privilege of not having to be in a hurry. The paved road was deserted. Joan looked both ways, twice, then started out left, toward town. As luck would have it, a pickup truck came into view to her right. She quickly braked to avoid pulling out right in front of it. This wasn't good. She was partially in the road, and it was a blind curve in both directions. Instead of going around her, the truck slowed and the driver waited, gesturing for her to enter the two-lane roadway ahead of him. After an awkward moment of indecision, Joan nodded at the bearded young man and moved her foot from the brake to the gas pedal. Both vehicles needed to get out of the way before anybody else came around the bend. Now, the awkward thing was the sense of obligation to drive with purpose so the motorist behind wouldn't be annoyed at her rate of speed. *So much for casual exploring.* Joan glanced in the mirror. If this guy was a local, or local enough to know exactly where he was going, it would have been so much better if he had gone on ahead. Because, of course, now he was tailgating. Had he pretended to be gallant, allowing her to go first, just so he could play "how close can I get"? Joan sighed. *Just ignore him, the way you always try to ignore tailgaters. They don't deserve to get you unnerved.*

The truck made the same right turn as she did, toward town. Of *course* it did. Was there a reason to feel this creeped out? She watched for any parking lot to pull into so this annoying guy could get out from behind her. *Good!* The pickup slowed and veered off to the right, where a sketchy-looking steel building stood on a sad-looking lot. High weeds overlapped the edges of the gravel parking area. The building seemed to go with the old truck. A weather-worn sign read "Mueller's Garage." Joan put the garage and the truck behind her, relieved to do so, but not before noticing in the rearview mirror that the driver was out of his truck and seemed to be staring after her.

At a T intersection about half a mile past the garage, Joan stopped at Hill Street. To the left was the Crook Mountain Diner with a general store across from it. Beyond those buildings, Hill Street, true to its name, went uphill and curved out of sight. Directly ahead was a pretty park. Joan turned right onto Hill, then left onto Crook Mountain Street, passing the park, a bank, a strip shopping center, the Post Office, and the town hall. A picturesque church building begged to be photographed in the late afternoon sun, and

Joan answered the call. She parked, shut the engine off, gripped her camera bag, and gracefully slid out onto—*Thank God!*—solid pavement for a change. One other car, an older gray sedan, was on the premises. Either it was left there by a parishioner, or someone was presently in the building. A custodian, maybe, doing the weekly cleaning before Sunday activities? Unlikely that anyone else would be at work this late on Friday afternoon, unless the pastor found this the quietest time to prepare his sermons.

Ten minutes later, with some twenty new images in tow, Joan was back behind the wheel, feeling invigorated by the steps and the couple of deep squats it had taken to get the pictures. Very little appeared to be going on in town, including at Crook Mountain Diner, whose parking lot was almost deserted. But, according to the lighted sign that wasn't especially bright yet against the waning daylight, the place was open. *Is there something everyone else knows that I don't? Was "Diner Disaster Leaves Ten Dead" the front-page story in the last issue of Crook Mountain Monthly?* Why not find out right now? She parked near the door.

———◆———

Yellow can be a difficult color for many women to wear well, but the woman behind the counter, who appeared to be the only person in the place, had no trouble there. She almost glowed in her trim, yellow uniform dress with white apron—a very springy look. Odd. A food worker's uniform shouldn't be that spotless and wrinkle-free at this time of day. Maybe she was just starting her shift.

"I've been expecting you." The brunette surprised Joan with those words and a broad, pretty smile. "Cora Haskew phoned me from the church. She saw you out taking pictures and predicted you'd end up here sooner or later if you're looking for local color." She filled a clear plastic tumbler with ice and water and set it on the counter. "Cora is the church librarian. Thanks to her sharp eyes and good memory, I could have *really* surprised you by naming the color of your car and asking which of your two camera lenses worked better in this light!"

The name *Cora* suggested a senior adult. Joan pictured the stereotypical "little, old lady librarian" with white hair up in a tight bun. "She would be the owner of the gray Buick, I suppose." *Let it be known that your librarian isn't the only observant person in town today.*

"That's right. Have a seat, if you're here to eat, that is." The one-woman staff gestured to the seats on the other side of the counter from where she stood. "Or did you want to take more pictures?" She gave an extra-brilliant smile, fluffed her hair, and straightened her collar, which didn't need straightening. Joan couldn't help but laugh. "Seeing as how you're the only customer I have right now, why not sit right here? I'll be that much closer if you need anything." The woman in yellow spritzed the counter with a colorless liquid and wiped it with a thick paper towel.

"Sure." Joan settled onto one of the dark brown stools. That feeling of good fortune from earlier—before the run-in with the truck driver—crept back as she glanced around. A large menu board was mounted up high. Also mounted around were modern, flat-screen televisions and antique odds and ends in the Cracker Barrel style of décor—old washboards, military caps, license plates and such. A framed document boasted the number 99 in large script. "Nice health rating. At least *that* wouldn't be the reason you don't have any other customers right now."

"Oh, thanks." The uniformed woman offered a genuine-looking smile which, with her neat, long hair, steady gaze, and manner of speech, could have placed her in a boardroom chair or at an attorneys' table just as easily as here. "That one point off was an unfortunate circumstance. Not our fault. But it does no good to dwell on it. It may be a needed reminder that perfection is still just a little out of reach."

Right. I'm betting she wasn't born and raised in these parts.

"I'm Dove, by the way."

Okay, maybe I'm wrong. "Dove"? Joan's phone beeped and she checked it immediately. The other woman turned tactfully away. Joan smiled at a brief, sweet message from Lee acknowledging her safe arrival. She stowed the phone in her pocket and regarded the woman named Dove. Joan had known of a Lark, once. And some Robins, of course. She'd run across a female or two who ought to have been named Vulture. But she'd never met a *Dove.* It was unusual, but it seemed to fit. The pretty brunette working efficiently behind the counter was well-spoken and hadn't been using those awful endearments "sweetie" and "baby." Maybe she owned the place. An M.B.A. entrepreneur, perhaps.

Joan raised her eyes to the menu board. There were unhealthy items at all eateries that, normally, she instantly ruled out, like French fries. There were others that, normally, she instantly zeroed in on, like salads. This trip wasn't normal. Joan landed between the two extremes.

While waiting for her food, she sipped delicious, peach-flavored iced tea and gave her surroundings a closer look. A notice was tacked to a support post, too far away for reading the content, but close enough to see it was printed in color ink on white copy paper that had started to curl in the humidity. Out of curiosity and the desire not to sit any more than necessary, Joan eased to her feet and walked toward the bulletin. It advertised a community event on the Sunday upcoming, March 30. "After Easter worship," it read, "stay for the best home cooking anywhere & come back to the park at 6:00 for a benefit concert by Blueberry Creek Band for our town's little sweetheart, Laynie Key." The photo showed a young girl, maybe eight or ten years old, seated, with one leg extended in a full cast. She had long, dark hair and a sweet smile. The couple standing behind her would be her parents. At the bottom of the page was the name of where Joan had just come from, Crook Mountain Church in the Wildwood, along with its street address and time of the Sunday service.

"I'd forgotten it's Easter this Sunday." Joan made the bland comment almost to herself as she returned to the counter. More loudly, she asked, "Are you the owner here?" When no answer was offered immediately, no reaction given at all, she added, "It's none of my business, of course. Just curious."

"Are you a curious person, generally speaking?" The question came over Dove's shoulder as she put Joan's order together.

Interesting twist on small talk. And sly, answering a question with another question. "I guess I am. Most people are curious by nature. People who don't ask questions have been conditioned not to by one thing or another. Lack of encouragement to express themselves, fear of a stern authority figure, fear of being embarrassed, or having been rebuffed after asking too many questions or indelicate questions at the wrong times." She heard herself sounding as though she were sitting on a panel of experts, which, as it happened, she'd done numbers of times.

"Are you a counselor?" Dove still had her back to Joan.

"In a way. I counsel with people about their eating habits and food choices. I'm a registered dietitian." She left off the fact that she did also have a Ph.D. in clinical counseling.

Dove turned now and glanced down at the plate she was setting in front of Joan. "Oh, my!" Her well-shaped eyebrows rose. Joan bent her head. The large cheeseburger suddenly looked extra-large and the potato chips seemed decadent, even though they *were* baked, not fried.

Joan lifted her head and grinned at Dove. "Not to worry.

Dietitians indulge, just like everybody else. I'll have fruit, low-fat granola and skim milk for breakfast."

"That makes me feel much better. I'd hate to think I was an accessory to something."

Joan laughed and popped a chip into her mouth. "As long as we're getting acquainted," she said after swallowing, "I'll let you in on something else. Dietitians don't think about food twenty-four-seven. Though I'm fairly sure, and sad to say so, that there are a lot of people who *do*. Last time we walked the beach together, my daughter and I saw a family applying sunscreen that legit smelled exactly like apple strudel. As sure as I sit here!"

Dove's laugh rang out as she refilled Joan's glass. "So, what brings you to Crook Mountain, Mrs.—?"

"Oh. Ryan. Joan Ryan."

"Pleased to meet you."

"I actually didn't *plan* to come here at all. It was very spur-of-the-moment."

"I see." Dove almost visibly switched gears then, launching into some of the chattiness that helps people connect with their customers. Business tonight was slower than on a typical Friday night because some of her regulars would be at home, cooking what they'd be bringing to the annual "dinner on the grounds" after church on Easter Sunday. The pleasant, even voice was lulling, especially when combined with Joan's inevitable energy lag after her hasty packing and road trip. So Dove's next question caught her off guard. "Think you'll want to attend church on Sunday morning and then have one of the best meals you'll eat this year?"

The Diner's door opened with a jingle. *Saved by the bell.* Joan turned her head toward the sound. An older man was stepping over the threshold. He was polished-looking, with neat, gray hair, a tastefully-patterned sport coat, gray slacks, and a pale blue dress shirt just open at the neck. He wasn't a tall man. Probably about her own height, five-eight. Or maybe five-nine. "Hello, Miss Dove." He stayed near the door. "Everything all right with you?"

"Hi there, Mr. Givens." There was a kindness in Dove's smile that looked to be all about respect, not flirtatious in the slightest. Joan's eyes went directly to Dove's hands. No rings. "Going very well. It's kind of you to ask. Won't you sit down and have some fresh coffee?"

"Oh, no, thank you, dear. Edith will be expecting me at home shortly."

If the man had taken any notice of Joan, he was either too courteous or too uninterested to acknowledge her. But Dove took care of that. "Mr. Givens, please meet a new friend of mine. Joan Ryan. She and I are just getting acquainted. Mrs. Ryan, Mr. Gerald Givens."

Joan moved to stand up, but was gestured to stay put. "No need to get up, young lady. Don't interrupt your meal. But thank you for the thought. Proper manners are always a blessing to see, nowadays."

Dove stepped swiftly from behind the counter and approached Mr. Givens with a brown paper bag. "Please take these sweet rolls to your wife and tell her I look forward to seeing her at church on Sunday."

"I'll be pleased to do that." To Joan, "A pleasure to meet you, ma'am." He left.

"There is a true gentleman, and one of the best things about this town." Dove stopped by one of the nearby tables to straighten the salt and pepper shakers on her way back behind the counter. "Mr. and Mrs. Givens have a charming old house just up the street here. If you're wanting to take more pictures, you ought to get by there. They wouldn't mind a bit. In fact, they'd be delighted. Edith has quite a green thumb, and their place shows it."

Joan continued to wonder about the well-spoken woman facing her. Each "-ing" was coming through loud and clear at the end of words. No drawl. No dialect. "I'll definitely try to do that." Joan took another bite of the juicy cheeseburger and lifted a napkin to pat any stray ketchup or mayonnaise from the corners of her mouth. "Mmmm!"

"Cora said your license plate was from Gwinnett County. Did you drive from Georgia today? Unless I'm being too nosy. Just say so."

Joan kept chewing, which was a great cover for taking time to consider her answer. Was there any particular reason to share personal information with this woman? Was there any particular reason *not* to? Dove hadn't answered the question about whether she owned the restaurant. Joan hadn't said whether she might attend church and the potluck. The score was even. "Yes. I drove up today." She nodded toward the posted notice. "What is the benefit need for the little girl?"

<hr/>

With several pillows supporting her back, Joan lounged on the bed, chatting by text alternately with Lee and Melinda, mostly with the latter, since Lee was up to his neck, having said in his last message that his departure for Corpus Christi would be the next morning.

To Melinda Joan described the pickup truck and its driver; the waitress named Dove; the nice Mr. Givens whom she guessed was a lifelong resident and probably was in sales, brokerage, accounting, or life insurance; and the elusive spy, Cora Haskew, who was masquerading as a church librarian but was probably a C.I.A. agent in her forties, wearing flowered dresses, sensible shoes, and a gray wig. Melinda's answer was punctuated with "LOLs" and funny emoticons. It was good to see that. Joan sent a much briefer version of the same information to Lee, adding, "Wish you were here. Did I say that already? As I left the town diner tonight, 2 rough-looking blokes were coming in. One of them was the guy who stared me down from his pickup truck. Creeeepy!" She threw in extra letters E for emphasis.

"Prob been a while since they saw as fine-looking a woman as you in their burg."

"Sweet. Thanks. This Dove woman invited me to church Sunday."

"And?"

"Didn't answer. Another customer walked in just then. I forgot about Easter. Might go. Could be interesting if rest of the locals are as varied as those seen so far. Waitress also asked me if I'm a curious person." Joan added a smiley face emoticon followed by another one with eyes round like saucers.

"Your reputation precedes you."

Joan grinned at that but didn't respond. Instead, she demonstrated the validity of Lee's remark by typing, "Must remember to look up population of this town. In knowing of 6 locals so far (well, 9 counting the poster family), I may have met or heard of half the town already."

In a few seconds she received the next text from Lee. "Crook Mountain, TN. Pop. 212."

"Beat me to it. Showoff. If I find a dress I can't resist in Cluny's Ridge TOMORROW...YES, I DROVE RIGHT PAST IT TODAY...I'll go to church and stay for the potluck meal. A bluegrass band is giving a benefit concert for a young girl who's had multiple leg surgeries w/big expenses. Hey, one can be a Cluny's Ridge tourist any day, but this lineup sounds like a whole 'nother brand of fun." Joan kept her chat lighthearted, but underneath that she did feel twinges over what the little girl, Laynie, and her parents must be going through.

"Enjoy your fun. Meanwhile, I'll have fun my own way, sweating it out over this bridge."

"It'll be the greatest bridge ever built, with you on the job!"

"Right. Need to run now. 'night, sweetie." He even sent a "kissy face" image.

Aww! That was sweet. Joan replied simply, "Out", and let him go. He had a lot on his plate. She pulled up her browser and located the town's website. "Focus on Crook Mountain" was in large, white letters against a dark green background. Below that, a not-too-special clipart image of a person aiming a camera. Then more text, smaller, in black type on stark white. *No web designer on this town's payroll. Or, an overpaid one.* "Mayor Teddy Dyle welcomes you to Crook Mountain, nestled in the breathtaking southern highlands of Tennessee. Enjoy natural beauty, secluded quiet, and small-town friendliness all just minutes away from Cluny's Ridge with it's large-scale attractions." Joan rolled her eyes at the all-too-common spelling of "it's" where the writer meant "its" as a possessive pronoun. *If only someone would pay me to rid the world of every case of that!* Besides the typical sidebar listing a handful of municipal departments and a contact name under each, there wasn't much more. A new search brought up business listings for Crook Mountain. There was the general store she had seen across from Crook Mountain Diner. It was called, just as unimaginatively, Crook Mountain Gen. Mdse. An ice cream shop, a beauty salon, and a bank came up, as well as Crook Mountain Church in the Wildwood and Mueller's Garage, each with phone number and street address. *"Mdse." Gotta love abbreviations that are impossible to pronounce. I guess they could just call the store the "C.M.G.M."*

Earlier, at the Diner, Dove had greeted the two young men coming in, using the word "twins" in her remarks. If another party, a family of five, hadn't been climbing out of their car in the parking lot, Joan would have been uncomfortable about Dove being there with only those twin brothers, for some reason. But, surely Dove knew them and had dealt with them before. She hadn't sounded anything but genuinely pleasant as she had greeted them. Still, that Mr. Givens had stopped in just to "check on" Dove. Wasn't that a bit odd? Was he protective? Dove had been there pretty much alone, except for Joan. Maybe the older gentleman had driven by and seen the CRV, a strange car in town, and had felt he must check it out. Small towns could be that way. Or, maybe he just found the waitress too pretty to resist.

Sipping occasionally from an oversized mug of hot herbal tea, Joan spent the last of her day's energy importing, viewing, weeding, and cropping the photos of the church building. *Hang on.* Maybe Cora Haskew was peeking out of a window and had made it into one of these pictures. Zooming in, Joan studied each one eagerly. Photographers always loved catching random content that might prove some law case or at least spark a laugh. But, no. No face in any window. The spy had stayed out of sight.

Joan set her phone and laptop aside to recharge overnight, and, after not having to set an alarm—*ah, vacation!*—fell asleep to an impossibly loud chorus of crickets.

Chapter 3

Carrying a bottle of room-temperature spring water, Joan unlocked and slid open the glass door leading to the wood deck off the back of the cabin. Neat shrubbery edged the smallish plot of lawn. Beyond that, there were woods to the south and, as the planners of the house would have known, a broad view to the west for sunsets. The early-morning air was chilly and the sky overcast, but it was supposed to clear beautifully with highs in the upper sixties. Joan's strongest sensory images from past trips to Cluny's Ridge were of gorgeous blue skies, clean air, and temperatures like this. Really, the overall sensation was almost as distinct as the one called "that Christmasy feeling."

After the healthy breakfast she'd told Dove she would have this morning, she showered and dressed, then held her breath as her faithful Honda carried her down the steep incline and over to the Diner, where the parking lot was almost covered up with cars, in contrast to last night. Joan stepped from the brisk morning air into warmth and into aromas of coffee, bacon, and biscuits. Maple syrup, too. This morning's customers, eating, chatting, tapping and swiping mobile devices, had disheveled the salt, pepper, sugar packets and napkin holders left in neat order by Dove last night. Joan drank in the scene with roving eyes. The Diner seemed to have everything that ought to be going on in a good restaurant on a Saturday morning. Crook Mountain folks had no need to drive to the pancake houses in Cluny's Ridge so long as this place stayed in business.

Dove wasn't working the breakfast shift solo. Several other employees, all in red T-shirts and jeans, were on the job. But Dove wore a uniform again. This one was white. Joan waved at her, but didn't make a move to be seated yet. For the moment, just to stand here and survey the room was all she needed. How many times had she blissfully vacationed seven miles south of here, unaware that this town existed?

Just one person—a man—sat at the counter. He seemed very engrossed in his side of the conversation he was having with Dove, who looked as serene as Joan was already disposed to expect her to look even under stressful circumstances. Was this man a tourist, like herself, animatedly describing how he had happened upon Crook Mountain? Maybe a local fellow enjoying a captive audience in Dove while, somewhere nearby, his wife was tending to children and housekeeping? Men, married or single, would tend to enjoy sharing the mundane details of their lives with someone as pretty as Dove.

It wouldn't do to take up a table in the dining area just for coffee. Joan slid onto a seat three places down from the grand talker, picked up a menu, and listened. It didn't matter just now what her personal scruples were about eavesdropping. There was no possible way to avoid hearing the mostly one-sided conversation. For almost a full minute, which any food service employee could little spare at such a time, the man continued regaling Dove with details of a certain personal escapade, and the story required broad gestures as well as rhetorical questions which, if answered, would stroke his ego. The event seemed to have happened some years ago. As memory had faded, the grandiosity of the feat had probably expanded. Joan tried to focus on the menu even though she wasn't going to be ordering from it. Sure, it was a good thing to hear a confident person speak on a subject about which she or he was passionate. But, not so much when the subject about which the speaker was so passionate was himself.

"Good morning, ma'am." Dove greeted Joan as soon as the man monopolizing her attention provided a tiny window for it. For some reason, Dove had spoken as if she hadn't already met Joan. *She's concealing my name in case I don't want it broadcast. Nice going.*

"Good morning." Joan smiled at Dove and just managed to keep the smile from escalating into a laugh.

"What can I get for you?"

"Just coffee, thanks." But omelets, biscuits, bacon and grits on plates being prepared behind the counter were dimming Joan's memory that she'd just eaten a sufficient breakfast.

Dove was already pouring coffee from a black-rimmed glass carafe into a sturdy, white mug. "Help yourself to creamer and such over there."

By this time, Mr. Big Talker had turned his eyes from Dove to Joan several times, and Joan's peripheral vision was sufficient to tell her that his gaze hadn't stayed exclusively in the general area of her face. As she moved off the seat to go doctor her coffee, the man began to twist around. At the condiment station, Joan sprinkled one packet of sugar into her cup, noting one more thing that raised the Diner's status: black plastic lids for the to-go cups. *White* lids always showed lipstick marks. Turning around and idly stirring for longer than necessary with a narrow, wooden stick, she surveyed the room again. Appropriate to the locale, an energetic highland reel sounded over the speakers, with a steady beat and strains of fiddle and accordion. The volume was set just loud enough for listening if you wanted to, but not so loud as to prevent conversation. Joan automatically attributed this pleasing circumstance to Dove, who, if she wasn't the Diner's manager or owner, ought to be.

Joan happened to lock eyes briefly with a scowling blonde who looked to be in her late twenties. A man seated opposite the blonde had his back to Joan, but even from that angle he appeared considerably older than his tablemate. His pinstriped, short-sleeved shirt had "Mueller's Garage" lettered across the back in dark blue. Returning to her seat and replacing her handbag by her feet (she never left it unattended), Joan pulled a couple of paper napkins from the metal holder and sipped her coffee that was now tinged with hazelnut flavor from a pump dispenser. She also managed to sneak a few glances at the front side of the garage man. He bore a resemblance to at least one of the young men Dove had addressed last night as twins when Joan was going out the door. Fraternal twins, most likely. Was this man their father? The one twin in the Ford truck had turned off at Mueller's Garage after tailgating her. It all seemed to fit.

When she rested her coffee cup on the counter again, there beside it were a fork and a small dish of fresh fruit she hadn't ordered. She looked up inquiringly. "On the house," Dove explained quietly, and Joan smiled her thanks before piercing a beautiful strawberry with the fork. The enthusiastic talker was now bringing to a close a different rousing account of a different amazing accomplishment. Then, without seeming to stop for breath, he invited Dove to be his companion during the special events on the town calendar for Sunday. It sounded as though this wasn't the first time he had asked Dove out. Joan almost laughed over the sudden sensation that she was in the middle of a television sitcom. That, or a commercial for a men's health supplement.

Dove caught Joan's eye with a subtle expression. "I'm sorry, Mr. Kidd, but Mrs. Ryan here has already agreed to be my guest on Sunday, so I'm not available to be *yours.*"

Oh! This was a new wrinkle. *And so much for my anonymity. But, for the sake of kindred womankind, I'll go with it.* Joan couldn't help herself. She liked Dove and wasn't put off by the fabrication. *I guess I owe her that much for the free bowl of fruit.*

A white coffee cup, then a blue-sleeved arm, then a shapely form topped with long, blonde hair inserted itself between Joan and the man whose wooing of Dove hadn't gotten off the ground. With a none-too-gentle *thunk*, the blonde set her cup on the counter and, with few words and fewer manners, ordered Dove to refill it. Her stylish spring blouse was low-cut. She left the cup, already steaming from the prompt refill, untouched. "What's yer business in town, Mrs. Ryan?"

Joan turned her head slowly and cast a quizzical look at the unpleasant creature. Clearly, the woman had heard Dove say "Mrs. Ryan." Joan assumed a businesslike expression that stopped just short of a smile. "I don't believe I've had the pleasure."

The other woman reset her lips, colored bright pink, into a smile—a very plastic-looking one. "Marilyn Mueller Walker." She flipped straight hair that was longer than Dove's, but not as pretty, behind her shoulder and extended her right hand for Joan to shake. Joan took hold of the brightly-manicured fingertips reluctantly, and as briefly as possible. "I'm sort of the unofficial welcomin' committee around here."

Crook Mountain needs to elect some new unofficial officers. With an effort, Joan kept her tone bland and her amusement contained. "That's nice. Thanks for the welcome."

"Have friends in town?" The interrogation continued by Marilyn, née Mueller (of the Mueller's Garage Muellers—it had to be). Here was the twin boys' sister. Older sister, it appeared. Married older sister. But the polished-looking Mrs. Walker, who clearly didn't work on cars in the family business, wore no wedding ring on her left hand. Was she divorced? Or widowed, her late husband being one of the unfortunate townspeople, hypothetical, whose tires had skidded in gravel to his demise?

The town's welcomer had glanced pointedly toward Mr. Kidd while asking Joan if she had friends in town. Joan shook her head a little at the absurdity that was threatening to derail her peaceful morning. Continuing to ignore the question, she turned her eyes back to the dish of enticing-looking fruit. It didn't deserve to be neglected on account of present company. Sinking her teeth into another strawberry and several blueberries in one bite, she reached down for her purse and rummaged for pen and paper with her head bent. "Forgive me, Ms. Walker. I must jot down my shopping list before I forget it." Joan started to write and was glad to see the offensive young blonde turn away.

"Gavin, honey! Yeh look just *terrific* this mornin'! I'm sure I've never seen a man look better in that color than you do."

"Well, yer lookin' mighty fetchin' yerself, sweetie. Big plans fer the day when yer through with the old man?"

A giggle. "None that cain't change if they *need* to."

Joan wanted to keep her first breakfast down, and the fruit as well, so she hastily prepared to escape. Underneath a bill that would cover the coffee plus a nice tip, she handed Dove the piece of paper on which she had been writing. It was not in fact a shopping list, but a short note. "No change needed. It was delicious!" Dove thanked Joan sweetly and wished her a good day.

"Bye, now," Gavin Kidd called as Joan made for the exit, pulling her sunglasses down from the top of her head and not acknowledging the wolfish-sounding farewell. She did turn her head in time to see the bold Ms. Walker place a hand on Kidd's arm for support as she wiggled herself and her snug-fitting ecru trousers onto the stool beside him.

The conversation Joan had intended to pursue with Dove apparently wasn't meant to be. So she had written the note, giving her phone number and asking Dove to call during a free moment. As Joan settled into her CRV and got warm air blowing, Gavin Kidd and Marilyn exited the Diner together, all but holding hands. They laughed and flirted down the couple of wooden steps and stopped next to a red sports car. He aimed his key fob, and the lights flashed. She leaned against the car in a provocative pose and gave his arm a squeeze. Her mouth continued to move with conversation; her head, shoulders, and tight blouse, with laughter. *Maybe I should take notes. I could give Lee a laugh with my Marilyn imitation.* The Mueller's Garage man came out the door and down the steps with what looked to be a bit of stiff-leggedness. He folded some dollar bills and slid them into a front pocket of his dark blue pants, then made his way toward Marilyn, immediately appearing to exert some persuasion. The brightness falling off her face as if by the flip of a switch, Marilyn left Kidd's side and sauntered, behind the man who by all indications was her father, to that same green and white Ford pickup. Mueller looked as though he had worked hard all his life, but somehow had missed out on the American dream of life becoming gradually more comfortable.

Joan didn't leave the lot until after the truck did. If any following was going to happen this time, she was going to be the one in back. The truck went right, then right again, but it didn't turn in at Mueller's Garage. Farther out from town, Joan watched the pickup turn left. The same direction as her cabin. Wait. *Mueller.* That beat-up mailbox with only the letters M-u-. Joan hypothesized without lightness of heart that her current residence was close to where the Muellers lived. If the mailbox was any indication, the general state of their property was probably in sharp contrast to her attractive rental cabin with its tailored landscaping. Just a guess. Joan turned the other way and headed toward Cluny's Ridge, suddenly needing contact with home. It was disappointing to get the recorded greeting, but the fact that it was in Lee's voice was enough comfort for the moment. "Hi, honey," she said into her phone. "Just wanted to say I love you. Everything's good here, and I hope there, too. Talk to you soon."

———⬥———

Joan planted on a bench in downtown Cluny's Ridge and set several parcels down beside her. She rummaged through her large purse and removed the wherewithal to add a packet of powdered vitamin mix to a bottle of water. Shaking the closed bottle with one hand, she pulled her phone out with the other and dialed Melinda to ask about Catherine. The situation was hard, but the experience of ministering in such a time of difficulty was precious and irreplaceable to all concerned. "A mixed blessing," Melinda called it.

"I know they're very grateful to have you there."

"They are."

Melinda sounded tired. Joan gathered her things and walked as she talked, pointing out that Melinda was not only serving her brother's family, but was showing her children a wonderful example of sacrificial love. Divorced from the children's father, Melinda needed encouragement, though most people wouldn't guess that. She was the one who always seemed to be lifting others' spirits. "When you get back and pick up your kids from the farm, tell your parents I said they did a wonderful job raising you. Tell them I want to come and stay with them myself!"

That's funny timing. Here she was standing in front of a nail salon she and April had used before, just as she'd been imagining herself learning to milk a goat. She looked at her hands, laughed, and went inside. It appeared she would be first in line, but it wasn't going to be easy to pick a polish color to go with a dress she hadn't bought yet, to wear on Sunday to a church she'd never visited before. She looked back and forth over several narrow shelves of little, glass bottles.

"Need help choosin' a color?" The short-haired and slightly-pierced manicurist was seated, already holding a wad of cotton soaked with enamel remover.

The pink that had been saying "choose me" suddenly looked too much like what Marilyn had had on her pointed nails. Joan wheeled from the array of colors and settled into the padded chair. "If I can just get this old polish off and a neutral shade on, that would be perfect. I'll let you recommend a color."

Forty-five minutes later, Joan gently ran her newly-manicured fingers over feather-light wool roving and, in contrasting texture, over smooth cotton strands, tightly wound and labeled with circular, brown paper wrappers. While the yarn shop's proprietor, a Mrs. Abernathy, was recommending products for the stitchers on the Ryans' Christmas list, an incoming call made Joan beg pardon. The unknown number had the local area code. She touched the green circle, whispering a "sorry" to the woman who had been describing where and how one of the fiber collections was dyed. "Thank you for calling." Joan stepped through the wooden doorway and onto the sidewalk so she could talk with Dove. "I had wanted to ask you a question this morning, but it wasn't possible."

"It sure wasn't! Apparently it was the morning for characters on parade at the Diner."

That intriguing manner of expression again. "Yes. During my time as your Easter guest tomorrow, we should talk about some of those characters."

"Oh, my goodness. I'm sorry for dragging you into something without warning, just to put off Gavin Kidd. It was a sudden impulse. Please forgive me."

"Don't worry about it."

"But you mustn't feel obligated to follow through."

"I admired your quick thinking. I'd *like* to talk with you more, in fact. I decided last night that if I found a dress today, I'd go to church and the whole nine yards. I mean, the potluck meal and the outdoor concert. That's what I was going to ask this morning. Assuming that you are familiar with Cluny's Ridge, is there a store you would recommend?" Besides being a perfectly reasonable question from an out-of-towner, that was a subtle bit of bait cast in hope of learning more about Dove. *Was* she familiar with Cluny's Ridge? "Those little boutiques tend to come and go, and it's been a while since my last visit here. Being a local, maybe you know of some dress shops the average tourist might miss." Joan switched from the call screen to her note-taking app so she could get a record of Dove's answer. "Great. I'll check it out and plan on seeing you tomorrow. Am I expected to bring food?"

"Oh, no, not at all. There will be plenty."

Joan chose hanks of hand-dyed wool for a cousin on Lee's side who was an accomplished knitter. The amount would be enough for a long-sleeved sweater, Mrs. Abernathy assured her. Then, because the yarn was too beautiful to resist, Joan selected more of it in a different color family to take home for herself. What would she do with it? That would have to be a topic for another time.

A couple of blocks down and around a corner, Elegant Looks By Rita was right where Dove had said it would be. Dove appeared to be fifteen or twenty years Joan's junior. Maybe shopping at a place the younger woman liked would prove to be a good style move.

A late lunch and *two* new dresses later, not to mention a very smart pants suit that would do nicely for a certain upcoming dinner party, Joan made her final stop at a grocery, using her phone to find a couple of recipes and purchasing what it would take to fix at least one full dinner. The cabin had a nice range and good cookware.

Joan's lighthearted satisfaction over her day's shopping fell off a notch as her car approached the start of the cabin's driveway. *Gravel coming up!* The tires crunched again, and Joan grimaced again, already anticipating the point where the slope would change from uncomfortably uphill to stupidly steep. Finally, the cabin came into view, and Joan's body relaxed out of its tenseness as the gear shift went into Park.

However, as if fate fiendishly grabbed the opportunity to kick her while she was down, some bit of movement happened at the edge of the woods. Joan glued her gaze to the spot where she thought she'd seen it. Images of black bear had just been surrounding her in Cluny's Ridge on T-shirts, hats, and art prints in the shop windows. Was she about to be reminded why?

She reached forward to grasp and detach the vial of pepper spray that was always on her key ring or in a front pocket. *Pepper spray for a bear?* She stayed right where she was and asked her phone that question. It seemed there was a different product sold specifically as bear spray. Who knew? However, any port in a storm. She made sure the dispenser's nozzle was turned in the proper direction. How many times had Lee insisted she act out this defense process as fast as she could? *I need to make him proud of me.*

For several minutes, nothing she could see of the leaves or of the undergrowth betrayed the presence of anything alive, large or small. And nothing seemed amiss in the open spaces of the yard. Joan started to laugh at her overreaction. She'd probably imagined the whole thing, or else it had been a harmless bird flapping its wings. This was spring, after all. Small mother birds often swooped and squawked at larger ones they feared were threatening the nest. Nevertheless, after Joan stepped out of her vehicle, she hurried over the stepping stones to the porch, all the while darting glances in every direction.

Inside the cabin, she set bundled purchases on the sofa, then turned and shut the door and locked it. Above the deadbolt was one of those metal loop gadgets that would catch on a peg if someone started to open the door. She moved that over and, finally, set the security alarm. It wasn't just that she was alone in a cabin, in the woods, in a remote area. These locks and the alarm system were precautions everyone *everywhere* ought to use every day of the year, no matter where they were staying. Sad, but true. That was just the way the world was.

"Okay," she said out loud, gathering groceries for the kitchen and picturing herself in the pretty, new clothes that had been delivered into her arms at Rita's. She passed a window, and something moved again, outside, over at that same spot. Joan watched, limbs frozen, adrenaline wreaking havoc with her heart rate. Someone was out there, watching the house. Watching *her*. Almost casually, the figure looked down and lifted a hand to brush something off a blue pant leg. Then, it turned slowly and disappeared between the trees. And Joan got a pretty good look. It was that Mueller twin! The same one who had tailgated her.

Her new clothes forgotten and her cold groceries staying off refrigeration a while longer, Joan was at the front door, checking it again to be sure it was very locked. Knob. Deadbolt. Peg and loop thing. She touched each one in turn, then looked at the alarm system's control panel. The locks and the security system hadn't made any special impression on her when she had moved in, nor when she had left the cabin this morning. Now, they seemed much more significant. *Were* they just a matter of standard precaution? Or had they been installed for very specific reasons?

Chapter 4

Beside Joan's open laptop on the glass-topped kitchen table, steam from a cup of mulled cider gently billowed its comfort. Over the speaker setting on the phone in Joan's hand, Dove's voice was calm. "It's nothing to worry about, I'm quite sure." Thankful that the shopping advice had given her Dove's number, Joan had called shortly after seeing the young man lurking and watching. Calling Lee or Melinda might have produced a sympathetic ear, but neither of them could have helped in a practical way. Dove, on the other hand, might shed light on the matter. And she did. Dub Mueller was "slow," according to Dove, although people in the small town didn't really say that openly. And they didn't call him "special."

"Dub is just Dub, and everybody seems to take it in stride how he is."

Apparently without the prospect of ever living independently, the young man nevertheless was very good with cars, and his father, Jesse, quite depended on both Dub and his brother Luke in the family business. Dove went on to say that Joan bore a slight resemblance to Sarah Mueller, the late mother of Marilyn and the twins. Before her death from cancer five years ago, Sarah had been the peacekeeping, nurturing parent. From Dove's account, that woman's death had left a gaping hole in a family structure that could scarcely afford such a blow.

Hearing she might look like Mr. Mueller's deceased wife was unsettling, but the most important thing right now was Dove's assurance that the son, Dub, was harmless. If he were acting like a peeping Tom or a stalker, it was much more likely about his loss of a mother figure than about any intention of harming Joan, Dove said. Not for anything would she believe him capable of that toward a nice, pretty stranger or to anyone else. "Okay. I'll take your word on that." Joan thanked Dove and they hung up.

Her cider stopped steaming and finally went cool as Joan sat. *Dove has been in Crook Mountain long enough to be sure she knows this Mueller boy pretty well, but not long enough for her speech or accent to adapt to local patterns.* The laptop went to screensaver, making the almost-blank page that was supposed to be the start of her September presentation disappear. Somewhere out there was a young man who needed the care and the presence of a mother— of *both* parents. Needed their support and provision past the usual age of separation. In her roles as registered dietitian and counselor she'd seen many people with destructive behaviors and eating disorders that were directly related to unhealthy or unfortunate family dynamics. Her few minutes' observation of Jesse Mueller that morning had suggested he wasn't exactly the nurturing type.

Dove had reported on Marilyn's background, too. At twenty-nine, she was back under her father's roof after a fairly brief marriage the chief goal of which had been an escape from Jesse's tyrannical control and from the meager living conditions his income provided. As for the boys, Luke was his brother's greatest friend and champion, having felt his whole life the special twin bond plus, from as early as Luke could grasp Dub's special needs, an obligation to act as encourager and protector. Finally, Dove had confirmed Joan's suspicion that the Mueller home bordered the property she was occupying. But, how would Dub have known she was here? Until they had talked tonight, she hadn't told Dove where she was staying, nor told anyone else, so it couldn't have gotten around town. Maybe wandering around in the woods was just a daily thing for Dub. Or, maybe there were so few rental places in town that anyone curious about a stranger just naturally thought of this cabin first.

Joan dressed for Easter service at Crook Mountain Church in the Wildwood, glad the forecast promised this would be the prettiest day of her trip so far. She turned in front of a large mirror in the bedroom. The multicolored dress fell just above the knee; its white chambray shirt-jacket had bright buttons that matched the dress. Mapping out the day in her head, Joan set out her all-weather coat to take to the concert. In these mountains, the mercury could plummet dramatically after sundown.

Besides telling the rather sad story of the family that lived adjacent to Joan's cabin, Dove had revealed another interesting fact on Saturday. A narrow walking trail led from the cabin's lot down to a paved road. Dove had offered to pick Joan up at the foot of it, saving her the trouble of driving to church. It was the least she could do, she'd said, after coercing Joan into joining her for the day's events. Somehow, the fact of a walking trail had been left out of all descriptions of the property Joan had seen. Maybe it was a recent improvement. Maybe the owner had added it as a secret escape route against trespassers. Or bears. Regardless, its existence meant Joan didn't have to navigate the steep gravel this time. *Good!* Besides that, her shoes were comfortable, her dress was pretty, her hair was behaving in spite of being washed in strange water, the Mueller boy wasn't out to get her, she'd slept great, and the morning was beautiful.

Easter. Back home, she and Lee hadn't been seen at church for a while. If together at home today, they probably would have made the effort, enjoying the large crowd, new clothes, majestic music, and proclamations of resurrection from the dead and hope for the world. Otherwise, whether in Crook Mountain or at home, had it *not* been Easter, Joan might have been in sweats and sneakers, out for a brisk walk, or else cuddled up with coffee and her laptop in the bright sunroom, binge watching a smart, new series. She had several on her watchlist, including a period drama April had been urging her to try. What was it called? Something that sounded like Mozart. But it started with…P. That was it. Poldark.

———⬥◆⬥———

The little, stone bench was shaded enough for Joan to see her phone without glare, but situated so the sun's rays warmed her feet and ankles nicely. In text messages, Melinda was getting a quick account of Easter morning at Crook Mountain Church in the Wildwood as, somewhere in the caverns of the building, the hospitality ladies were getting all of the food ready to be partaken of. Reverend Gene Kirkpatrick's sermon had run a bit shorter than usual, by his own admission, so that everyone might enjoy the good food and fellowship all the sooner—which remark had met with grateful grins and nods of approval, also with an enthusiastic whoop from a youngster promptly shushed by his embarrassed parents. The church service had seemed genuine and sweet, the music offering in sincerity what it might have lacked in "quality" (as usually defined).

Joan stopped reporting to Melinda for a moment, raising her head and rotating her neck a few times and continuing to debrief the church experience within herself. Marilyn Mueller Walker had not been possible to ignore. Though by sitting with her father and her brothers she had made their family unit complete, Marilyn hadn't appeared to be emotionally close to her relations. The twins, beards trimmed, Sunday clothes and manners on, hadn't seemed to deserve the term Joan had used before in describing them to Lee: *rough-looking*. Of Jesse Mueller, Joan couldn't make the same concession in light of what Dove had said last night. Regardless, none of the four Muellers had paid Joan any attention thus far.

She bent to her phone again and ran her thumbs over the letter keys. "A certain young 'lady' blessed the holy day with an outfit I'd rather expect to see in the infield at the Kentucky Derby. OK, I exaggerate a LITTLE." Whether the setting was a church or a convention or a restaurant, there was a standard of appropriate dress that decent people adhered to. Marilyn Mueller Walker had been absent—or in the restroom fixing her makeup—the day they'd taught that.

"Gross. But I know YOU looked beautiful & classy, judging from the pics you sent of your new spring duds. I hope you're glad you went."

Joan was typing her answer to Melinda when a supercilious voice accosted her over the clack of heels on the sidewalk and the competing clink of bangle bracelets. "I don't see your Georgia license plate in the parkin' lot, Mrs. Ryan. Don't tell me you *walked* here from the McCain cabin." Marilyn stopped in front of the bench, and Joan couldn't help but stare for an unpleasant moment at the tight dress that didn't go high enough at the bustline or low enough at the hem. Even so, she caught and immediately filed the name *McCain*, in fact typed it in the middle of her text in progress before pressing the lock button on the side of her phone. How should one respond to that? Joan *wanted* to say she hadn't been aware until today that Frederick's of Hollywood had an Easter dress collection. And Marilyn's brother Dub must have told her where Joan was staying, so it seemed that family did have *some* communication. "Walked here? In these shoes?" Joan kept her tone mild as she regarded her accoster, who appeared to be a couple of inches shorter than her brothers and was distinctly curvy in contrast to *their* builds, which looked on the undernourished side. Rising from the bench, Joan smoothed the front of her dress though it didn't need smoothing. The frock was simply cut and very flattering. It draped but didn't cling. The fabric's rich shades of grape, fuchsia, and bright yellow were flattering to her skin tone. Those facts made her stand a little taller. She was done here, but she lingered just long enough to deliberately portray a false picture of herself just for the fun of it. "Excuse me, please. I think I'll go in and try to be at the front of the line. I'm a guest today, after all. And, you did tell me yesterday that you want me to feel welcome in town." Regally, she left Marilyn behind.

———◈———

Dishes of chicken pie, vegetables like sweet corn frozen fresh from last summer's gardens, cornbread, blueberry cobbler, and much more had been raided appreciatively by old and young, including Joan, and those who remained were engaged in quiet conversations around the long tables in the social hall. A comforting and happy din it was until a familiar voice rose above it in a squeal. *"Gavin!"* Joan, and Dove beside her, and virtually everyone else occupying a metal, folding chair or standing along a wall, halted at the disruption. Gavin Kidd ambled through the room with a sportcoat folded over one shoulder, as if in a cologne commercial. Now, to be honest, Joan had to admit that the man's features were handsome. However, his personality made all the difference. She resolved to be amused, not revolted, by both him and his ardent pursuer.

Kidd heaped a plate with food while heartily explaining his tardiness to his curvy shadow, whose responses included "I'm so glad yeh got to come *by*, darlin'!" and "Can I get yeh some tea or lemonade?" He swept the room with his eyes, then headed in the direction of a single empty chair that was nearly opposite where Joan sat beside Dove, with Miss Cora Haskew next to Dove, and Mr. and Mrs. Gerald Givens across from the threesome of ladies.

"Good afternoon, good people!" There was no perceivable warmth in the words or on the face of the man speaking them. He sounded like a game show host demanding the audience's attention. *He ought not to expect everyone to hang around while he eats. Naps may be calling most of these people home soon. Not to mention, it's kind of tacky to show up for food when he didn't attend church.* But, wait. Seriously, who was she to begrudge the man a tasty meal and some socializing within his familiar community? Today, of all days in the year, sitting in judgment of another human being over something so utterly trivial was completely out of line. And, beyond that, what difference did it make to Joan *how* these people she'd never see again conducted themselves? Kidd's eyes met hers then, just as her appraising expression might have been misinterpreted as interest. *That* kind of interest. Another man, a more confident or astute man, might have found the eye contact completely incidental. But this wasn't another man. This was God's gift to women in Crook Mountain and points beyond. Single women and married women. Equal opportunity. To him, a skirt was a skirt, apparently. So, in spite of Marilyn's relentless bids for his attention, Gavin Kidd zeroed in elsewhere. "Happy *Easter*, Ms. Ryan."

Joan gave a slight nod and the tiniest upturn of her mouth, then immediately turned her head toward Dove and Cora. Joan had met the mysterious Miss Haskew that morning on the way to church when the elderly lady had been a passenger in Dove's car. Just now, there unfortunately was no time for new conversation between the women. "I managed to get away from a business round o' golf so I could rush over here where I wanted t' be all along." Gavin Kidd was still looking at Joan. *I don't care.* Mr. Givens started to say something to the late arrival, and so gallant it was of him to step in and redirect Gavin's attention toward himself, but Marilyn thwarted that by forcing her way into the group. She leaned in—*Oh! That neckline!*—and placed a full glass of iced tea on the table for Gavin. Then, the demanding tone in her voice not disguised by a syrupy "please," she asked a feeble-looking lady if she wouldn't mind moving down one place to create an open spot just there.

I'm done. Joan stood and gathered her silverware, soiled paper napkins, plate, and large plastic tumbler. Dove and Cora followed suit. As Joan waited behind a few other people to dispose of her trash and to hand actual flatware over to the ladies in the kitchen, Gavin Kidd strode toward her. "That's a mighty fetchin' dress, Ms. Ryan."

"*Mrs.* Ryan." Too bad Melinda with her striking red hair wasn't here. At least *she* was single! Joan grinned in spite of herself and hoped not to be misinterpreted.

"I was hopin' to show yeh around our fair town this afternoon, *Mrs.* Ryan. I've got a convertible!"

Seriously? What answer would be unmistakably dismissive without being downright rude? "Mr. Kidd, as tempting as that sounds, I am *Dove's* guest today, remember. And she has already asked me to afternoon tea at her place." *Wherever that is.* That tea invitation was totally bogus, of course, along the lines of Dove's fib yesterday morning, and Joan hoped she wasn't about to learn that Dove commuted to the Diner and to church from a number of miles away. Dove was standing right behind. If Joan's words surprised her, she was covering the fact flawlessly when Joan stole a look at her.

Outside in the fresh air, Joan, Dove, Cora and the Givenses stood in a silent though contented-looking group, having finally succeeded in leaving Gavin and Marilyn to each other's devices. Joan's only regret about rushing out was that she didn't thank the ladies in the kitchen for organizing the meal and for cleaning up. She said as much and asked any of present company to convey that message when they could.

Dove's car, with its three occupants and some mostly-empty dishes of casserole and dessert, soon slowed to a crawl less than a mile from the church. Up the short driveway they went. "Up," so to speak, that is. This driveway was nothing to the steep grade of Joan's, nor to its length. And, it was paved. *Totally jealous of that!* The one-level, brick house was old and quaint. Big, square support columns on the front porch were painted white and appeared, from Joan's vantage point in the car, to be in need of repainting. A script letter "H" decorated the screen door. Dove stopped the silver Elantra in the driveway and turned the engine off, then stepped out and walked around to the passenger side to open the door for Cora. Cora promptly fussed in a kindly way about not needing help. "We all get out," Dove said to Joan, who sat quietly in the back seat, safety belt still buckled. "This is where I live."

———◆———

The back porch was comfortable with homey cushions and a smattering of antique bric-a-brac. Joan slipped her sandals off, Cora and Dove having already exchanged their Sunday shoes for comfy house slippers. What ice remained after everyone's feet were made comfortable was broken with small talk about the day. When Marilyn's name came up, as it must, Cora simply shook her short, gray-white curls back and forth and uttered some *mmt-mmt-mms.* That seemed to cover it, and Dove changed the subject, laughingly referring to the grandiose ways of the town's mayor, Teddy Dyle, which had been upstaged by the late arrival of Gavin Kidd. The mayor had sought Joan out to introduce himself and had seemed in a fair way to begin bending her ear until Gerald Givens had tactfully distracted the rotund politician with some or other question about the local business climate.

Accepting a second cup of tea, Joan gazed through a large window screen. Sunlight played on leaves that were swaying in the breeze. Here she sat, taking tea in a private home, two days into her trip. The letter on the front door screen would be for Haskew, of course, but Joan still hadn't heard *Dove's* last name, nor whether Cora happened to be a relative of hers. The cat of the house, Emily, purred audibly from between Cora's feet and a leg of the painted wooden settee softened by cushions in faded floral chintz. Somewhere in the yard a bird warbled in sweet, melodic tones. Joan closed her eyes and concentrated on the feel of the gentle breeze. There was a magic in the springtime beauty of the area that really did cast a spell. One could get one's feet planted in a place like this and want to stay forever, or, at least, stay for "the season" in summer, the way the "snowbirds" migrated to Florida in winter. But, it wasn't awfully polite to sit here so disengaged suddenly, especially after inviting herself over. She set her cup gently on its saucer and pressed her fingers daintily, afternoon tea-ishly, on a napkin to remove oily traces left from a homemade butter cookie. One was all she could manage after the large meal at the church.

Dove looked prettier than ever in her smart skirt suit of pale lilac with its narrow, black velvet trim. The front strands of her long, dark hair weren't clipped back from her face as when she was serving patty melts and coffee at the Diner. No-last-name Dove, stalwart citizen of Crook Mountain, Tennessee, was hosting her for Sunday afternoon tea as if it were the most natural thing in the world, as if they were old friends. But they weren't. What was that woman's story?

"Something in a hill child dies when he goes down to meadowland." Cora's sudden statement was a bit off the wall, especially since she'd been the least talkative of the three for most of the day. "That was one of the favorite sayings of a teacher I had in my teens. Miss Mildred Cantrell was my inspiration for becoming a teacher myself. Her memoir of life and work in the southern highlands in the late 1940s is one of my prized possessions, Mrs. Ryan. I hope you will let me show some of it to you while you're in town. It's stored in the church library."

Cora went on to share, at Dove's prompting, that in her retirement years she continued to be involved in the public schools, reading to elementary-aged children as part of a program she had developed herself, called Liberty Through Literacy. "I love that name!" Joan interjected. This house had been Cora's parents', and she had lived here all her life. An only child, she had stayed close to her parents, caring for them until they had passed on. She hadn't married and had no children. "This dear young lady goes with me to put fresh flowers at my folks' places in the cemetery once a month." Cora seemed to regard Dove as a valued friend, maybe as the daughter she'd never had.

"It's time I started my nap." Cora's statement was abrupt, as if an internal timer had just gone off. As she left the porch, carrying her tea dishes with her, Emily followed. The cat's slightly fat, gray-striped midsection swayed left and right.

"Any unwanted attention from Dub Mueller at church today?" Dove asked Joan as soon as it was just the two of them. Joan shook her head. "I hadn't expected you to receive any. Neither of the boys puts a toe out of line with their father so close at hand. And it's seldom that he isn't. Jesse Mueller rules his family with an iron fist, though Marilyn manages to duck his authority every way she can. Jesse indulges her, at least compared with how he controls the boys. I think Jesse hopes Marilyn will catch another husband, one well fixed for money. But he wants the boys' eyes only on carburetors and spark plug wires. Did you pick up on the accidentally-on-purpose contact between Luke and a sweet young thing named Bonnie Jarvis, going for their desserts at the same time, that sort of thing?" Joan hadn't noticed. "Take a look during the concert tonight. If Jesse weren't so nearsighted, he would see more of that than he does. Too much manly pride to wear glasses. Or he just can't afford any."

"How do you know he is nearsighted?" This small-town gossip was intriguing, as was the fact that Dove was especially free with it just now.

"When he's in the Diner, he reads the menu, when he needs to, off a card in his hand instead of from the board. We change the specials around to keep life interesting. And I hear the boys talking sometimes. Their father's worsening eyesight is one reason he says he needs them both as mechanics. There was talk of Luke getting training for something in electronics, but Jesse squelched that. It's a shame, too, because Luke deserves his chance. I believe he would stick around and help his family, not use a higher paycheck as a ticket out of town. They're good boys, both of them."

The conversation and the setting suddenly felt like an episode of *Murder, She Wrote*, with Dove an expert on everyone in "Cabot Cove" and having answers to most all of an outsider's questions because of her keen powers of observation, like that town's notable resident, Jessica Fletcher. Joan made the observation out loud, then begged Dove's pardon in case she wasn't flattered by a comparison to a senior adult detective/novelist.

"I haven't watched more than a few episodes, but I know the general storyline. It's really interesting you should bring that up."

"Why?" Joan covered a Sunday afternoon yawn with one hand.

"Because, speaking of *murder…*" Dove paused after that dramatic intro, stretching her arms and nestling a little more comfortably into the cushions of the settee's matching chair.

"Please don't tell me the town's saga includes *that!*" The response was automatic and cliché, but was what Dove seemed to be hinting at really so outlandish? In another case of "sad but true," didn't homicide visit most places sooner or later? In fact, hadn't she herself once heard rumor that a friend's distant cousin had done away with her first husband, somehow or other—probably poison or withholding proper medications—and had gotten away with it? It did happen. And real-life Jessica Fletchers and Aurora Teagardens didn't always show up the guilty parties, the way they did in novels and mystery movies.

Dove stood and carried the plate of cookies away. *Good. Out of sight, out of mind.* Through the open door that led into the kitchen came the sound of dishes clinking. Then, that stopped and in its place wafted soft strains of dulcimer and other stringed instruments. Whatever else this Dove woman was, she was a shrewd hostess who knew how to use food, atmosphere, and personality to meet core needs in the average person.

"How's your tea holding out?" Dove was back.

"Warm it up a little." The words came out like a command instead of a request. "Sorry. That's a line from *White Christmas.*" She laughed with Dove, who had said the last two words with her.

"What a great movie. It's funny which parts of a script will stick with you."

Joan actually declined the tea in favor of directions to the bathroom. On returning to the porch, she inquired for the second time whether Dove owned the Diner. If Dove was about to bend her ear with Crook Mountain's latest murder case, *she* was going to get at least this one question answered first.

"No. Heavens, no." Dove laughed and flipped some hair behind her shoulders. "The Diner is owned by a small business partnership. Names of McCain, Stillman, and Dyle. Yes, Mayor Dyle. No, I don't own anything here, except my car and my clothes. I'm only staying in Crook Mountain temporarily."

That would explain a thing or two, like why her speech didn't sound like everyone else's. But it also raised questions. Maybe Dove was the mountain version of those who would pick up and move into apartments or tiny cottages at the beach, waiting on tables or working as lifeguards, and working on their tans, until the naïve idea of endless paradise wore off. Except that Dove did not seem naïve. "Are you related to Cora?" *A niece or a once-removed cousin, maybe?* No relation, Dove said. "How did you happen to start renting from her?"

"You *are* the curious one today." Normally, that remark meant someone was tired of nosy questions and was saying so in as nice a way as possible. But Dove actually looked pleased as she continued, "I drove into town one Saturday morning and happened to see Gerald and Edith Givens out in their flower garden—you do need to make sure you see their place—and told them I was looking for some information and a place to stay. One thing led to another. They connected me with their friend Miss Haskew, who had spare rooms, a kind heart, the need for some extra income, and the onset of a few mild geriatric issues. And so it was arranged." Joan simply nodded, and Dove added, "I like it here."

"I can understand why. But where did you come here from? I get the feeling you weren't born and raised in these hills."

"We 'Army brats' typically live all over. My parents ultimately decided they wanted to go back to Germany, and I settled in Florida. That was several years ago. I eventually left an office job I didn't like, sold my condo, and worked as a full-time, live-in caregiver to an elderly woman in Vero Beach."

"I hope that went well. You do seem to have a way with people."

"Thank you, Joan, but I don't take any credit for that. It's how I'm made, I guess. I care about people." *I do, too. Is that what seems to be connecting us?* "May I call you Joan?"

"Certainly." They weren't waitress and customer today. And, even if they had been, did she in any way "outrank" Dove, except by age? Of course she didn't. There was more to Dove than an unattached (that was an assumption) passer-through without any long-range goals, content to work as a short-order cook while helping to look after an aging landlady she hadn't known very long. She had just said she came to Crook Mountain looking for information. *Maybe she cares for the elderly in hopes of being named in their wills. There's nothing wrong with caring about people* and *reaping that kind of reward, if fate hands you that, I guess. Great work if you can find it!* Maybe Dove wasn't as saintly as she appeared to be. "Speaking of names," Joan uncrossed her legs and recrossed them the other way, "I've never heard your last name."

"It's Sechrist." Dove spelled the name for Joan, then said that her somewhat unusual *first* name came from parents who had named her for the white doves released at their wedding. "I was a 'honeymoon baby.' Any more questions?"

"Yes, a couple." Joan shifted naturally into the demeanor she assumed during nutrition consultations or when sitting on a panel of experts. "Marilyn called the place I'm staying the McCain cabin. Same McCain who owns part interest in the Diner?"

"Yes. Serena McCain. Stillman is her married name. Her father runs the bank. He had the cabin built new for Serena five or six years ago, but since then she has left town, apparently for good, though she doesn't live very far away. She married a man who came from Kentucky and has business interests ranging from race horses to real estate. Very successful. If you judge success by money, that is."

"And you don't?"

"I don't."

Joan believed her. Maybe she wasn't trying to weasel her way into extra inheritances, after all. "There's just one more thing I'm curious about, Dove, and then I really need to go." Though, of course, she was at the mercy of her hostess for a ride home. *Maybe I can dodge her murder tale, after all. She brought it up but then dropped it.* "How long have you been living 'temporarily' in this town?"

"Almost two years now." Dove turned her head and gazed through the porch screen. Her eyes looked wistful. And... burdened? "I came here to fulfill a dying woman's last request, and that request could be connected with a murder. I don't *know* that, but it's what I came here to try to find out."

Chapter 5

"Yes, sweetie, I'm having a nice time! The weather is perfect so far. I did the shopping thing yesterday, knocking out some of our Christmas list. And, I have to say, there are some interesting people around here." *And how.* Even if Lee had had the time to listen, in one phone call it would have been impossible to bring him up to speed. The details of her trip thus far would have to wait. They would be better in person, anyhow, when she could spin them with lively antics and make him laugh. Right now, grateful to hear his voice "live" at last, she stayed with small talk. "I can't say I've made entirely stellar eating choices, but blame that on there being this one good place in town that keeps calling me back. That and the potluck after church today."

"Oops. What was that you said about your derrière before you left home?"

"Ha ha." Joan's weight hadn't varied much more than seven or eight pounds her entire adult life, not counting two terms of baby weight. Lee knew that. He wasn't criticizing her; he was just backing up what she'd said herself. *Good husband!* "I plan to do some walking tomorrow."

After the call, Joan set an alarm on her phone and stretched out on the bed. *Newman.* It was an intriguing tale Dove had told. *A missing man named Larry Newman.* His mother Harriet, at whose side Dove had sat, whose meals Dove had prepared, whose troubled hands Dove had held comfortingly, had extracted from her young caregiver a solemn promise. Dove had vowed to do her best to find out what had happened to Mrs. Newman's only son, a bachelor in his late fifties who had gone missing two years ago, after being last seen in Cluny's Ridge.

Eyes closed, Joan mulled over the story. Dove hadn't gone into great detail, insisting that the utmost secrecy was crucial. If she was on the right track and let it be known too soon, to the wrong people, all hope of exposing the guilty parties could be lost. Over lunch tomorrow, she would explain more. Joan yawned, plumped the pillow, and turned onto her side. Monday lunch. Did she need to start using a calendar for this vacation? And her Reminders app to be sure she told Dove about the wisteria? Coming home from tea today, she'd found a surprise on the cabin's front porch. Twigs of purple wisteria had been left on the wrought iron table, with a tin can serving as a vase. Some considered that plant a pest to be squelched, but she and Lee had a natural area in their back yard where the growth was carefully managed into a thing of beauty. She yawned again. *Wisteria* sounded like *mysterious*...

A peppy jazz tune rudely interrupted the good nap. *Snooze.* Joan tapped the convenient and tempting word on the screen of her phone and slipped straight back into never-never land. At the second alarm, she pressed "OK" with a groan and started the drill, rehearsing what she would do when her feet hit the floor. At home, this ritual meant picturing her outfit piece by piece, right down to the jewelry, and remembering (or deciding) which meals of the day would be eaten in and which ones out. But this was *vacation*. It sure was tempting to ditch the concert. Nevertheless, the call of adventure finally won out. Coffee would help. Some enticing flavor names had spun by when she'd twisted the carousel of one-serving cups beside the Keurig in the kitchen Friday night.

Twenty minutes later, Joan refreshed her makeup and brushed her teeth, hoping to look as perky as the "Sumatran Sizzle" had her feeling. That exuberance was tempered, though, as she unbolted the front door. *Peeping Toms and bears not allowed.* She looked and listened carefully around before scooting from the front porch to her car. *Safe.* She managed to reach the road below after making only one little skid in the gravel. *Whew!*

The park in the center of town included a grassy amphitheater, and nearby businesses, closed until Monday morning, offered plenty of parking. What a refreshing change! Atlanta was known for many good things, but also for its unrelenting motor traffic. Parking at venues like CNN Center, Fox Theatre, and Turner Field was never like this. Imagine it! Just rolling up at your own, leisurely pace, a little while before start time, and finding this many empty spaces. *Life in a small town!* Immediately, an echo seemed to reply, *Can't beat it!* Joan grinned upon understanding. Her memory had just served up a slight variation on dialogue exchanged by Bing Crosby and Fred Astaire in *Holiday Inn.*

Advance flyers about tonight's concert, like the one in the Diner, had attracted people from outside the town limits, Joan learned after locating Dove. Outsiders were easily spotted by the home folks in a small town. In his ostentatious way, the mayor was doing his utmost to greet everyone, while the ladies in charge of hospitality fluttered around in their denim shirts and high-waisted khaki pants, making sure locals and strangers alike knew just where the garbage cans were ("Please use them!") and where hot chocolate was being sold for three dollars a cup ("Yes, dear me, that *is* high, we know, but do chip in to help our wonderful Key family if you can. That's why we're all here tonight!").

Dove had brought a couple of blankets, and Joan an old quilt kept in her car for use at places like Stone Mountain. These would ward off the mid-fifties night air and also pad the hard, concrete seating of the outdoor theater. Cora was going to be made even a little more comfortable than that in a folding chair with armrests and a cup holder. The Givenses were at home, Dove mentioned, being quite regimented in their sleeping and eating. Plus, Edith wasn't quite as robust as most women her age were. Gerald, a couple of years older than his wife, was still working full-time even though he was certainly retirement age and past. *Town gossip flowing freely again!* Joan breathed deeply of the cool air and took her cues from her hostess, content just to be along for the ride.

Dove greeted a slender, young woman and gently tugged on her arm in order to bring her over to the others. This was Bonnie Jarvis. Dove launched into a short soliloquy praising the girl's qualities, one of which was an impressive knowledge of area plant life. It took quiet urging by both Dove and Cora to start Bonnie talking, but in answer to their questions and Joan's, she quietly began to tick off some of the more interesting names of local wildflowers, shrubs, and trees: jack-in-the-pulpits, little brown jugs, and violets, for starters; plus devil's walking stick, hearts-a-busting, wild hydrangea, mountain holly, mountain laurel, azalea, and rhododendron. Bonnie, who didn't appear to be older than eighteen, seemed to blossom *(appropriate metaphor!)* as she warmed to her subject. Names like partridgeberry, trumpet-creeper, catbrier, greenbriar, muscadine, and wisteria clearly brought her pleasure. Bonnie was learning the botanical names for plants, but couldn't always pronounce them, she said. Besides, most folks'd find those names too hard. Several of the trees Bonnie named were familiar: fraser fir, varieties of maple, beech, poplar, and pine. Sometimes you'd run across a weeping willow, Bonnie said, and there were lots of other kinds of that tree, too: Carolina willow, dwarf willow, prairie willow, and silky willow.

By this time, Bonnie's voice had risen with her growing enthusiasm. But, just as soon as the words "silky willow" were out of her mouth, she stopped abruptly and a frightened expression replaced her pretty smile. Her eyes were fixed on something beyond the three ladies who had been her rapt audience. Now, they all turned. A few feet away stood Jesse Mueller, glaring—maybe not specifically at Bonnie, but in their little huddle's general direction. A moment later, the twins Luke and Dub appeared, falling into place behind their father, heads down. The three moved off toward the higher rows of seating. Marilyn was conspicuously absent, not just from her family, but from the amphitheater altogether, so far. *If she were here, I'm sure we'd all know it.*

As the band warmed up, it was Joan who took charge of the conversation. "Let's get seated before we're crowded out of our spots." It was second nature to worry about saved seats being encroached upon in general admission seating. They had set Dove's blankets and her quilt at the end of a ledge, low and up front, beside Cora's folding chair. Bonnie left them and scampered over to sit with her parents and a number of younger siblings, pulling a little one onto her lap and bouncing him gently up and down.

Dove sprang for hot chocolate all around. Joan took a cup and thanked Dove for it, settling into her place and wondering about that uncomfortable moment with Jesse Mueller. Oh, well. Whatever it had been about, it wasn't going to spoil this evening. She studied the musicians for a few minutes so she could tell Sam about them later. Then, she turned to Dove and asked her if she had any hobbies.

"Oh, I walk, I try painting a little, though I'm no good at it. And I explore around Cluny's Ridge some. I'm learning things about mountain life from Cora and the others around here, and I write letters to my parents."

"Letters?" That was old-fashioned. "Not e-mail?"

Dove shook her head. "They like real letters. It may be the stamps they like better than what I write. I'm afraid each letter tends to cover the same ground as the one before it."

Hmm. That was sad. It spoke of stagnation. Were the opportunities around here that limited? But, in view of what Dove's purpose here was, some such limits must be at least partially self-imposed. Imposed by that promise she'd given. And Joan hadn't missed the bit about exploring in Cluny's Ridge. Why hadn't Dove rented an apartment *there*, invested herself in the community *there*, where this missing man apparently was last seen? Instead, she was a fixture here in Crook Mountain. Maybe there was a particular tie-in to this town, or a suspected one, related to Larry Newman. Unless it was simply that Dove didn't want the people she suspected in Cluny's Ridge to see her enough to catch on to what she was about. Joan studied her. What facts or leads was Dove working from?

Dove apparently noticed the scrutiny. She volunteered quietly, "Some people find me an oddity, for sure, showing up in town and staying. It takes a long time for an outsider to be accepted. But the wiser folks have warmed up to me and taken me under their wings." She patted Cora Haskew affectionately on the arm. Did Cora know about Dove's promise to Harriet Newman?

The four members of Blueberry Creek Band, all male, gathered in the concrete stage area up front and led off with some impressive dueling breakdowns complete with physical antics that grabbed the audience's interest in a hurry. Then, guitars and banjo struck up some chords and the lead singer leaned close to his mic. He was a thirty-something-looking blond of average height and muscular build, sporting long sideburns and a separate, short beard. He wore a black vest with his jeans and white shirt. "This next piece is a Scottish air called *John Roy Lyall*. Some of you might recognize the tune, but we've put some words to it especially dedicated to Miss Laynie Key, tonight's guest of honor." Applause and a few shrill whistles answered his mention of the little girl, and over that the musicians began their intro, launching into a ballad version of *The Itsy Bitsy Spider*. They managed to make the story told in a silly children's song, of a little spider's difficulty and ultimate triumph in climbing a waterspout, engaging and almost visual. The tune was emotive; the delivery, mesmerizing. At the song's end, Joan clapped as enthusiastically as anyone and immediately searched for the band's name in her browser so she could look later at what recordings they had for sale.

Mayor Dyle hefted his rotund frame from a folding director's chair just off the stage area and took over the microphone. After needlessly requesting more applause for the band, he invited the Key family, parents and three children, to join him. With more inane remarks that could have been edited to half their length, the mayor thanked the town and community for responding so wonderfully to the benefit. When Laynie's father was finally invited to speak, he reported on his daughter's condition and said how grateful they were for all of the money raised and the prayers and encouragement. The family started to move off, a younger brother importantly pushing Laynie in her wheelchair. The lead singer asked the guest of honor from the microphone if she would like to stay down front and sing a number with the band. Applause was loud as Laynie, all smiles, nodded.

With the wheelchair positioned and the mic lowered, the handsome singer squatted down to whisper some instructions. The band struck up the familiar tune of *The Itsy Bitsy Spider* then, strumming soft, simple chords in order that Laynie's young treble would be showcased. The effect was…affecting. Sniffles could be heard from here and there in the audience, and Joan, though she didn't have the emotional connection the others did, but already planning to put a contribution in the bucket, decided to increase the amount of her gift. It was touching, this town's longstanding support for a family whose daughter had had to undergo multiple, expensive procedures to help her lagging right leg catch up in growth to her left one. Joan took a bill from her wallet and folded it, then stood and made her way toward the table where the Keys were now receiving the public. Meanwhile, the band slowed things down with *The Kentucky Waltz*. Joan did her best to miss as little as possible of the entertainment. The banjo player was singing the lead this time:

... I was the boy that was lucky, but it all ended too soon.
As I sit here alone in the moonlight, I can see your smiling face.
And I long once more for your embrace and that beautiful
Kentucky waltz.

She closed her eyes. This fellow might not be the lead singer, but he sounded just as capable.

Laynie and her family sat behind a portable, folding table that had no covering. Just the basics for the occasion: the money box, one vase of flowers, and a poster taped to the front edge of the table, with photographs of Laynie bearing up in various medical settings and doing rehab exercises at home. Her younger brother and sister proudly wielded their own posters reading "Thank You From The Keys" (his, with drawings of keys) and "Your $upport Makes A Diffrence" (hers, with a spelling error). Behind Joan in line, someone started singing along with the band. "As I sit here alone in the moonlight, I can see yer smilin' face. And I long once more fer yer embrace..." Good grief! The worst! How could *anyone* be so selfish as to ruin another's listening experience by singing along, out loud? The voice was way too close to Joan's ear now. Muscles in her stomach catching, she moved forward a step and turned around. *Of course.* It took all her self-control not to roll her eyes at Gavin Kidd. *Lee would chew you up and spit you out.* She'd seen her tall, steel-built husband halt worthier-looking men than this one with a look, a stance, and very few words, when he'd wanted to nip a foolish business proposal in the bud or to ward off someone who believed the college football experience was enhanced by being too intoxicated to know what was going on. *And this unfortunate soul thinks I'm smiling because of his pleasing attentions.* "Mr. Kidd, I don't blame you a bit for liking that song. This band is *really good.* Do you know any of them personally? I wouldn't mind an introduction."

"Wish I could help ya there, darlin', but don'tcha fret. Yer so fetchin' I bet those git-tar players wouldn't mind one bit if yeh marched right up and interduced yerself."

"Well, aren't you *kind?*" No time like the present to practice her Marilyn imitation. "Maybe I'll do that. You have a great evening, now. I've seen at least one young lady here who would just love to have you sing in *her* ear." Gavin was left to puzzle on that total fabrication as Joan turned from him to speak a few encouraging words to Mr. and Mrs. Key and to each of their children. She pushed her money through the slit opening of the collection box.

Laynie thanked Joan and grinningly said she would keep busy writing thank-you notes to all the friends who had done things for her and her family. This couldn't be easy on the youngster, nor on her siblings. The pain, the missed fun and the immobility due to her cast, and all of this abnormal attention.

As Joan made her way back toward her seat, a friendly-looking stranger stopped her. "Mrs. Ryan, I'm Sherry Kirkpatrick. My husband, Gene, is the minister, and this is our daughter, Kelley."

"Hello." Joan made eye contact with mother and preteen daughter in turn. "I am enjoying my stay in your town." It seemed the thing to say.

"I'm sorry I didn't get to greet you earlier today. I was helping in the kitchen after church. But I wanted to tell you that we will be keeping your friend's sister-in-law in our prayers."

That was a surprise, but it had to have been Dove or Cora who had shared that information. That afternoon, over tea, they'd heard the circumstances that had brought Joan here. "That's good to hear, Mrs. Kirkpatrick. Thank you."

"Oh, we don't stand on ceremony. Please call me Sherry. I get kidded about my name. You know, a pastor's wife named *sherry*. But it breaks the ice."

"Thanks again, Sherry. Enjoy the evening."

"We intend to. School's out all week for spring break, so we're glad it's not a school night tonight." Kelley Kirkpatrick seconded that by bobbing her shiny-haired head up and down. She said she and her brother would get extra time for TV, and for her to beat him at computer games.

Joan moved on. Almost immediately, another woman stopped her and told her virtually the same thing Sherry had, expressing concern for Joan's sick friend. This was the town's hairdresser. "I'm in the strip mall 'cross from the Post Office. Come see me if yer here long enough t' need a trim er some highlights. We do nails, too!"

The concert continued. Joan slipped her slightly-tight shoes off, keeping her bare feet warm under the quilt. The banjo player urged the crowd to its feet and called a series of simple, stand-in-place dance motions to the old classic, *She'll Be Comin' 'Round the Mountain*. Much smiling and laughing made its way through the audience as most joined in. Afterward, while the band took a break, Joan settled back onto the blanket and couldn't find her shoes. Her stomach tightened the way it did if her purse or her diamond ring or something important of Lee's that she had temporary custody of wasn't where it was supposed to be. She moved the quilt around with her bare feet. She lifted it up with her hands. She looked farther left and farther right, irritated not only that the shoes were gone, but also that having to look for them was taking her attention from her *raison d'être ici*. Had the shoes been stolen? Stolen right out from under her in this sweet, small-town gathering on this idyllic Sunday night? Joan knew the stories about impoverished families in Appalachia needing shoes. *I would gladly* buy *a barefooted person their own pair!* Maybe Dove had accidentally kicked them aside, not knowing they had been there.

A thin, young man with longish hair and shortish beard leaned in close to Joan, over Cora. He was wearing faded jeans, a brown, button-up shirt, and all-purpose work shoes. "Here, ma'am." He held her taupe Vince Milo flats out to her. "I seen who got 'em, so I went an' got 'em back."

Tongue-tied, Joan reached out and accepted the shoes from where she sat, bare feet folded again inside the lower edge of her quilt. "Thank you," she said finally, studying the young face of Dub Mueller. "You didn't by any chance also bring some purple flowers and leave them on the porch of my cabin today, did you?" Dub gave an embarrassed grin before turning and disappearing into the crowd. Joan pulled her shoes on, shaking her head. Had the boy taken these himself and then returned them, just to make her feel grateful, or just to have an excuse to talk to her?

"Mrs. Ryan." It was Cora Haskew addressing Joan directly, for almost the first time that evening. "Gavin Kidd took your shoes. That buffoon has the finesse of a sixth-grader." This unexpected barb by the quiet octogenarian broke the tension, and Joan and Dove burst into laughter. Cora's eyes twinkled. "Mr. *Kidd* is aptly named."

Joan's phone vibrated in her coat pocket as Blueberry Creek Band cranked up again. They weren't being stingy, but giving a full-length concert. Melinda was asking how the vacation was going. Was Joan having a restful time? "Restful? I guess." Joan texted back. She certainly had not exerted herself much. Except mentally. Her thumbs glided back and forth over the phone's letter bank. "Bluegrass band pretty awesome. Guitars, banjo, fiddle, drums. Sam would love them." Not too conspicuously, she hoped, she raised the device and took a quick photo of the band from her relatively close vantage point. "Here's a pic! Sorry to be taking the fun you were supposed to be having. I'll try to get you one of their CDs." The temptation struck to rattle off something, even something vague, about a new acquaintance having told her quite a story. She wrote three or four lines and then read over them. Secrecy was absolutely crucial, Dove believed. Joan went the way of caution and erased the message. "Going to check out the gen. store in the morning. More later."

She stowed the phone, not wanting to miss any more of the music. But her mind wandered, anyway. Sweet Melinda was sacrificially serving her extended family while Joan was here, having gladly seized the opportunity for leisure. *Oughtn't I to have insisted on going to lend two more helping hands, even though she assured me it wasn't necessary?* Then, there was this whole Newman thing. Joan pictured that elderly woman in Florida, bedridden, distraught as no mother should ever have to be, with Dove constantly by her side. Then, Dove had uprooted herself and come here to pursue her serious mission. Would she, Joan, be found doing the same? Making such a far detour from her own goals in order to fulfill a promise to someone who wasn't even a relative? Dove was indeed under a heavy burden. *A burden she has suddenly decided to unload on me. Why me?* People often found it easy to confess their deepest hurts and confusions, even their sins, to someone they didn't expect to see again. No names. Just a chance meeting, during an airplane ride, maybe. A desperate moment of venting to a total stranger with the hope that that person would provide a needed murmur of sympathy or a practical suggestion that hadn't been tried yet. In the midst of this "interlude" in Dove's life—a life that apparently was without family obligations like the ones Joan had—the young woman seemed to have found a present niche for herself in Crook Mountain. "I like it here," she had said this afternoon. If one was duty-bound, best to be so in a place one liked.

As if these serious ponderings weren't enough to distract her from what remained of the bluegrass, Joan noticed a hubbub across the way. Marilyn Mueller Walker was putting in a grand entrance very late in the game, as Gavin Kidd had done at lunchtime. Even over the music, Joan could hear Marilyn greeting Gavin, then the mayor, and then the Keys, all of whom were milling around on the periphery of the amphitheater. After dropping a few bills into the money box, Marilyn bent down and spoke to each of the Key children. Her pink top's neckline wasn't modest enough for children's eyes at that range. Joan sighed and was glad when the band announced they would be wrapping up with a couple of final numbers. It had been a very long day. Even so, she tapped her feet to *Earl's Breakdown,* a lively salute to Flatt and Scruggs. The closer was a gentler selection called *Memories of Maybelle.* The tune washed over Joan like a sweet sedative. There was no question about it. These musicians knew their stuff. *Life in a small town… Can't beat it!*

Chapter 6

Cross-legged in comfy pajamas on top of the bed, Joan sipped from a glass of the merlot she'd grabbed from home at the last minute, when packing. "Crook mountain general merchandise." The microphone on her tablet's keyboard took the words she spoke and typed them in the search field. She'd go there in the morning for more bottled water and some backup batteries for the camera. It never hurt to have a little advance info on a place one planned to visit. The store's name popped up in a short list of results, including the store's page, the Crook Mountain official page, and an independent business directory. The C.M.G.M. home page—well, *only* page—was pretty basic. A "glass brochure," her daughter would call it. No slide shows, no feeds, no share buttons. The predominant item was one large photo of the store's exterior, taken in autumn, the default season for mountain vacations. Below the banner picture were the street address and phone number, directions from Cluny's Ridge, and the words "Billy Oden, Prop."

Joan scrolled down to a filmstrip-style grid of pictures representing the range of goods for sale: staple groceries and produce; jeans and overalls; toys; flower and vegetable seeds; cookware; spades, shovels and power tools. Different in composition from all of the others, the far right picture was of five or six adults gathered around an old-fashioned metal Coca-Cola cooler supported by four legs. It was the kind powered by ice and human effort, not by electricity. Each person clutched a refreshing-looking soda in a glass bottle. Joan leaned closer, squinted, and then zoomed in the view. *Ah. Thought so.* One of the men grinning at the camera, and raising a bottle of orange soda as if in a toast, was Gavin Kidd. "And, on *that* note…" Joan swiped all apps closed and put the tablet away.

Ending a Sunday that in no way could have been called a day of rest, Joan slept, dreaming that she and Lee and Sam and April were listening to a bluegrass band in the Falcons football stadium. A woman seated just behind them and wearing a patchwork quilt as a shawl around her shoulders was crying and rocking her body forward and back. "My son is missing!" she moaned over and over again.

Next morning, with only the sun for an alarm clock, Joan stared absently at the open-beam ceiling. Twice now, Dove had recommended a visit to the home of Gerald and Edith Givens. Last night during the concert, she'd given Joan the address. Mr. Givens should be at work. A small potted plant would make a thoughtful gift for his wife. Or, maybe a jar of preserves, since it sounded as though the Givenses were well fixed for greenery by virtue of their own talents.

Joan pushed the covers back with the kind of sigh that meant "it's time to start another day whether I want to or not." Besides the Givenses' place, Dove had described a certain vantage point she wanted Joan not to miss on an unoccupied rental property. "You'll thank me once you've seen it," she'd insisted, to the point that Joan now had the keys to both the house and its padlocked gate on a key ring in her purse. Dove was acting as caretaker at the moment, watering the plants and checking to make sure no pipes had chosen to spring a leak. "If you'll let yourself in and water the plants for me Monday morning," was the proposition, "I'll gladly feed you lunch. And dinner! Most tourists interested in picture-taking would never have access to this view. What's the use of having a friend in town if it doesn't get you some advantage over the general population?"

"How do you know you can trust me with these keys? What if I were to go up there and rip the plants out of their pots, leave the water running, and spray-paint graffiti all over the walls?"

"I have more faith in my own judgment of character than that. How many people do you know who are registered dietitians, Ph.D.s, and sought-after lecturers living double lives as common vandals?" At Joan's questioning expression, Dove had shrugged and smiled. "I Googled you."

Once dressed for the day, Joan broke her fast with granola-topped yogurt, a banana nut muffin, and more Sumatran Sizzle. She sent Lee a quick "good morning" text and attached a "selfie" with her lips pursed as if in a kiss for him. His reply pinged in a few seconds later. Good. They each knew the other was alive and well. She pulled on sturdy and stylish cross-trainers and scooped up the matching jacket that completed the ensemble of kiwi green jogging pants and sleeveless, white knit top. *Now, just in case any next-door neighbors named Mueller come wandering up here...* She double-checked the security alarm and headed out.

⟫◆⟪

True to its representation on the internet, Crook Mountain General Merchandise was the go-to for just about everything from applesauce to zinnias. Joan found her water, batteries, and hostess gift along shelves of canned goods, stationery, kerosene lamps, gardening supplies, and clothing. At the counter, a balding, middle-aged man turned each of her selections over in his hands. He wasn't looking for the barcodes to scan. He was reading actual printed prices off actual stick-on tags. One by one, he listed Joan's purchases by item name and amount on the top sheet of a pad of lined paper. Then, he punched each price on a small calculator. Joan watched as he multiplied the subtotal by one-point-something to add the sales tax. This man wouldn't come in first place, or even fifth, in a competition for speediest cashier. *I guess it helps to pass his day, each sale being such a long process.* With customers he knew, and that probably described most of them, there surely was homespun talk that made the ordeal last even longer. Only, everyday conversation wouldn't be an ordeal to longtime friends. It would be life.

Joan paid, and the man said, "Thank yeh kindly."

"Are you Mr. Oden?" Joan smiled warmly and introduced herself, then asked permission to leave her car parked in that lot during her walk, tacking on a word of thanks for his having allowed public parking there during the concert. Then, finished with doing ninety percent of the talking, she left. If Proprietor Billy Oden *was* given to homespun talk to pass the slow hours in a slow town, he'd been acting out of character with her.

She set her purchases in the floor of the car where they wouldn't be in the sun. Spying some pretty wildflowers at the end of the park opposite the amphitheater, she headed straight for them and snapped several pictures. Then, ready for some honest-to-goodness exercise, she set out jogging on Main Street and on down toward the highway that had brought her into town. It would be about a mile round trip from the general store to Mueller's Garage, but she would turn back before reaching the garage. A warm fifteen minutes later, she drank deeply of her water and used a small towel to wipe the perspiration off her face as she sat in her driver's seat with that door, plus a window on the passenger side, open to encourage a breeze. Next, it was off to the cabin for a quick shower and change of clothes before running Dove's house-sitting errand and then meeting her for lunch.

Navigating the old-fashioned way seemed more in keeping with the remote setting around here. Joan went by Dove's instructions and watched for a white mailbox on a bright red post. It proved easy to spot. She wheeled the Honda onto a well-shaded gravel driveway—*of course, more gravel*—and slowed it to a crawl in anticipation of the barrier several yards ahead. With the lock undone and the metal bar moved aside, she pulled ahead, stopped again, and got out to reposition the long, yellow-painted bar and lock it. That seemed the cautious thing to do. *The times we live in.* After all of that effort, however, she ultimately decided to walk, not drive, up. And "up" was the word! Good. Exercise was one of her big goals for the day. Her sturdy sneakers prevented all missteps but a skid or two, and a large, brick house finally came into view. It was situated serenely, and aspects of the yard resembled the McCain cabin. Maybe the same people had landscaped both places. On the porch were a couple of rocking chairs and some of the plants she had agreed to water. She went right to that task, finding the wherewithal just where Dove had said. The interior looked new, clean, and tastefully decorated. Not rustic. The three-bedroom house would make a very comfy rental for a family group or a girlfriends' getaway.

Out back, through a clearing at the edge of the high property, a classic red barn was visible down a ways. A scattering of cows stood as motionless as the barn. This would be east, and the hills stretching far beyond would ultimately be western North Carolina. The blue nuances of the Smoky Mountain ridges were, in a word, majestic. Joan aimed the camera and snapped while knowing that the view was one that a camera could never capture adequately. She spent a few more minutes drinking it in with the lenses of her two eyes.

To the south, those eyes were arrested just as effectively, but by scenery very different. The clutter of rubbish and rusty metal strewn across a fenced-in, overgrown lot was in such stark contrast to the earlier beauty, it was almost physically dismaying. Wasn't there a feel-good chick flick a few years ago, where the main character chose household and industrial garbage as her specialty photography subject? The photographer hoped that players in the fine art world would notice her unique work and that gallery patrons viewing the pictures full of "subtext" would be moved to take better care of the earth.

This junkyard was behind a somewhat dilapidated building. It was crawling with high weeds, not just because recent spring showers had caused everything with chlorophyll to be "busting out all over," but from apparent, extended neglect. Large, rusty odds and ends, piles of old tires, and old cars in part or in whole littered the space. Was that a 1970s Chevy Nova, its signature broad, flat trunk lid all rusty?

A relatively clean-looking pale green cover was fitted over the shape of another automobile. It appeared to have shiny, new hubcaps. Instead of resting in the high grass, this car was on a platform of plywood sheets. *Hey. Wait a second.* Joan glanced around her. Grasping a sturdy branch of the nearest likely tree for climbing, she hoisted herself up, thankful for all of that diligent strength training with weights. Just a little higher. Now, she could see the upper edge of a sign attached to the front of the corrugated steel building. She'd seen that weathered sign before. This junkyard was the back side of Mueller's Garage.

As if on cue, Dub Mueller appeared, striding across the cluttered lot with more purpose than Joan had seen him exhibit at any other time. He went to the front of the covered car and began peeling the tarp back. Whereas, before, he'd been walking with some speed, he now appeared to be moving almost in slow motion. Although his back was to Joan now, she supposed that the young man was acting with a deliberate lack of haste so he could admire every successive inch of the automobile. She imagined an expression of delight on his face. She knew a little about how men sometimes felt toward their cars.

This automobile was a dark color. The distance and the sun's glare made it impossible to tell if the paint was black, or else midnight blue or dark green. *Green?* That color had been mentioned sometime yesterday. Something green on one of the food tables after church had been referred to as Dub's favorite color. Joan kept watching. Dub was folding the protective tarp now. *Folding* it. Not bunching it up. Next, he didn't toss it aside, but *set* it aside. He'd handled the cloth reverently, as one might do the white covering from the Lord's Supper table or the flag that had been draped over a departed one's casket.

He wiped the soles of his shoes with a large, blue rag before opening the driver's door and seating himself behind the steering wheel. The car's model wasn't distinct enough to identify from this distance. It was a sedan. It did look newer rather than older, and that right there would explain the special care it evidently warranted. Joan pulled her camera up by its strap and peered into the viewfinder, pulling on the zoom lever. The car's radio was on now, turned up loud enough for the sound to carry that far. It was talk, with music underneath. Probably a commercial. Now, the windshield wipers were moving back and forth over washer fluid. The driver's door had stayed open this whole time, and Dub moved his hands over the steering wheel as one might caress the fur of a beloved dog or cat. If the Muellers had any pets at home, they wouldn't likely be lap dogs. Just a guess.

A text message alert vibrated. Checking her phone, Joan was suddenly very aware of how uncomfortable she was, perched a bit contortedly in the tree. *Yeah. I'm in a tree in Tennessee—that sounds like a country music line—in my khaki capris, spying on someone through my zoom lens. Stories to tell the folks back home.* Carefully she climbed down, then shook her muscles out gingerly, crossed the yard, slipped a little on the gravel's downward slope, and headed to her next appointment. She soon passed the front of Mueller's Garage. If Dub's impairment, whatever it actually was, kept him from passing the standardized driver licensing test, maybe he had a special car of his own, nonetheless, just to play with. And, licensed or not, he obviously drove the family truck sometimes.

When Joan arrived for lunch, she studied the exterior of Crook Mountain Church in the Wildwood again. There was at least one good camera angle she'd missed on Friday evening, but Dove was already waiting for her there in the parking lot. Joan commented on the apparent amount of food as she took some of the bundles Dove was pulling from the back seat of her car. "Enough for four," was all Dove answered.

Joan followed as they carried the food inside and down a corridor toward the social hall. Who were the other two going to be? The Givenses? As they passed the open door of a lighted room, Joan glanced over. Someone was working at a computer. "Wasn't that Bonnie?"

"That's right." Dove stopped and turned around. "Let's make a short detour by the library." She stepped in and greeted Bonnie. Joan did the same. "Bonnie is Cora's able assistant."

As if summoned by the sound of her name, Cora Haskew appeared from behind a shelf of books. "Indeed, she is. I dread the day some clever employer snaps this one up for a full-time job. For now, she's busy *almost* full-time helping her mama take care of five younger brothers and sisters. Bonnie, would you help

Dove take the food and things down the hall? I'd like to show our new friend my pride and joy."

"Yes, ma'am." The slender girl lifted her fingers from the computer's mouse, took Joan's load from her, and followed Dove out.

"That nineteen-year-old is a sharp young lady. Computers are just a little over my head still, but I aim to learn. Bonnie is using this one for research when there's not much library work to be done." Joan glanced around. There shouldn't be much library work to be done in so small an operation. But, that was probably naïve. A certain amount of administration was necessary everywhere. "She doesn't have the resources at home. Or the quiet. She is going to join us for lunch, and I want her to tell you about her project. But, first, a quick tour for you."

The church library might be a comparatively small shop, but the responsibility for it was something Miss Cora Haskew obviously took seriously. She briefly explained what holdings were kept where, and how the church went about acquiring materials at the lowest possible cost. Then she opened a file cabinet drawer and brought out a blue folder. Cora opened the folder and tapped the topmost typewritten page, which identified the work as the memoir of Mildred Cantrell. "This is a store of Appalachian history, written by a former schoolteacher of mine. You are not the first visitor to whom I have shown this prized possession, Mrs. Ryan, and I trust you will not be the last. The words in these pages are my heritage as a highlander—a picture of life in these hills when things were slower and simpler. A time long gone, I'm afraid." Cora gestured toward a reading table. "Please."

Joan accepted the folder and sat down dutifully. Carefully handling the historic resource, she turned the title page over and soon caught unusual words like "clannish" (used to describe the southern highlands settlers that came mostly from Scotland and

Ireland) and phrases like "dry humor and gunpowder tempers, and pure water, pure air, and a far view from the front porch." It was poetic. She asked Cora if the document was published.

"No, but it needs to be. I believe Bonnie is going to get it scanned and offered to a larger library, where folks who are more connected can get it 'out there'."

"Good. I'm all for history of this kind getting out there. I hope the school children of Crook Mountain are aware of this. I can just see them being assigned to draw pictures based on these descriptions!"

"I have read from the pages of this folder to them myself, and will do so for as long as I am able and welcome to."

Joan read on, a glance or two at Cora telling her the older woman was pleased. But Joan wasn't reading just to be polite. She was a voracious learner. She smiled at descriptions of "homes hidden deep in the hollow," people who were "lovers of song and respecters of God," and homesteaders making their own sweetening (not "sweetener") using a sorghum press, as opposed to buying white sugar. The writer, a teacher who had been a key influence during Cora's formative years, told how the eventual influx of store-bought goods led some of the mountain dwellers to feel embarrassed about their homemade clothing and hand-wrought furniture and housewares. But tourists admired and coveted items like handmade quilts and weavings, and home-forged ironwork—*We still do!*—so much that the artisan products of the highlanders came back into popularity. Out came looms and bellows again, though modern machinery and the availability of manufactured goods had made their use optional. "You really do have a treasure here, Cora, and what a gift that you knew this woman personally!" It was probably time they should go find the others, but Joan lingered over the memoir a little longer. County and federal farm agents, Miss Cantrell had written, had encouraged growers to rotate crops and to plant "cover crops" that would be plowed under to replenish the earth so that "the soil farmed today will be rich and sweet for the farmer's sons."

After returning the file to its place, Cora walked Joan to the social hall and invited her to share the task of filling four cups with ice. Having an inside track by virtue of her position as church librarian, Cora had squirreled away and now produced a few servings of dessert left from the potluck: banana pudding, brownies, and apple pie.

Shy Bonnie Jarvis was plainly dressed but a natural beauty. She hadn't the advantages of expensive cosmetics and more stylish cuts in clothing, but she had great skin (from the pure, mountain air?), inquisitive eyes, a pretty smile, and a sweet voice. Joan looked from young Bonnie to elderly Cora, and then to Dove. In this unlikely foursome it was plain that true beauty was less about physical features, makeup, and wardrobe, and more about the glow that comes from a kind spirit, confidence, humor, love of life, a desire for knowledge, and dedication to worthwhile purposes.

"This clever young lady is putting together a program on identifying this area's foliage," Dove bragged on Bonnie. "It will be used this summer at a day camp for children over near Ellis Creek. It's great that people around here are starting to discover her abilities. And children love her!"

Bonnie looked pleased yet embarrassed by the praise. "That last part comes easy, what with havin' a house full o' young'uns t' help mama with."

Joan contributed to the topic a mention of the mimosa she'd seen so much of. Back in Georgia, too, it thrived along the interstates and in woodsy side or back yards except where people chose not to encourage it. Mimosa was also called silk tree, Bonnie told them. It tended to take over, and she didn't care much for it. "There're prettier things that th' mimosa likes t' crowd out."

The talk got around to Dub's favorite color with a little help from Joan, who brought it up casually on the heels of the plant topic. "Speaking of everything being so green…" She winced at the lameness of her transition. "Wasn't there something here yesterday in a green dish? I overheard someone say it was somebody else's favorite color, but I didn't know who they were talking about."

Bonnie lifted her head, but she didn't say anything until after Cora encouraged her with a small nod. It was Dub who was partial to that color, Bonnie said, "even when it comes t' pickin' out a bar of soap at the store." Joan smiled. *Irish Spring, then, maybe.* She loved guessing games. The green container was a crock pot of chili brought by Edith Givens. Cora said Edith had a soft spot in her heart for the twins, particularly since the death of their mother, and because Gerald and Edith never had any children of their own. "It wasn't only the color that's a favorite with Dub. Edith's chili is, too."

Over dessert, Joan asked 'of anyone who might know the answer, "Does Dub have a driver's license?"

"He ain't got any license," Bonnie said quietly. "But 'is daddy lets 'im drive that ol' truck sometimes."

"Coffee, anyone?" Dove went for the carafe and brought it over with some Styrofoam cups. "Tell us about your morning, Joan."

"Well, I took some pictures of the wildflowers at the park."

Surprisingly, Bonnie spoke right up. "One o' my brothers helped plant 'em. It was a school project."

Joan nodded and praised the work. "Before that, I browsed through the general store and went for a good run."

Dove said *she* needed to do more jogging—or walking, at least—being around so much good food all the time.

"You're too good a cook for your own good?" Joan kidded her.
"Could be!"

But Dove's weight didn't look to be a problem. Like most
people, all she probably needed for better overall health was
to step it up a little with regard to exercise, moderation in diet,
and common sense when it came to portion sizes. There was
something else of greater interest that Dove could probably shed
light on, namely that awkward moment on Sunday night when
Jesse Mueller had looked daggers at them, but, with Bonnie sitting
here, now might not be the time to bring that up. So, Joan said,
"And I dutifully watered all those plants you're looking after."

Dove coughed. She coughed some more, then scooted her
chair back and sputteringly apologized, saying some of her coffee
had gone down the wrong way. Cora reached over to rap Dove
firmly on the back a few times. Funny. Dove had drained her
small Styrofoam cup a little bit ago, right after she'd mentioned
jogging. Now, she was up. She gathered what she could in one
load of the plates, coffee cups, and the pans of pasta and salad
she'd brought from the Diner. Joan did the same, followed by
Bonnie, and then by Cora.

"Four ate. Four clean up! I raised my children on that." Joan
offered the small talk, underneath it wondering what was so
secret about her going over to water plants that Dove had had to
cover it up with a fake coughing fit.

Chapter 7

Bonnie and Cora returned to the library, and Dove showed Joan into the pastor's reception parlor. Was Reverend Kirkpatrick in his office? Dove said he wasn't, Monday being his regular weekday off. "We can talk freely here." She shut the door.

"Obviously, there's something about my going up to check on that house for you that you wanted to hush up. For whose sake? Bonnie's? Or Cora's?"

"Bonnie's."

"Why?"

"I'll get to that. But first, I want to hear about your errand. I suppose all was quiet at the house. No evidence of water leaks, nothing else unusual?"

"Nothing at all." Joan sat in one of the two wingback chairs upholstered in a woven, maroon fabric. "You didn't send me there expecting me to encounter something unusual, did you? To stumble upon a hidden passageway you've never found yourself, where a dead body just happens to have been hidden, maybe?"

Dove took a seat in the matching chair. "Of course not. It's just that I accepted a responsibility to keep an eye on the house while it's vacant. Incidentally, it and your cabin are owned by the same people. Serena Stillman and her husband. Serena and I have become friends even though she was married and living away before I moved here. Her father connected us, us being similar in age."

"Well, if she's the one who decorated or landscaped either or both places, you can tell her I said she has good taste."

"I'll do that. And the yard, and the lot—did you find that amazing view I wanted you to see, off to the east?"

"I did. I took some pictures I hope are good, though I'm not a good enough photographer to do the subject justice. My friend Melinda will enjoy them. She'll be glad I got to see that view. That's the way Melinda is, not begrudging of it when someone else is benefited instead of her."

"The world needs more like her, then."

"I ran across another interesting view, to the south." Joan paused for effect. "Quite a sentimental little love scene."

"Really? Some picnicking couple on a blanket in a clearing, thinking they were the only people in the world?"

"No. This love scene was between a young man and a car."

Dove blinked. "Okay…that sounds weird."

"Well, not so weird when you consider it was our young mechanic friend, Dub, out behind Mueller's Garage."

"Behind the garage? I thought they worked on most cars inside the building."

Dove's tone sounded normal enough, but Joan was trained to notice nuances of facial expression and body language. This conversation was increasing in significance to the other party. Dove hadn't expressed any surprise that Mueller's Garage was visible from the elevation of that lot. "If you've been up there yourself, which, of course, you have, and if you've seen down to Mueller's Garage from there, maybe you've noticed this car yourself. Assuming it's not a brand-new arrival, that is. Who knows? All I can say for sure is, from the way Dub uncovered it and treated it, he is very enthralled with it."

"You saw him *uncover it?* This *has* to be providential! In all this time, I've never seen it, but *you,* on just your third day in town..."

Joan needed no more convincing that Dove had a very particular interest in said car, and that the car had been there for some time. "Yes, I watched him peel the tarp off, sit inside the car, listen to the radio, run the wipers, and caress the steering wheel."

Dove leaned forward and lowered her voice a shade. "Joan, this is *really, really* important. Please tell me everything you can about what you saw. Every detail you can remember about that car."

Joan described the dark color. Dark green, maybe, but it had been impossible to tell, even through the zoom lens. The hubcaps looked to be sporty add-ons, but the make and model hadn't been identifiable. "It was a two-door, though." The door had looked abnormally long when Dub had swung it open.

There were several adjectives Joan might have scribbled down about her companion if participating in a first-impressions exercise prepared by a group facilitator: Intelligent. Patient. Good-humored. "Excitable" wouldn't have made the list. Until now. Dove was leaning forward, literally sitting on the edge of her seat. "Don't go anywhere." Her tone was urgent. "I'll be right back. I have to go see Cora for just a second." She hurried out of the parlor, slowing down only enough to shut the door quietly behind her.

Joan took the opportunity to stretch her legs, examining the small room from every angle. A stack of blue paper cards rested on a polished table along with a box of facial tissue, a copy of the Bible, and an assortment of small pamphlets intended to help those going through different crises: divorce, grief, loss of income, serious illness. Joan took a card off the stack. *How may we pray for you?* was its heading. Below that, in smaller type: *We are pleased to join you in praying for specific needs.* There were blanks for one to describe a need, plus a checkbox to indicate whether the request was confidential or not, and a line, marked "optional," for the name of the person completing the card. The hint was pretty clear, that anyone using one of these forms ought to be participating in the praying instead of expecting other people to do all of it. It might be good to write Melinda's sister-in-law's situation on a card and turn it in. Joan wasn't sure she could hold up her end of the implied bargain, though. Besides, hadn't both Sherry Kirkpatrick and the hairdresser already told her the church would be praying for Catherine? Joan put the card back. Sitting down again, she pulled a powder compact out, but now Dove was back, picking right back up as if she'd never left the room. "Let me ask you something." She sat. "If you were trying to disguise a white car, might it be a very natural decision to paint it a dark color?"

"That sounds like most people's first impulse, yes. Unless you knew that anyone looking for the car would *expect* you to do that, and so you would do something different, like paint it tan or light blue."

"Precisely. *But,* if you were *simple-minded…*" Dove let her sentence hang unfinished. Her eyes were wide. Her palms rested flat on the tops of her thighs.

"You might go for the dark," Joan finished for her in a bland tone. "Dark *green,* maybe, especially if green was your favorite color. Is that what you're getting at?"

Dove nodded. "I just pulled Cora aside to hear her say what kind of car the late Mrs. Mueller drove. Sarah Mueller drove a Ford Taurus. A four-door sedan, about ten years old. It was gold. This is information I already looked into, naturally, but I just asked her again, to be absolutely sure. Cora has sharp eyes and a sharp memory, you know."

"What's your point, Dove?"

"I asked you to go up there this morning on the excuse of checking the house and watering the plants. I was hoping, *praying*, you would see something helpful to me. Yes, I've been up there several times, but, short of standing on that hillside day in and day out with binoculars, or being able to set up a surveillance camera, there's little chance for me to get such a break myself. I've seen that car, but always covered. For all I knew, it was Sarah Mueller's gold Taurus. It would be just like the Muellers to make her car a kind of shrine to her memory. All of them miss her terribly. But, from what you're telling me, it can't possibly be or ever *have* been a four-door Taurus. But it *could be* Larry Newman's two-door Mercedes."

"Sure. I mean, I guess it could be. But why *would* it be? Why would these people have the missing man's car? Would they have killed him in order to steal the car? Why not just steal the car and hide it or change its color, and let the owner use his insurance to get *another* car? Mechanics ought to be good at breaking into cars. Do you seriously think these Muellers are *murderers?*" Joan wasn't trying much to mask her incredulity. Who could possibly take such a notion seriously? And, if they did ("they" being Dove), why were they living and working and going to church side by side with suspected dangerous felons? If there were any real evidence, any solid grounds for suspicion, why weren't the Feds all over the Muellers' home and place of business with search warrants? Joan sensed Dove's desperation and pitied her. She *must* be desperate to be entertaining such unlikely notions. What stress the young woman was living under! Joan checked her attitude and assumed a gentler tone. "Why don't you tell me about Harriet Newman?"

Dove told more of the story. She'd come to live with Mrs. Newman about three and a half years ago because the woman had begun to need personal help that was impractical for her son, living away, to try to provide himself. Larry was devoted to his mother, though, and checked on her frequently, seeing to it that she had all she needed in terms of medical care, daily necessities, and little extras. "He had put an ad in the paper for a live-in caregiver, and I interviewed. I was a good fit for Harriet, Larry said later, my being a good cook, and kind and caring."

"I can see all of that. So, you spent some time with the son?"

"Yes, I saw him just a few times after I took the job. He would come for short visits. I cooked for them. Well, for the three of us."

Had Dove fallen for the man, maybe? Was it that, as well as her promise to his mother, that was fueling her search? Maybe the two had e-mailed frequently about Harriet. People sometimes formed attachments that way, unfolding their personalities freely and growing to depend on each other's sense of humor. "And he went missing when?"

"Two years ago in January. Naturally, a missing-person report was filed right away. After that, Harriet died, and I closed up her house and ended up here."

"What record is there of Larry's movements on the day he was last seen?"

"He left Cincinnati, where he lived, and was headed home to Florida. It wasn't a birthday or a holiday, just a convenient time in his schedule. It would have been a two-day trip. He was coming through Tennessee and had intended to stop in Cluny's Ridge, and *did* stop there, if a certain shopkeeper told the truth the first time he gave a statement. The police have records of Larry's credit card transactions. He bought gas in Lexington, Kentucky, and a meal in Knoxville. And he made a purchase in Cluny's Ridge. A Mr. Coffey first confirmed having seen Larry in his store, but later he retracted that, saying he couldn't be sure."

The shopkeeper, Neal Coffey, had been rather self-important while being interviewed by reporters, Dove said. He claimed to have seen Newman and maybe to have been the last person to see him alive. "Not too bright, if you ask me. Who would make a big show of having been the last person to see another person alive? On TV, isn't that usually the person who ends up being arrested on suspicion of murder?"

"Yes, until a Jessica Fletcher or a Hannah Swensen outshines the authorities by exposing the *real* murderer."

"Hannah Swensen! I like her. Cute movies those books have been made into. Yes, maybe Hannah would have weaseled the truth out of Coffey after bribing him with jam tarts or mint cream bon bons. Anyway, whatever his reason was, Coffey changed his story, saying he'd gotten carried away by being in the spotlight, which caused him to sound more certain of the facts than he really had been. He said he thought it was possible someone else had found or stolen Newman's credit card somewhere along the way."

"Then he's admitting to not asking for a picture I.D. before approving the sale. Or, he's admitting to having a poor memory for faces. But are you saying that some or all of the *Muellers* might have done this? And that for some reason this Coffey can't or won't identify *them* as having been in his shop using Newman's credit card? Why the Muellers, if Newman's trail can't be shown to have come to this town?" Dove might be wanting to fulfill her promise so badly that she would believe anything, would invent an answer out of a clear blue mountain sky.

"January a year ago, on the anniversary of the disappearance, a news story about the case aired on TV while I was at work. Later, I found the same story on the station's website and printed it." Dove reached to the foot of her chair and picked up her large, yellow handbag. Setting it on her lap, she unzipped an interior section and pulled a folded piece of copy paper out. She handed the page to Joan.

"It was one year ago in January that a Missing Person report was filed on Clarence 'Larry' Dean Newman," Joan read aloud, "last known to be driving from Cincinnati, Ohio, to Vero Beach, Florida, with a planned stop in Cluny's Ridge, Tennessee. Newman did not reach his destination, and reports of his being seen in Cluny's Ridge have proved unreliable. No traces of Newman or of his white 2010 Mercedes CL550 have been found." There were a few more lines about Newman's tenure with the same company, his general physical description, and his address in Cincinnati. Then, "Persons with information are urged to contact authorities in Cincinnati or Vero Beach."

"When this report aired on TV, Jesse, Luke, and Dub were in the Diner. There was a definite reaction on their part. Jesse saw to it that they got quiet in a hurry. And then they left."

"Did you report that to anyone?"

"No."

"Why not?"

"At first, I guess I was acting like one of those TV or storybook detectives we were just talking about. I wanted to solve the mystery without help." *Right. Hannah Swensen with a dark wig. Even the diner part fits! A diner and a bakery are almost the same.* "I checked the same leads as the police and came up empty. I moved into Cora's house because that just fell into my lap while I was exploring the area. Rent is high in Cluny's Ridge. Then, after the TV thing and how the Muellers reacted, I couldn't help but begin to believe I was led to *this* town instead of that one or any other. As for my not reporting what I suspect, well...the longer I stayed here, the more stories I heard about the Muellers. You'd have to be very sure you wanted to cross them—well, not the boys so much, but their father." Dove lowered her voice almost to a whisper. "Jesse Mueller is rumored to have killed his late wife's oncologist by running him off the road."

What kind of a town have I landed myself in? This has to be my punishment for not refusing the cabin and going to help Melinda. "Rumored by whom?"

"Well, I doubt anyone could tell us, now, where or when the rumor started. You know how things get around."

"And how things get *exaggerated.*"

Dove shrugged and looked a little deflated by what Joan had just said. "I know how all of this must sound, but I don't mind telling you, I *am* afraid of Jesse Mueller."

"What about the daughter? Miss 'welcoming committee'?"

"Marilyn does have a mean streak, like her father, but I don't have a clue whether she would be in on whatever the others might know. She was away with her husband—now ex-husband—at the time Larry disappeared. But I believe her fully capable of concealing something like this if she does know. People do what they have to do. Would you or I necessarily turn a relative in? How do we know *what* we'd do?"

"If you truly think the Muellers are dangerous, maybe you should talk to the authorities, then get out of town fast."

"But I made a promise."

"What exactly *did* you promise?"

"To do my best to find out what happened to Larry."

"Does anyone suppose he simply wanted out of his responsibility to his ailing mother, after being tied down so long with her health issues and, I assume, handling all her financial business, and he just went away? No foul play? I mean, he drove a pretty sporty car. Maybe he was in his first or second midlife crisis and just decided he'd had enough. Wanted more freedom." This explanation sounded at least as plausible as murder did. "What kind of company was Harriet?

What did she do in her younger years?" If the woman had been tiresome to be around, if she had been crotchety and cantankerous, that might support the theory that her son had simply ditched her.

"I don't believe for a minute that Larry abandoned his mother—and his home, and his job. No one who knew him seems to think that. I interviewed people who worked with him. Harriet was very dependent on others, but with me there, Larry was able to let go of most of the caregiving. He *loved* his mother. It wasn't that he merely felt obligated to try to make her happy and comfortable. To me, at least, he seemed *glad* to do that. After all, Harriet was *his* only family, too. She was a stay-at-home mother most of her adult life, but worked some as a tour guide and a secretary. Near the end, she had the usual aches and pains and fears of old age, but to my knowledge she always kept her complaints to herself when her son visited."

That seemed to shoot down the abandonment theory, all right. Joan shifted her weight and glanced at the time. If Newman had had a good-paying sales job for a long time with the same company, it did seem unlikely he would leave that without a word to anyone. It wouldn't be like him, everyone connected to him had said, according to Dove. And to not even come to the funeral after his mother died? To not claim his inheritance, whatever it amounted to? "You said Larry expected to be on the road two days." Joan was still trying to get the whole picture, trying to see any obvious angle that hadn't been covered. But, if two women could sit here and think of something in twenty minutes that had gone overlooked for two years, her confidence in police work was going to plummet.

"He had a hotel reservation in Atlanta in order to break up the trip. It would have been another eight-hour drive the next day to Vero Beach."

"Some people might have flown instead of driving such a long way. Was Larry scared of flying?"

"Not scared, to hear Harriet tell it. Of course, she wouldn't be the first doting mother to shy away from admitting her beloved son was afraid of something. I think he was just accustomed to driving a lot in his work and didn't especially care for flying."

Joan angled her head and grinned, raising her eyebrows. "Yeah, well, if *I* drove a Mercedes, I might feel the same way!"

Dove laughed with her. "Harriet knew he would be traveling close enough to stop off in Cluny's Ridge and asked him to take a few photos there to bring and show to her."

"That sounds odd." *And demanding?*

"Well, it had been a favorite spot in her younger years. It's where she and her husband spent their honeymoon. And it was pretty plain she would never be well enough to see it again in person."

"And why have you suddenly chosen to confide all of this in *me*, a complete stranger? Especially since you believe secrecy is so vital?"

"It wasn't a sudden decision. I've been waiting for the right person to come along. Someone who can help me in just the right way. I believe you're that person, Joan." Dove shook her head. "I'm not sure I can explain why, so that it would make sense."

The whole scenario sounded absurd. This was the twenty-first century, when murder, kidnapping, and other major crimes were investigated by competent professionals in federal agencies, not covered up in mom and pop towns by power-hungry officials or by citizens who intimidated other citizens. Right? "What could *I* possibly do to help?" Couldn't Dove see how silly her request was? "I'm headed out of here on Thursday. Unless you think there's something I can do from home. I'm not sure I have the kind of connections to put a fire under law enforcement officers."

Dove sighed. "If you want to help, I think a way of helping will present itself if we put our heads together. Working alone, I feel I've run into a stone wall."

Joan shifted her weight again. It was time to wrap this interview up. "Look, Dove, I really should be going." *Didn't I say the same thing to her just yesterday?* "I need to head back to my place and clear my head, check in with Lee, and figure out what I'm doing the rest of the evening." The visit she had expected to work in, with Edith Givens, wasn't going to happen today.

"I understand. But maybe we can talk about it more, later?"

"Maybe. Just tell me one more thing. Does anyone else in Crook Mountain or Cluny's Ridge know why you came here and what you suspect?" Dove had said she'd been working on the matter alone, but that didn't necessarily mean she hadn't ever told some or all of the story to anyone else.

"Cora knows. She's the only other one who knows my whole story, but even with her support, I haven't made any real progress. You might say my efforts have gone dormant. However, Cora and I believe Bonnie Jarvis is going to be a key, ultimately. That's why it's really helpful to me that Cora and Bonnie spend time together. Cora and I are trying to gradually build our rapport with her in the hope that she will come to understand that if she wants a future with Luke Mueller, she needs to find out if he's involved in this case. If he's an innocent bystander, and Dub or Jesse, or both, have done something criminal, Luke needs to stop believing he's required to help cover it up just because they are family and because his father rules with such an iron hand. He might think he's doing the honorable thing *now*, but will it serve him in the long run?"

⊲◆⊳

The aroma of the beef tenderloin in its red wine sauce was mouthwatering as well as comforting. Joan stirred the wild rice and snuffed the gas heat under the broccoli, which was steamed and ready. Cooking was such a great "unwinder"! Dove liked cooking, too. Maybe it was Dove's "happy place," her anchor cord of solace in a world that was otherwise rather out of control. Joan ate her meal slowly, savoring each bite. Then, after putting the kitchen to rights, she sat on one chair and propped her feet, one at a time, on another, to touch up her toenail polish. She stroked on a single extra coat of the same bright pink that was wearing off at the tips. It wasn't a very neat job, but she followed the pink with a coat of clear hardening glaze so her sloppy paint job would at least stay on well. With an exaggerated sense of accomplishment, then, she rewarded herself with part of the thick slice of mint chocolate chip fudge from Saturday's visit to a Cluny's Ridge confectioner. Luxuriating in the smooth decadence on her tongue, she messaged Lee to see if he could talk for a few minutes on FaceTime. *Yay! He said yes.* Joan initiated the connection and grinned at her sweetie when his face came up. "Hey, there!"

"Hello, yourself, gorgeous."

"Look what I'm indulging in." She showed him the fudge and described the meal she had just cooked. Lee told her not to be too smug, that the seafood feast *he* had just had was…well—he summarized it by simply kissing his fingertips and patting his stomach. Joan's dream from Sunday night came back to her again. "Oh! I just remembered something. After hearing that bluegrass band last night, I had a crazy dream." What it was about the present conversation that had triggered the memory, she couldn't imagine. Maybe just seeing Lee's face.

"Should I be jealous? Was a good-looking drummer the subject of your dream?"

"No, sweetie. The only good-looking drummer who has *my* heart is our son, who is as handsome as his father. In my dream, you, me, and the kids were seeing this band in concert. Not *this* band, the one that played *here,* but *a* band. They were playing in the new Atlanta stadium. It was a sellout crowd, and we were sitting up high." More details were coming back now. "Sam was holding a giant cup of Coke." Joan and Lee both laughed. That part was true to life. Then Joan relived turning around and watching the quilt-wrapped old woman rocking back and forth, wailing, "My son is missing!" Her own son Sam, who in the dream had been grinning over a Coca-Cola and watching a pro work a set of drums he could identify by brand name and probably by part numbers... What if *he* were missing? What anguish it would be if she didn't know his whereabouts. Or April's.

"Something wrong?" The distortion of the video connection apparently didn't hide that her expression had gone distant and somber.

"Sorry." Joan looked at Lee, and somehow the sweetness of the love they shared made her dream, and the real-life missing-person case that had triggered it, all the more sad. "I was remembering more of that dream. It took a sad turn. And it's connected to something that really happened, according to a woman I've met here. Dove. I've mentioned her." Lee nodded. "She says she came here for the sole purpose of fulfilling a promise to a dying woman in Florida. Dove was her caregiver. She promised to try to find out what happened to the woman's son, who went missing two years ago. And the whole thing is supposed to be a deep, dark secret, for fear of this one family of garage mechanics here in town that she thinks has the man's missing Mercedes hidden away and might have killed him in order to get it."

"Wow."

"I know! It sounds completely crazy. And *Dove* doesn't seem crazy, aside from this. She seems very smart, in general. I can't help admiring the commitment she made. It just seems she's been moving really slowly on it. What hope does she have of keeping that promise, trying to solve a case the authorities haven't been able to? I mean, really. What are the odds?"

"That's a tough one. A promise to 'try' isn't easy to gauge. You can't assign a number or a percentage to 'doing your best.' Statements like that are always thrown out when you sit through a class on how to set good goals."

"I love it when you talk like an engineer." And she did.

"Still, her commitment is admirable, as you said. I'd like to think that any of us would try our best to keep such a serious promise, provided we had taken careful thought before giving it."

"The woman depended on Dove like a daughter, with her own son living far away. Dove probably felt a similar attachment. *Her* parents live out of the country, and she isn't married. Has no children. At least, that's what I assume."

"Yeah. Well, as I said, it's admirable."

"She asked me to help her." Joan finally got around to the point on which she wanted Lee's input.

"She *is* desperate, isn't she?"

"Very funny."

"What did you say to her? Do you think you *can* help her?"

"I don't have any idea how, at the moment. I'm happy to give it some thought and offer her any suggestions I can, I guess."

"Sure. Why not? I think solving a missing-person mystery sounds just up your alley. You've risen to a lot of other challenges." Joan smiled, immediately picturing her first and only skydiving experience, on her fortieth birthday. That was a very different sort of challenge from this one. "If it's another brain she needs for the task, she couldn't get a sharper one than yours, honey. You're a born problem-solver."

"Flatterer." Was Lee serious? Did he truly think she'd be phoning him in a couple of days to say that the Newman case had been cracked wide open, due in large part to her logic, fortitude, and luck? Or was he just making light conversation? Maybe he was praising her sharp intellect mainly because he was missing her.

Later, in bed, Joan couldn't keep from thinking on the unthinkable again. How terrible it would be if Sam or April disappeared without a trace! She would want every imaginable kind of help from every imaginable source. Her thoughts bounced between trying to put herself in Harriet Newman's shoes and admiring the rare degree of altruism in what Dove was doing. Joan's being in Crook Mountain on vacation (no matter that in some ways it was the oddest vacation ever) was the direct result of *another's* altruism—her friend Melinda's. With these two examples of service to others staring her in the face, could she remain unmoved? What would be the harm in trying to help Dove for these remaining few days of her stay? Even if they accomplished absolutely nothing together, maybe the support would give Dove some hope as she stayed her course.

Chapter 8

Joan groaned. Tuesday morning. She wasn't feeling up to a new day, much less a new month. It had been a restless night. First coffee and then an especially long wake-up shower helped, apparently enough that Dove's story seemed to merit some investment of energy by a random passerby—*her*—today and tomorrow. *Melinda said on Friday that I'd find some useful purpose here. Who knew she was clairvoyant?* And hadn't Lee encouraged her to pitch in? It was two against one. So…she'd pitch in. First, though, would be her visit to the Givenses', bearing a jar of muscadine jam as a gift in exchange, she hoped, for a tour of the yard and permission to take pictures.

From the closet she pulled the second new dress, solid white, ankle-length, sleeveless, and accessorized by a long-sleeved cotton sweater in army green. Paying a call on Mrs. Gerald Givens might not necessitate being this dressy, but the temptation to enjoy the new frock right away was strong. Feeling bright and pretty in it, and still getting her arms into the fitted sleeves of the sweater, Joan glanced out the front window. "Oh, *no!*" Dismay deflated her outlook just as something had deflated the left front tire of her CRV. It was almost completely flat. There was a spare in cargo, and a tire repair kit, but she would have to take her new outfit right off again before trying to discover a nail or a gash, or to inflate the tire enough to drive on it. She squared her shoulders.

To tell Lee she had changed a flat all by herself—now, *that* would impress! Herself, as well as him.

On impulse, Joan stepped outside and snapped a picture of the tire and texted it to Dove with the caption, "It's an April fool joke on me." She added a frowny-face emoticon and said she'd be in for a large latté after conquering her car trouble. Back inside the cabin, she removed sweater, sandals, and jewelry. Then, with the grubbiest jeans she'd brought in hand, she sat on the bed in her white dress and took a few minutes to read and respond to a colleague's e-mail that had just popped in. Engrossed in wording her answer just so, she was startled by the sound of a car horn outside. She moved quickly to the window. Gerald Givens was stepping out of a dark blue Lincoln Town Car. Joan slipped her sandals on and got to the front porch.

"I heard about your flat," her caller said. "I'm here to help."

"How kind of you, Mr. Givens! News does travel fast."

"Well, I was by the Diner, and Miss Dove mentioned your trouble." The gentleman's business attire made Joan protest. She, at least, had other clothes to put on. But her rescuer was already rolling up the sleeves of his white dress shirt. Joan did manage to insist he wait long enough for her to place a thick bath towel down to protect his trousers and to cushion his knees against the pea stone.

Joan doubted this was Mr. Givens' first time stopping on his way to work to help a stranded motorist. As he worked, he offered to take the tire straight down to Mueller's Garage to be repaired. Joan flatly refused. "You've done too much already." Besides, if *she* ventured to the garage, as a customer, maybe she could learn something that would help Dove.

The spare was on, the flat was stowed, Gerald Givens had gone, and now Joan had even more reason to call on Edith. She would offer the jar of jam as a token of thanks for Gerald's good deed. She gathered her essentials for the second time, then stopped. Why not grab a pair of flip flops in case there was time to duck into the beauty salon for a pedicure to replace yesterday's amateur touch-up job? A small, plastic shopping bag with handles that would go conveniently over one wrist would do nicely for the flip flops. Then her hands would stay free to use the phone or the camera about town after she went visiting. *Bingo*. There was just the thing. One of Saturday's gift purchases had been at Addison's Pipe & Tobacco. This parcel wasn't stowed in her car for the trip home because she didn't want it exposed to the heat. The sampler set of tobacco pouches in intriguing-sounding flavors like rum cured and cherry Cavendish was for a friend who had been her hospital administrator once upon a time. Selecting the tobacco for Jerry (over options like fancy lighters, stem polishes, and tobacco flavorings in little plastic bottles that resembled vials of eyedrops) had been an educational shopping experience, with little to no help from the man minding the store. Jerry would never have seen the dark brown plastic carry bag, anyway, because the gift would go into a pretty Christmas box. She removed her purchase from the bag and slid her flip flops in.

⋙◆⋘

"They say knights in shining armor gallop in on white horses. This morning, mine arrived in a blue Lincoln!" Joan was sitting on the porch swing and Edith Givens, in comfortable slacks and a collared pullover knit top, perched delicately on the shiny yellow glider. The vintage glider was an attractive piece, and Joan expressed her envy that it had been taken care of so well. Her gift for Mrs. Givens rested on a glass-topped table beside what must be the healthiest-looking Christmas cactus in existence. The porch was the perfect accessory for this house of traditional red brick, and it didn't appear to have a grain of pollen or a speck of dust anywhere. Even so, the lady of the house had taken care to place a quilt from her linen closet over the seat and the back of the swing to protect Joan's white dress.

They were less than a quarter of a mile up the road from the C.M.G.M. and the Diner. It was clear now how convenient Gerald Givens would find it to patronize the restaurant or to pop in and "check on" Dove as he had done on Friday evening. Edith, according to intelligence, was a capable cook but suffered from arthritis, and Gerald wanted her to exert herself at what she loved most, which was caring for the roses and other shrubs and plants that so obviously loved her touch. To save work in the kitchen, therefore, he picked up ready-to-eat meals and casseroles for the two of them often, sometimes from the Diner. After thanking Edith for her husband's help with the tire, Joan said she was sorry the two of them hadn't been able to attend Sunday night's concert.

"I wouldn't have been up to sittin' so long outdoors at that hour. But we made a donation. Gerald is very generous, and we are thankful to be able to help others whenever we can."

"The town seems to be very supportive when someone has a need."

"Yes. It was that way with Sarah Mueller's funeral bill."

Joan's eyes widened. "The town took up a collection?"

"The town, and some parties bore the largest part of it. Gerald. He wouldn't say so, though. The Bible says, 'Let your givin' be done in secret.'"

Then it's good that your husband has you to say so. "I understand she died of cancer? It happens way too often. In fact, I'm here in Crook Mountain only because my friend, who was staying in the cabin, had to leave here to go help her brother's family. His wife is very weak from her chemotherapy treatments."

Edith murmured sympathy and a comment about the fragility of life, and Joan felt the mood turning gloomy. "You certainly have added a great deal of beauty to life in this town!" She gestured across the front yard. "I found out that Bonnie Jarvis knows quite a bit about local plant life." Joan dropped the name deliberately, wondering if it would prompt the other woman to mention any connection between Bonnie and the Muellers. It didn't. At the risk of sounding too one-track, she fished once more. She told Edith Givens about the disappearance of her shoes during the concert and how Dub Mueller had returned them to her. And the cork on her "fishing line" went underwater.

"That boy is a sad case. Don't let your head be turned by his havin' recovered your shoes, seein' it's likely he also flattened your tire."

Oh. "Do you think so? I wouldn't have expected that." It *was* a disappointing thought, attacking a general faith in humanity, but it might go hand in hand with some of those entries in her cabin's guest book, come to think of it.

"You *wouldn't* expect it, since you don't live here, Mrs. Ryan. But a good many folks believe there's a certain amount of business that the Muellers get for their garage by their own hands."

"That's terrible! Is there any proof of that?"

Edith shrugged. "Not that anyone cares enough to wave under the nose of the law."

"But suppose someone were to get hurt?" In spite of her first impression that Luke and Dub were creepy and scruffy, Joan had since come to doubt that either was really malicious. If a sharp girl like Bonnie had set her cap for Luke, she must believe he was of good character. "Maybe their father puts them up to it. As the one who bears the responsibility of family provider, maybe it's *his* idea." It seemed natural to root for the sons, the ones who had the most opportunity left to better their lives.

"Maybe. And maybe it's the *daughter's* idea. *She* would be one to be thinkin' in terms of whatever brings in more dollars.

That one tries to *write* fate instead of just acceptin' it. You know, imagines herself livin' someplace where the house numbers have five digits instead of three. Now, don't get me wrong. We don't hate that family! Feel kind of sorry for them, losin' Sarah and all. If ever a family felt the loss of its brightest star, it's them. The boys and Marilyn—they all have the potential to make more of themselves, but aren't makin' much progress."

"Hmm." That could be said of a lot of people.

"When Sarah was alive, even Jesse could be almost civil. And what good she couldn't pull from him, she tried to do herself."

"Do you know what 'Dub' is a nickname for?" Joan stuck with the Mueller topic but changed the sub-topic. "A name that starts with W, maybe?" Not that the answer to that question should have any bearing on anything. She was just curious. If it really mattered, there was always the hall of records. Or an online people search.

"I don't recall any other name."

"I was just curious." She hoped her interest in the Muellers didn't appear out of the ordinary, for Dove's sake. But Edith voluntarily kept the subject going.

"Well, Gerald—and I don't know that there's any real grounds for it—Gerald feels protective towards Dove, being alone sometimes at the Diner the way she is, and Jesse Mueller is a big part of the reason for that. Since Sarah passed away, he seems to have an eye towards certain ladies, and not all of them in his own age bracket."

Joan hadn't picked up on that wrinkle. Maybe Jesse Mueller had at least one thing going for him (as little a laurel as it was)—that he was more subtle than Gavin Kidd. The thought was perversely amusing, but Edith Givens wasn't the one to share it with. But Dove hadn't dropped a hint of *that* kind of concern with regard to Mueller. Maybe she thought it would make her sound conceited to tell a new acquaintance that she thought she was being eyed in that way. But, if Dove *was* being eyed that way, it would make her doubly wary of Mueller, and rightly so. If she sincerely believed him capable of murder, other crimes might be in his line, too. Joan shuddered. Maybe it was time to wrap this visit up. She planned to visit one more source of local gossip before having her tire looked at. And she still hadn't taken any pictures of Edith's thriving shrubs and flowers. She did so hurriedly before thanking Edith for the chat, a chat that enabled Joan to leave knowing several things—potentially important things—she hadn't known before. Whether any of them would prove helpful to Dove's cause, only time could tell. But some of them might prove helpful to *her* as an imminent patron of Mueller's Garage.

She left her shady spot at the Givenses' and parked at the Diner in order to walk down a couple of yet-unexplored streets. Rain was in the forecast for Thursday—just her luck, the day she was driving home—so now was the time to enjoy being outdoors. In front of the Lickety-Split ice cream parlor, appropriately located on Rocky Road, she stood idly gazing through the window when a distressingly familiar voice rang out.

"Well, if it isn't our very own Jaw-ja peach still in town!"

Joan rolled her eyes before turning around. "Mr. Kidd." *Doesn't the man have a day job? But maybe he's on his lunch hour.*

He moved closer. She backed up a step. "What say we elevate this establishment with the presence of a very handsome couple? How's about a banana split?"

Honestly, a banana split sounded very appealing—no pun intended—but not across from *this* guy. And not when she hadn't had lunch yet. This last thought she expressed aloud, considering it a most logical and inoffensive reason for declining.

"Great! This can *be* lunch! Cheaper than a burger and fries, too!"

"A banana split."

"Sure! Why not? You only live once."

"And *longer* if you eat from actual food groups."

"Well, then, how about a stroll around town?"

Joan narrowed her eyes at him and quickly clasped her hands in front of her body, next repositioning them to put her engagement ring and wedding band topmost. She was never one to flash her jewelry (which was not meager) in front of someone just to show it off. But, now, she deliberately lifted her left hand in front of her face, artificially high, on the pretext of checking her watch. Could he possibly, this once, prove himself astute enough to catch on to the fact that she was a married woman, on whom he should not be hitting? "Mr. Kidd, I'm sorry, but I have plans, including making a phone call *to my husband.*" That wasn't true. She had no plans to call Lee. She reached out and held the door open, gesturing as if to usher the man inside the ice cream place. "Please, enjoy a banana split if you will. I have to be going."

Gavin shrugged and grinned. "Suit yerself, sweetie." Joan shuddered at the "sweetie" as Gavin walked inside, presumably to take her suggestion. What had her encounter with him looked like to whomever was on ice cream scooping duty? More fodder for local gossip. *Whatever.*

Joan almost immediately crossed paths with someone who should have tied with Gavin Kidd for Person That Others Are Most Likely Not To Want To See Again After High School. Joan recognized Marilyn after a moment's delay. It wasn't the dark glasses, but the hair, that was the stumbling block. A brassy blonde when last seen, Marilyn now sported long locks that were as dark as the lenses in her sunglasses. Instinctively, Joan looked up at the sign to see what business Marilyn was exiting. Yes, it was the beauty salon, Good Hair Day. *Clever name.* Whoever had opened this salon and the ice cream parlor next to it had worked a little harder than those who had named the Diner and the general store. How fortunate that Marilyn had been in the salon first and was already out again. It wouldn't have been any fun to be captive there, her feet soaking away for a pedicure, and have this one show up for a lengthy dye job. On the other hand, maybe the dark color was the *natural* Marilyn.

The brunette spared Joan a scowled greeting and demanded, "Don't you love my *new look?*" Joan looked and had no answer to offer. "The man I'm interested in seems to prefer brunettes at the moment," Marilyn elaborated, and Joan thought back to Saturday morning, the first time she'd seen Gavin Kidd. He had been trying to convince beautiful, dark-haired Dove to go out with him. "I'll set you wise, Mrs. Ryan."

Joan bit her lips to stop the smile that would betray her considerable amusement. "Go right ahead." *Isn't that what Edmund Gwenn as Kris Kringle said, also with considerable amusement, to the toy department manager who was about to instruct him in how to be a good Santa Claus?*

"I've seen Gavin playin' up to you. He's so charmin' that way, liftin' the spirits of *older* women that he couldn't possibly have a serious interest in. Besides, you're only a *tourist.*" Marilyn's petulance was teenagerish. Bratty. *Older* Joan was flattered that this young woman considered her a rival. And *tourist* Joan hoped Marilyn Mueller Walker would be standing close enough to catch some of the dust when a certain Honda CRV left town. Marilyn was ridiculous, but her insecurity was sad, just the same.

"Well!" Marilyn exclaimed, and Joan was at a disadvantage because the dark glasses hid the upper half of the younger woman's face. *What now?* "I see you've been to Addison's. Quite a nice, little, *expensive* shop!"

Ah. It's the bag I'm carrying. "Well, it does look that way, doesn't it? I've been there at one time or *another,* or else I shop at thrift stores in Georgia that get their shopping bags from all over."

To that, Marilyn replied nothing. Instead, she lifted the sunglasses and set them on top of her now-dark hair. "Pop," she said rather tonelessly. Her eyes were looking past Joan.

Joan turned to discover Jesse Mueller behind her. "Mr. Mueller." With so much of his history—and his *suspected* history—known to her, she wasn't thrilled at the prospect of making his acquaintance. "I'm not sure we've been introduced." But Mueller didn't meet her eyes, nor did he react to Marilyn's revised appearance. Maybe by now he was accustomed to his daughter's caprices.

"You smoke cigars, miss?"

What? That was from left field. Jesse Mueller was looking at the Addison's bag. Like Marilyn, was he impressed with the idea that she had spent money in a shop they considered high end? What was the big deal? "Indeed not." Joan pulled the plastic drawstring open to expose the ends of her flip flops. "I'm just using this to carry some spare shoes." *Not that it's any of your business.* "And, by the way, Mrs. Walker, yes, I do *love* your new look!" Leaving off the customary and courteous "excuse me," Joan left daughter and father to deal with each other and made her way toward the Diner to retrieve her car.

To walk to Cora Haskew's house had occurred to Joan, but it was almost three-quarters of a mile away, and she was wearing a new dress and sandals, not gym clothes and sneakers. Dove was at work, and Cora's regular schedule at the church didn't include Tuesday afternoons. Now was the perfect opportunity for some straight talk with someone besides Dove about this Mueller business.

Joan still hadn't eaten lunch. She pulled a granola bar from her purse and ate it as she walked. The strange stories and annoying citizens of Crook Mountain notwithstanding, it was a fine day to be alive and outside. Chirping birds and the gentle breeze shared that opinion.

⋙◆⋘

The screened-in porch was just as pleasant as it had been on Sunday afternoon. This time, Joan felt comfortable enough to get right to her point with Cora, from whom Dove had no secrets regarding Larry Newman or Harriet Newman. Or the Muellers. Could Cora shed any light on Jesse's odd behavior before the start of Sunday's concert? "I can't imagine what he was offended by. Does he just hate to see other people enjoying themselves, or what?"

Cora smiled, but it was a sad smile. "I might be able to explain that."

"I wish you would, Cora. It always bothers me to see people who seem incurably unhappy, or mean. Or both."

"Meanness and sadness are closely related." The older woman was about to wax philosophical, if Joan's cue reader was in good working order. Sometimes the elderly felt an understandable urgency about imparting wisdom, as if right now might be one of their last chances to do so. "As our Reverend Kirkpatrick is fond of saying, 'Mean people are unhappy people, and that's why Jesus commanded us to love our enemies. Mean people need the love they didn't get somewhere along the way.'"

"And does mean, unhappy Jesse Mueller sit under the reverend's sermons on a regular basis without recognizing himself in statements like that?"

"He does. But don't you think many of us hear general criticism or instruction and believe it applies to everyone around us, but not to us?"

Joan laughed. "I can't argue with that."

"But, back to your question. If you recall, at the moment to which you were just referring, Bonnie was listing types of plant life. Remember any of the names?"

"Well, let me think." Unsure what Bonnie had actually said, Joan started by calling out foliage she knew to be in the area: mountain laurel and rhododendron. She thought a moment, and "catbrier" came back to her. In spite of all Joan knew about growing herbs and about caring for the azaleas and other plants that made her yard back home a tiny bit of Eden, a lot of the words Bonnie had tossed out on Sunday night had been unfamiliar.

But, like a good teacher, Cora praised her pupil's effort. "Good. What about trees?"

Trees. "Pine. Beech. Maple?"

"And willow."

"Yes." Was this to the point, or had Cora just gotten caught up in the game? She was obviously enjoying this little memory test.

"We have several varieties. Bonnie named dwarf willow, prairie willow, Carolina willow, and silky willow. I guess it was kind of hard on old Jesse to hear his firstborn son's name—the son who has turned out to be such a challenge and, frankly, such a disappointment to him—spoken that many times in a row."

Joan blinked. "Wait. *What?*"

"Dub is short for *W*." Cora spoke slowly, as if she were explaining remedial fractions to a fifth-grader. But Joan had already theorized the *W* initial. "And the *W* stands for *Willow.*"

"*Willow?*" Was Cora serious? Not William, Wesley, or Wayne? Not Wyatt, Wallace, or Wright? Not even *Wyoming?* Parents had been naming sons geographical words like Dallas and Dakota and Denver for years.

Cora was serious. "Yes. Dub is Jesse Willow Mueller, who preceded Lucas Jeffrey Mueller in birth by a few minutes." Joan processed the names and the birth order as the native Crook Mountainer unfolded more of the story. "Dub's middle name was chosen by his mother, and it is a biblical word, which pleased Sarah in particular. Maybe they didn't realize at the outset that in its English origins the name was known as a feminine one, but there was teasing that started because of it, or because Dub was slow to learn, or both. At any rate, they started calling him Dub back in the first or second grade. I suppose they didn't consider calling him Jesse, since his father went by that. Too confusing, two people answering to the same name in the same household."

"And I imagine that if the boy was lagging behind in intellectual development, that's all the more reason Jesse wouldn't want to have the son known as his namesake. How sad. But I wonder why they didn't just shorten Willow to 'Will' and let people assume it was for William."

"Maybe 'Will' was too close to 'Willow,' and that wouldn't have solved the teasing. What matters more is that folks don't know or remember the boy's real name any longer. Or, if they do, they don't mention it. People don't want to tangle with Jesse. He may not be proud of Dub in the usual sense, but family is family, and he can get ugly if provoked. He may not see the wrong in his own harsh treatment of the boys. I suppose he thinks it's his right as a father. Or his duty. But he won't sit for anyone else poking fun at either of them."

A telephone bell jangled in the house, and Cora went to answer it. Joan looked at the time on her phone. "Oh, dear!" Cora's dismay wafted from the kitchen to the porch. It didn't sound as though the caller bore good news. Given Cora's age bracket, that news might be about the death of a sibling, cousin, or former classmate. On the other hand, it was just as likely that Cora was sympathizing with a neighbor who had just said that her prize roses had aphids or that her sour cream pound cake for tomorrow's bridge game had fallen. Whatever the "oh, dear" news was, it was Cora's business, and Joan took the interruption as a convenient time to leave, which she did as soon as Cora was off the phone. It was almost 2:00. *Next stop, Mueller's Garage.*

———◆———

Joan watched for signs of guilt or any other emotion as she stood at the reception counter telling the Mueller twins about her tire. No dice. *I guess that would have been too easy.* Dub and Luke might be so practiced at dirty dealing by now that they were expert at appearing innocent. Or, maybe those rumors were entirely unfounded. Travelers on these gravel roads, herself included, might easily run over a concealed nail or some broken glass. *Her* misfortune could have happened on the drive up, resulting in a slow leak.

Joan looked past the young men. Was Jesse back there in the garage area changing spark plugs or inspecting brake rotors? She saw no movement and heard no noise. *Forge onward!* "Didn't you think the band that played on Sunday night was great? I certainly did." The brothers merely looked down. No, this wasn't going to be easy. That these boys seemed to smile so little felt more tragic by the second. So, Joan kept *her* face bright as she tried again. "I'm not sure I would have known you two were twins if people hadn't told me. Who is older?" It didn't matter that Cora had already answered that question. Men were supposed to like to talk about themselves. Right?

Right. "Me!" Dub grinned shyly and seemed to swell in height just a smidgen at being recognized as the senior twin.

And he had a great smile! Could she draw one out of Luke as well? To Dub, she said, "Well, then, would you like to carry my flat tire in and look for the leak? I'm sure you'll find the problem quickly. I just hope it's fixable! I can sure think of better souvenirs to take home than a boring new tire. For that money, I could probably buy about thirty big pieces of fudge in Cluny's Ridge, for example. Or ten buckets of Karmelkorn with the Georgia Bulldogs mascot on them."

That did it! Luke smiled and even offered his own example, though without eye contact. "Er take six folks t' the Ripley's Museum."

Joan laughed with genuine delight, not just because her attempt at conversation had finally succeeded, but also because of Luke's quick math. Dub laughed, too, then, perhaps because he simply followed others' leads much of the time.

Luke took charge in the apparent absence of his father. "We'll get yer tire patched up good. There's a seat fer yeh." He pointed to what amounted to their customer lounge, but it was a far cry from those at major dealerships. No complimentary coffee. No television. Just a couple of hard plastic seats, and some tattered-looking magazines resting on top of a dingy white plastic barrel. Should she be polite and sit? Edith Givens wasn't handy to offer a quilt to protect the white dress this time. Joan's phone rang. *Saved by a bell again!* Caller I.D. showed the name of her dietitian friend who'd e-mailed earlier. She answered the call, but the conversation had barely begun before an unreliable signal ended the connection. She stepped outside, followed by the Mueller boys. After giving them access to her tire and seeing them start back inside with it, she rounded a front corner and stopped on the shady side of the building. Still no signal. She walked to the back corner where the chain-link fence was attached to the building. The fence, considerably more rusty than she could tell from her distant view on Monday, was topped with three strands of barbed wire, also rusty. Her phone's signal display rose decidedly, and Joan laughed to herself at the disparity of the situation: surroundings looking bad, phone signal looking good.

She dialed back and apologized for the dropped call. As she listened to details of a proposed speaking engagement, her eyes fell on the very car she had seen Dub uncover and occupy. The light green tarp was in place. No surprise there, but the front grill and lower bumper were exposed as if Dub, or whoever had replaced the tarp last, had been careless or interrupted. A classic, oval-shaped, blue Ford emblem on the front of the automobile was in full view. Sarah Mueller had had a Ford Taurus, according to Dove. Could Cora and Dove be mistaken about the two-door/four-door thing, and was this two-door car in fact the Taurus? That would explain Dub's particular attachment, its being a vital connection to his late mother. As for its being dark green and not gold, Dub might have used some of the time on his hands to repaint his mother's car in his own favorite color. *Maybe.*

"Miss." An angry tone carried the word toward Joan, startling her out of her speculations. She turned her head. Jesse Mueller was making a beeline for her, sidestepping old tires and piles of rusty whatnot. Lost in thought, Joan had missed his apparent exit from the building by the back door, which now hung open. Mueller approached fast, not with the stiff-leggedness he'd shown the other morning outside the Diner. He looked extremely unpleasant and most territorial.

"Joan? Are you there?" *Oh!* She was still on the phone and hadn't heard a single thing since spotting the car and its front grill! Very quickly she cut in. "I'm so sorry, Ann. Gotta talk to this auto mechanic. I'll call right back." She slipped the device into an in-seam side pocket of her dress and mustered up a pleasant expression. Mueller now stood about five feet away, arms hanging by his sides, fingers twitching as if he were barely controlling the impulse to do violence to something or someone. In spite of the fence between them, Joan got a jolt of something she rarely experienced: intimidation. He was no taller than she was; she was looking him straight in the eyes with her head level. Logically, therefore, he shouldn't have any natural advantage, caged aggression notwithstanding. Still, it was pretty clear right now why Dove had said she was scared of the man.

Be professional. You've faced plenty of angry hospital patients and their unreasonable family members. "Don't tell me my tire is repaired already! But that shouldn't surprise me. Your boys seem very capable, and I imagine they've learned from an expert." Could she divert his attention from where her eyes had been focused when he'd called out to her? Maybe he hadn't noticed. Maybe he was angry only because she had left the designated customer waiting area, to which Luke had properly directed her. Repair shops and oil change places could be persnickety about that, on account of liability.

"What're yeh doin' out *here?*" The gruffness in Mueller's tone matched his scowl. He jerked his head toward the building. "Customers wait *inside.*" He must have arrived just now and learned from his sons that she *was* there as a customer.

"Certainly." Joan smiled without warmth. She was not going to be unpleasant, but neither was she going to apologize for having walked outdoors. "I simply came outside to get some phone reception in order to return a call from a fellow registered dietitian back home." Haughtily, she hoped some of what she had just said would be over the man's head. "If my tire is ready, I'll gladly be on my way." Picturing herself already driving away, Joan felt her insides lurch. Should she have left her car unattended in the front lot? She had locked it, but what if the Muellers had decided in a hurry to drum up some additional business from her? She hoped Jesse had not been there long enough for that, and she hoped his sons wouldn't undertake such sabotage on their own, especially after she seemed to have made some headway in befriending them.

Chapter 9

Joan ate a bite of blueberry muffin here and worked her phone there, seated at a booth in the Diner. Dove's message, late last night, had said that Laynie Key had fallen ill with a high fever and had been taken to the hospital. The concern was that she might have developed an infection after her last surgery. A second text from Dove, a few minutes after the first, had asked, "Road trip?" Joan wasn't the least bit shy of hospitals, having spent some years as a clinical dietitian. In fact, she was curious to see the Children's Hospital which served eastern Tennessee and areas of several other states. Besides that, and not discounting a genuine concern for young Laynie, she had several things to talk over with Dove. An automobile ride lasting the better part of an hour each way would provide the perfect opportunity to hear Dove's take on this latest uncomfortable brush with Jesse Mueller.

Dove poured coffee for a couple of guests at the counter while giving a few reminders to the employees who would handle things while she slipped away for the rest of the morning. She untied a chef's apron at the neck and behind her back, revealing casual slacks and a three-quarter-sleeved striped sweater. Sliding into the empty side of Joan's booth, she offered to drive the two of them in her Elantra. Joan accepted the offer, seeing as how the trip was Dove's idea. But, what about the Honda? Should it be left unattended for several hours, possibly picking up another mysterious nail or developing a sudden oil leak? If something were to happen that required a serious repair, that could mean she wouldn't be able to leave for home tomorrow morning. "Do you think it would be better if I moved my car to the church parking lot? There's plenty of shade there, and if I leave it here or at the cabin, it will be completely in the sun." *And vulnerable to sabotage.* "I try to avoid parking in full sun whenever I can." No one likely to be interested in eavesdropping was in the Diner right now. Even so, the women kept their voices low.

"I'm sure that would be fine, or maybe Mr. and Mrs. Givens would keep an eye on it at their place. He doesn't work on Wednesdays. And she, at least, is in the camp that thinks a flat tire here and there is not by accident, so she would understand your asking."

"I'm not sure I should bother them. I don't want to be paranoid." Joan mulled the matter over as Dove was hailed by a coworker across the way. As Dove started to get up, Joan made her decision. "I'll just leave my car here."

Dove stayed seated in the booth and took her phone out. She pressed a couple of buttons, then quietly explained to Gerald Givens that she and Joan would be riding together to the hospital and that Joan's car would be in the Diner's parking lot. And that was that. "He understood. I didn't have to spell it out for him." Dove conferred with the other staff long enough to review instructions about minding the slow cookers already simmering the pork that was a Wednesday night special and about which desserts to pull from the freezer when. Joan left a tip on the table and ducked into the restroom.

Outside, Sherry Kirkpatrick hailed the silver sedan before Dove could maneuver it out of the parking lot. Dove stopped the car and lowered her window. Sherry held forward a foil-wrapped plate. "I heard you're going to see Laynie today. Could you please take this for me? I threw something together after hearing the news last night."

"Glad to! But do you trust me with whatever's under this foil? We might show up there with only crumbs on the plate."

"Don't you dare! These brownies are Greg Key's favorite. Well, they're a favorite with most people in town." Sherry laughed.

Joan leaned over to wave at the pastor's wife, hissing to Dove, "Ask her how she heard you were going to the hospital."

Dove did, and Sherry answered, "From Edith Givens, who talked to Cora last night." Joan took the plate from Dove and stowed it on the back seat. They said goodbye to Sherry and were off.

Spending one's last day of vacation on an errand of mercy sounded all noble and sacrificial, but it didn't feel like any great sacrifice. Maybe it was selfish, in fact. It was a chance to spend a few hours away from people named Kidd and Mueller! Joan pulled her phone out and slid her thumbs over the screen. She scrolled through some search results, pressed "Call Now," then held the phone to her ear and placed an order through the hospital's gift shop. "It's always seemed more exciting to me when flowers arrive by delivery, versus the giver walking up and handing them to me." At Dove's remark that that was a very nice thing to do, Joan shrugged. "I don't mean to give the impression I would do the same for a virtual stranger every time, but I guess I'm caught up in this, after being at the concert the other night. I was very impressed by the caliber of band engaged to do that benefit. Don't take this the wrong way, but it was much better than I had expected it to be."

"Thanks to a couple of benefactors, namely Mr. Givens and the bank manager, Ron McCain. Most towns, even small ones, have their pockets of money. McCain and Stillman—that's the loud money in our town. And then there's quiet money, like Mr. Givens."

"Our town" was an interesting choice of words. Dove had no prior connection to Crook Mountain, and she believed a serious crime had been perpetrated by some of its citizens, against people she cared about. Still, she'd just called it *our* town and not *this* town. Crook Mountain was a picturesque pocket in the beautiful Smokies, to be sure. That was being reinforced with every foot of scenery they were passing. And the town had some very nice people living in it. But, to plant oneself here indefinitely, under such odd circumstances?

Traffic was relatively light, especially compared to what it would be in Atlanta on a weekday, even with the "morning rush" over. The thing was, the rush hour in Atlanta was rarely *ever* over. Next time she sat staring at a string of red taillights moving at a snail's pace on I-285, she was going to remember this moment, this scenery, and this calm.

"What have you got going on when you return home? Will your family get together soon, since you were away on Easter?"

"We'll probably have a family dinner for Sam's birthday in a few months. If Lee and I want to see him before that, we may have to show up at one of his gigs. He plays drums in a four-man rock band in his spare time. But my immediate goals are to organize the Christmas gifts I've just bought and to plan a special dinner for Lee when he gets back into town." Joan already had some ideas in the works for that meal, including red velvet cake, Lee's favorite dessert. "We'll see April pretty predictably. She likes her dad and me to pick up the dinner check when her cash runs low. And our house is still her free storage facility. But, we wouldn't have it any other way."

"Sounds like you have a great family."

"Have I not showed you pictures yet? Inconceivable! Wait until we stop."

"I have a picture to show *you*, as a matter of fact." Dove's foot was holding the brake pedal down at a red light where they were about to turn onto the northbound side of a divided highway. She reached into a storage cubby and handed an envelope to Joan. "Take a look, please." Joan pulled out a black and white glossy five-by-seven print. The man pictured appeared to be roughly sixty years old. He wore a tweed sport jacket, dark slacks, solid tie, dress shirt, and shiny dress shoes. He looked very professor-ish, seated in a wingback chair that appeared to be in someone's living room. One ankle rested on the other knee in the traditionally masculine way. He held a smoking pipe in his right hand. "Three guesses who it is."

Joan turned the photo over. "Happy Mother's Day" was written in black marker in a large scrawl, with "Love, Larry" below that. Joan turned the picture back over. He wasn't exactly George Clooney or Harrison Ford, but Larry Newman was handsome in spite of the fifteen or so extra pounds he appeared to carry. And, from the style of the son's inscription to his mother, it wasn't much of a stretch to imagine this being a movie star's autographed gift to an adoring fan. Joan held the picture gently by its corners, doubly thankful now for the Diner's rich, foaming soap, with which she had washed her hands after eating that muffin. "I imagine this was his mother's favorite picture of him. Is it the only one you brought with you to Crook Mountain?"

"Yes. I thought it best not to have much with me that relates to this. Just in case anyone might happen upon it, you know. That picture was taken the May before Larry went missing in January."

Joan set the picture on her lap and told Dove about seeing Dub and Luke, and then their father, on Tuesday. She repeated the conversation about things one might buy in Cluny's Ridge for the price of a new tire.

"Really? I'm impressed that you got that much out of them. Out of Luke, in particular. Dub has less inhibition. Less of a filter, if you know what I mean."

"Yes, I do. Being there in the garage gave me a glimpse beyond the curtain the boys seem to live behind." That proverbial curtain appeared to be held in place by Jesse. Had it been that way when the boys' mother was living? She put the question to Dove.

"It's my impression from Cora that Jesse has always been domineering, and meaner in the five years since Sarah died."

Joan resented having felt intimidated by Mueller out by that fence, and she resented any man's exercising harsh dominion over his family, including adult children who should have the right and the opportunity to escape that dynamic. The boys' lack of confidence, and even Marilyn's jealousy of other women and perhaps her ill-fated marriage, all could be the direct result of their father's treatment. If the ultimate outcome of Dove's quest for answers was that Jesse Mueller was proved to have caused the death of Larry Newman, and if Mueller was brought to justice for that, more people could benefit than just Dove and the restless spirits, so to speak, of the late Harriet Newman and of her son.

Joan told Dove she'd seen some of the front end of the mysterious, dark green car before Jesse Mueller had snarled at her for being in that area. "If you were hoping the car would turn out to be Larry Newman's white Mercedes repainted, wouldn't you say the Ford emblem points to its being Mrs. Mueller's gold Taurus, repainted, instead?"

Dove answered without hesitation. "No, because her car definitely was a four-door, and you definitely saw a two-door, right?"

"Yes, I did. It must be some *other* Ford that Dub is obsessed with." Unless it was possible to rebuild a four-door car into a two-door, or vice versa. It probably *was* possible, if you had the skill, the tools, and some reason for doing so.

Joan looked at the picture on her lap. It did make for a sad story, no one's knowing what had happened to this man. "Forget about the car at Mueller's for a minute. What if Larry had a heart attack while driving, and his car went off a cliff somewhere around here, and that's why nobody can find it? Do you know what kind of health he was in?"

"Yes, that's a possibility. But Harriet had the impression Larry saw his doctor regularly. You know. Lonely mothers of only sons tend to obsess about that sort of thing."

Joan smiled. "True. Then, too, only sons of lonely mothers might hide a medical condition in order not to cause worry." She gazed at the photo again, almost memorizing it. Then she turned her head toward the window. Here and there, light-colored houses stood out along the high ridge, some of them partially obscured by the lush green growth of spring. What views those places must have! But, how far to the nearest coffee shop or grocery store? Privacy versus convenience. It was a trade-off. Their house in Duluth was farther toward the convenience end of that spectrum. Maybe the wish to have it both ways was why some people bought a second home. Convenience in the city, seclusion in the country. That very topic was on the drawing board with herself and Lee. How many weeks ago was it that they'd driven through the Lake Oconee area with an eye to waterfront real estate? Three? Five?

Billboards were showing signs of greater civilization. Joan offered to get their final driving directions up on her phone. "Nice voice," Dove commented after hearing the Australian accent.

"He keeps me company," Joan laughed. They were crossing the Tennessee River, sun glinting on a surface that was rippled by the April morning breeze. The navigation took them successfully to the hospital, and Joan read to Dove off the hospital's website as the car climbed the concrete ramp of the parking deck. "Visiting hours are 'ten to nine, except for siblings under the age of 14, who are permitted to visit on Sunday afternoons and Wednesday nights.' I hope Laynie isn't here long enough for her brother and sister to come visit her on Sunday afternoon." That was four days away. "They could be planning to visit her tonight. I kind of hope not. It would be a late night. Of course, school is out, right? That could make a difference." *Or a "diffrence," if spelled by the little sister!*

"They'll stay with Bonnie Jarvis's family tonight and keep as normal a schedule as they can. They've done that before. Bonnie says her family has so many kids already that a couple more don't make much difference." Dove laughed. "Trust me. Between Bonnie and her family, and Sherry, and Cora, plenty of love and care will be showered on Zachary and Ruth Key."

They parked, gathered their purses and the plate of brownies, and found Laynie's room on the third floor. Dove knocked lightly, and Greg Key opened the door. He gestured the women inside and managed a weak smile. He looked tired. His wife was seated on the side of the bed, leaning toward Laynie, stroking her hand and murmuring softly. The little girl's eyes were closed. Joan and Dove moved farther into the room, politely declining Greg's offer of a place to sit down. Joan saw the flowers and the brown teddy bear she had sent. The card that was to read "With get-well wishes from your friends in Georgia, Joan and Lee Ryan" was in its envelope. It was unlikely Laynie had seen the gift yet. Several greeting cards lay near the flowers on the bureau, and a couple of mylar balloons, reading *Get Well Soon* and *Thinking of You*, stirred in the disturbed air.

Amanda Key seemed oblivious to the presence of the visitors. Her husband gently nudged her. "Honey, we got visitors. C'mon. Stand up. It's murder on yer back that way."

The patient's mother shook her head, unshed tears in her eyes. "Why would I care about *that?*" Greg Key shrugged and shook his head, aiming an expression of helplessness in the general direction of Dove and Joan.

Dove quietly set the plate of brownies on the bureau. "We brought you something from Sherry Kirkpatrick."

Joan wanted to ask how Laynie was doing and how long the doctors thought she would be here, but the girl's parents didn't seem to need questions just then. However, Greg volunteered a report as if that was what was expected of him. "We're jus' waitin' fer the medicine to do its job. Might take a few days."

The women nodded. "I'm sure she is in good hands." It was a lame-sounding remark, one that probably had been made many times by all of the Keys' friends, and that probably went in one of Greg Key's ears and right out the other. *You can do better, Joan.*

Dove stepped over to Amanda Key and leaned down to wrap an arm around her shoulders. "Won't you please come into the hall and talk to me for a minute? *Please?*" Dove gently gripped the woman's upper arm. "Come on, Amanda. Stand up." As if it were a relief to be given an instruction by an outsider, the weary mother relented. Heaving a large sigh, she made as if to stand and leaned heavily on Dove for support until she could ease her tense muscles and begin to walk. Just outside the door, which Dove closed behind them, Amanda Key's breakdown was easy to hear.

"Our sweet little angel shouldn't hafta be sufferin' this way!" The anguish caught at Joan much as the heartache had done in that dream about Harriet Newman. The sobs in the hallway soon were muffled, however, no doubt because Amanda had been enveloped in the arms of Dove Sechrist.

Joan stepped to the bedside and leaned near, launching into a cheerful-sounding soliloquy meant to distract Mr. Key and to encourage his daughter. "Laynie, hi! It's Joan Ryan. I met you at the park on Sunday night. I sure hope you'll be home and all better very soon. I see over here that someone has brought you a CD by Blueberry Creek Band. They were so good! And *you* were, too!" Joan could swear that Laynie's face reacted to that.

Greg told Joan that the banjo player had brought the recording himself, earlier that morning, and had autographed it. "Super nice people."

"That's really sweet." At a loss for what to do next, Joan was relieved when Dove led a composed Amanda back into the room. Behind them came hospital staff delivering trays from food service.

"We'll let you have your lunch," Dove said. "Gene and Sherry are planning to come and see you tomorrow. Meanwhile, enjoy Sherry's brownies."

As she and Dove walked, Joan didn't have enough motivation to look for the stairwell, her usual practice for getting some easy steps in for exercise. The visit had been pretty much a downer. Whatever Joan had envisioned—delivering the brownies, spreading cheer, visiting with brave little Laynie and encouraging her to eat well—hadn't quite materialized. Joan extended her hand and let foamy sanitizer fall into it from a dispenser near the elevator. "I'm sure you're big on frequent handwashing in your line of work."

"Absolutely." Dove reached out and availed herself of the same.

The elevator door opened, and the subdued pair stepped in to join a couple of chatty hospital staff wearing navy blue scrubs. Dining was on the ground floor, according to signage inside the elevator. Even though it was barely past 10:30, Joan suggested they check out the cafeteria. Food was almost universally a remedy for sagging spirits. They had passed viable restaurants on the drive in, including places for sushi, Mexican, seafood, and pizza. But Joan was curious about the food service right here. If an early lunch was the thing to cheer them up, there wasn't a more convenient option.

"Sure you want hospital food?"

"I confess I looked at the menu as we were driving. Between the grill, the hot line, and the salad bar, I think we'll be fine."

"Suits me. I'm just glad not to be doing the cooking!"

The cafeteria was mildly busy, with muted conversations, here and there the clink of a ladle against the side of a stainless steel soup tureen, and the sizzle of hamburger patties. One wall's large glass panes admitted natural light and afforded a pleasing view of some of the exterior landscaping. Food, and a decent view. Good planning by somebody!

"I can't help myself. I just have to try the grilled cheese. Spying on the competition, you know."

Joan ended up with a black bean burger and chicken tortilla soup after considering the panini du jour of turkey breast and pepper jack cheese. She used more hand sanitizer by the cash register after handling the community soup ladle and her own debit card.

"There's somebody I know," Dove said as soon as they were seated. "She used to live in Crook Mountain." Dove caught the attention of that person, who proceeded in their direction after handing some bills to the cashier. "Joan, I'd like you to meet the woman whose taste in buildings and grounds you've been admiring for the past several days. This is Serena Stillman."

Chapter 10

"Well, small world, isn't it?" To Serena McCain Stillman, daughter of the Crook Mountain banker, Joan gave her name and a short explanation of how she had come to stay in the cabin. The woman, who looked to be in her early forties, had somewhat angular features framed by shoulder-length hair that was chestnut in color and very wavy. Several clues suggested a person who'd been blessed financially: the quality of her clothing, the size of the diamonds in her ring set (enhanced by a flawless manicure), the name of a store printed on a gift bag, presumably for a patient she was planning to visit, and the fact that it was breakfast food, not lunch food, on her tray. If Serena's lifestyle was one of relative leisure, that would support the idea that she was not an early riser and that her breakfasts tended to happen much later than six or seven in the morning. The scuttlebutt was that Serena's husband earned well. Besides that, the couple had extra income from at least two rental houses—the so-called McCain cabin and the brick house of that special errand on Monday morning.

"I'll take a shot in the dark and say you're here for the same patient we just visited," Dove told Serena, who was moving her breakfast purchases from a blue tray onto the table.

"You got it. Dad called me this mornin' about Laynie. I live close, you know. I found some cute hair barrettes as a gift, plus a small toy each for the younger kids." Serena indicated the bag she had set on the table beside her fresh fruit, Danish pastry, and coffee lightened with creamer. Joan wasn't hearing quite the same degree of dialect in Serena's speech that was in Bonnie's and in some others', aside from dropping the Gs off her "–ing" words. Some of the townsfolk had come upon ways of broadening their worlds (and their speech, intentionally or not) through education or by living away for a while before coming back. Cora, for example. Gerald Givens. And, to a degree, even Marilyn.

Dove and Serena exchanged information about the Keys and hoped mutually that Laynie would improve very quickly. Serena had sometimes been a sitter for the Key children before moving away, Dove told Joan. Serena said she hoped Joan was liking the cabin. "I'm glad to hear that you find it attractive."

Joan nodded and smiled. "The cabin and the town make a very appealing setting. Quite off the beaten track. And," she made an effort not to inject any particular tone, "my stay has proved to be interesting." After all, to say that one's vacation somewhere had proved "interesting" didn't suggest cloak and dagger business. It could refer to anything from taking a trolley tour of the historic district, to finding one good book at the local library, to noticing that you were sharing your hotel with an array of tall athletes who turned out to be a professional soccer team in town for a tournament.

"If you ventured into the Diner, where most people meet Dove, I'll wager you've also run into some of the town's *other* fine citizens." Joan raised her eyebrows, but made no answer. "I hear my dear rival Marilyn Mueller has come back. I don't suppose she takes the presence of an attractive outsider like yourself quietly."

That got a broad smile out of Joan. "And I'm guessing she hasn't always taken the presence of an attractive *insider*, like you, well." Serena should be several years older than Marilyn. Maybe as many as ten years. The poise of that seniority, coupled with a natural grace and some of the elder's achievements that Dove had mentioned in earlier conversations—straight "A" student, musically talented, popular—would naturally set Marilyn up to be jealous.

"You're pretty much on target. If I tried to name the top five reasons I'm livin' here and not there, at least two of the reasons would have the name Mueller in them."

Joan tested the tortilla soup, trying not to slurp too loudly in her effort not to burn her mouth on the first spoonful. Was Gavin Kidd also in the top five? And was the second Mueller on Serena's "bad" list named Jesse?

Dove looked at Serena and softly asked if she would tell Joan her history with Jesse. *Bingo.*

"I don't mind. It's no secret. In a town that small, not many things *do* stay secret. It amounts to this: a couple of years after Sarah died, Jesse was showin' an interest in me that I couldn't live with. I tried to cope with it for as long as I could, but the problem wasn't goin' away. So I finally moved. My cabin—it was built as a gift from my parents—was too close to the Muellers for comfort." Joan nodded involuntarily and couldn't keep an audible exhale from escaping, having formed virtually the same opinion while occupying the cabin.

"I'm afraid my new friend here has had her share of first-hand experience with them since her arrival five days ago."

"Oh?" Serena looked at Joan. "Flat tire?" Joan nodded. "Peepin' Tom?" Another nod.

Serena's tone sounded fairly unconcerned. Here was yet another person who acted as if the Muellers' antics were nearly harmless. At least, Serena had been removed from the issues long enough that she could make light of them. But hadn't she also just said the Muellers had figured prominently in her decision to stop living in Crook Mountain? For this woman, whose family had means and influence, to have fled her hometown for reasons connected with Jesse Mueller didn't hurt the case Dove had been making, that the man was a scoundrel.

Joan spoke to that last question of Serena's. "I did see Dub Mueller lurking one day, yes. But just once, and I've had a few friendly words with him and his brother since." With the serious suspicions Dove had expressed to her in confidence about the Muellers, it was now a little muddy how much more should be said in front of Serena.

The women gave more attention to their respective meals, then, with occasional small talk on subjects including what each other's husbands did for a living, and what a future husband might do for a living, Serena kidded Dove. Her love life was a topic Joan had tactfully avoided with Dove, but Serena was a more intimate friend. As Serena made ready to go up and pay her visit, Dove hoped aloud that the mood in Room 312 might be a little less strained by now.

"Thanks for that!" Serena flashed a pretty smile. "Saves me havin' to go by the desk to ask the room number. Oh, before I forget—" She produced a business card and offered it to Joan. "If you or any friends ever wanta stay again." The card bore the name Stillman-Breck Realty, LLP, with contact information for three branch offices in the area. "My mobile number's on the back."

⋙◆⋘

Serena Stillman's statements in the hospital dining room were a springboard on several fronts, not the least of which was whether Jesse Mueller, a lonely widower, might actually have been trying awkwardly to make conversation with Joan for personal reasons. If so, he certainly needed to soften his approach! Maybe some women responded romantically to being scowled at, fussed at, and sneered at by a scruffy man in dirty work clothes, but not *this* woman. Twice now, Mueller had addressed her as "miss," but her diamond ring and wedding band, though not quite as flashy as Serena's (women were rarely able to avoid making that kind of comparison at close range), should have been a clear indication of her marital status. Jesse's eyesight wasn't sharp, according to Dove. Could it be that he didn't realize she was married? Or that, like Gavin Kidd, he didn't care?

On the way back to Crook Mountain, Joan asked Dove whether Serena could be trusted with knowledge of the Newman situation and with Dove's conviction that the Muellers were guilty of something connected with the case. Joan had invested plenty of energy in the matter by now. She wanted to leave for Georgia tomorrow believing at least that Dove had a strategic next step in mind. Maybe Serena, if made Dove's next go-to buddy in crime-solving, would come up with a detail that had gone overlooked or an approach that had gone untried.

Dove's eventual answer, that she'd have to think carefully on whether to recruit Serena's help, brought up another quote from *White Christmas*: "She's a real slow mover." That wasn't a quote Joan could voice, though. Several minutes passed in silence.

"Oh!" There was something a little less serious than missing persons and sick children that they hadn't talked about yet. "I know word gets around fast here, but is it possible you don't know yet that Marilyn got her hair dyed dark yesterday?" Slim as the chance of it seemed to be, Joan wanted to be the first one to inform Dove of one bit of Crook Mountain gossip.

"Well, if I *had* heard about that, it must be that Laynie's going to the hospital threw it out of my mind. How did *you* happen to get in the loop on an event of such earth-shattering consequence?"

Joan giggled. Then, although the lingering effects of the hospital visit took some of the energy with which she otherwise would have related the story, she gave Dove a reasonably spirited account of Marilyn's self-proclaimed reason for going brunette. From there, she described Gavin Kidd's invitation for banana splits. Dove laughed heartily. "Oh, and then Marilyn saw the shopping bag I was carrying from Addison's Pipe & Tobacco, and she started making a loud to-do over *that*, as if a roomful of people, and not a deserted sidewalk, was her audience. Then, I found out the sidewalk wasn't *entirely* deserted. Jesse Mueller was standing behind me." Since meeting Serena and hearing *her* experience with Mueller, Joan felt even more creeped out now than she had at the time. Still, she finished her report of the incident on a light note. "It's pretty awkward to discover that a man has been standing in back of you, and you don't know *what* he's been looking at." She tried imitating Mueller's voice. "'You smoke cigars, miss?' That's what he asked me." Joan looked over at Dove, expecting more laughter. But the car's driver wore a serious expression as she glanced at Joan a couple of times, then put her eyes safely back on the road.

"Jesse Mueller seemed interested in the fact that you'd been shopping at Addison's Pipe & Tobacco?"

"Yes, I'd say so. Of course, it was Marilyn who called attention to it first."

Dove shook her head in a rare display of annoyance. "I'd bet money that any comment of Marilyn's was purely for the sake of drawing attention to herself. If she saw you'd been trading at any place people consider expensive, chances are she'd talk about it, and loudly, to give the impression that she knows quality and can afford to shop at those kinds of stores herself. But what interests me is *Jesse's* take on it. *Listen*, Joan. *Addison's* is the store where Larry Newman was reportedly seen on the day he disappeared! It's the *last place* his trail can be traced. The shopkeeper, Coffey, positively identified Larry as a customer, by his picture, when questioned. But, later, he took it all back."

"Which suggests that Larry was robbed and likely killed somewhere along the way, after he left Cincinnati and before he got to Cluny's Ridge. Or that his car left the road somewhere, and somebody discovered him but never reported it. They broke into the car and took whatever valuables they could find. Like his credit card."

"No! There's a major flaw in that theory. Why would a random thief or killer take the route Larry was supposed to be taking? And just happen to go into a pipe and tobacco shop? Unless Larry had a shopping list next to him in the car and the guilty person thought, 'Oh! Good idea. I think I'll go there and buy that.'" Dove was getting worked up. "No. The only person using Larry Newman's credit card at Addison's at 6:02 p.m. on January 11 two years ago, to buy tobacco that happens to be Larry Newman's favorite kind, was *Larry Newman.* And if that shady character Coffey suddenly can't be sure it *was* Larry, then either he is guilty of something, or he was paid to change his story by someone, who did something or knows something."

Joan closed her eyes. The sign she'd seen on Saturday at Addison's, the one with the hours of operation, had given the shop's closing time as 6:30 on weeknights. That jived with the time of purchase Dove had just said. Who had waited on her when she'd bought the sampler pack for Jerry? Tattooed forearms had made an impression, along with the fact that the youngish man had had dark hair and a five-o'clock shadow. Beyond that, there wasn't much coming back. Had she really exchanged words and money with a man who was withholding information about a missing person? Not a comforting thought. The idea that Jesse Mueller could be seriously involved didn't sit well, either.

"Joan? Think back to yesterday afternoon. Picture Jesse's expression and tell me exactly what he did."

Joan opened her eyes, stretched her arms and legs, and looked out the window. They would be back in Crook Mountain soon. "Well, as I said, he'd been standing behind me for some amount of time before I knew it. But it couldn't have been long. Marilyn may not jump to do his every bidding the way her brothers seem to, but I'll bet she's afraid of him, just the same. I'm not sure she would have talked on and on with him standing there, before acknowledging him. And, when I turned around and spoke, he didn't look at me. He looked at the bag, and he asked me if I was a cigar smoker. I guess that was the first thing that popped into his head as a way of asking me how I happened to have that bag. It does seem strange."

"Yes. Doesn't it?"

"Maybe their whole family is fixated on that store, or on tobacco products, for some reason we don't know about."

"I doubt that. I *know* it's connected to Larry. And Marilyn making a loud fuss about Addison's in broad daylight tells me that *she* has no knowledge of a deep, dark, criminal secret connected to that shop's owner. If she did, she wouldn't sing out about it like that. I believe the key person is Jesse, and Luke and Dub are also involved somehow. Marilyn had married an elevator repairman named Chad Walker the previous August and was living in North Carolina until about six months ago. I think she is blissfully ignorant."

I won't argue with that. "But that didn't turn out to be her dream marriage, apparently."

"Afraid not. Walker made good money. Yeah. As an elevator repairman. Who knew? But he lost a lot of it at the casino in Cherokee. So the marriage certainly wasn't the pot of gold Marilyn had hoped for."

They fell silent again. Dove's cause was looking pretty hopeless right now. If law enforcement officials hadn't turned anything up in two years, and Dove couldn't or wouldn't go to them with what amounted to a flimsy notion and a strong feeling, which they would probably ignore, she might live the rest of her life here in Crook Mountain, flipping pancakes and hoping the answer to the mystery would miraculously fall into her lap. Harriet Newman's dying request sounded like a very selfish thing to have put upon her young caregiver. But then Joan pictured Amanda Key's tearful breakdown at the hospital as a long season of worry, sorrow, and exhaustion had welled to overflowing. A mother's heart was perhaps the most vulnerable thing on earth, and Harriet Newman's would have been no exception. Extracting that promise from Dove—maybe that had been desperation, not selfishness. That explained the asking, but what about the response? Many people might say just about anything at the bedside of a dying friend or relative. Anything that sounded comforting, just to let the person die in peace. Many people might put some time and effort, and even money, into making good on whatever nice-sounding things they had said: "I'll find your beloved Bitsy a good home." "I'll do my best to live by the things you've taught me." "I promise to get along better with my brother and sister." But "I'll give up my home, friends and freedom until I find out what happened to your son, even if I go to my own grave having tried and failed"? Had Dove really meant *that*? It appeared that she had. Maybe Dove believed this was the one true purpose of her life, the reason she had been born. Plenty of people in the world believed weirder things than that.

They headed toward town and passed Mueller's Garage. Joan refused to turn her head to watch it go by. "Dove." The time for talking was fast coming to an end. "How could you change the entire direction of your life the way you did? What keeps you from giving up and moving on to wherever you would be if you weren't here?"

Dove didn't answer until after she had put the car in Park under some shade in a remote corner of the Diner's parking lot. She turned to Joan with a slight smile. "Patience. Patience, and more patience. And the conviction that what I set out to do was the right thing—and still is." She leaned toward Joan a little. "You are the only person, besides myself and Cora Haskew, who knows what I'm trying to do."

"Then why not ask more questions? Involve more people? Gerald Givens, maybe? I'll bet you could trust *him*."

"I can't take that risk. His wife isn't exactly tight-lipped, and if she got wind of it, the whole town might know what I suspect. That could get really awkward. *Bad,* actually. I'd probably have to load up and move out of here in a hurry. People may not consider the Mueller family model citizens, but they *are* 'home folks.' I'd have a hard time making any more headway if it got out who I suspect."

"But why are you so convinced there was foul play?"

Dove reminded Joan about the Muellers' reaction a year ago to the news story, and about Jesse Mueller's strange interest in the bag from Addison's. Also about his nasty attitude when he had caught Joan staring at the mystery car. "I *know* the Muellers are involved. And, if it were just a matter of their *knowing* something, they would have no good reason to *hide* what they know, unless telling what they know would incriminate them. I can't imagine that Jesse Mueller has the kind of money to buy the silence of that guy in Addison's, but I *can* imagine that he might have been successful in threatening him." Honestly, Joan could imagine that, too. "A second ago you said I'd changed the entire direction of my life. I don't see it that way. 'The entire direction of my life' is to do what I believe God wants me to do. For now, that means living in Crook Mountain. There is a job to be finished here, and I believe you can help me finish it. I'm asking you. Will you consider staying a little longer? You don't seem to be on a fixed schedule. You're smart, you're curious, and your line of work tells me you have the desire to help people. Will you please help *me?*"

<hr />

After saying goodbye to Dove, Joan walked across the street and ducked into the C.M.G.M. to look for a quality word puzzle magazine. She came away empty-handed, though, not interested in a whole book of "word searches" suitable for third-graders. She crossed Hill Street again. Good. Her CRV was right where she had left it, and it appeared to have four firm tires and no stains of dark oil or greenish coolant on the gravel around it. Joan's phone told her it was 12:34. It also told her that Lee hadn't answered her last couple of messages.

She pulled her car onto the road and headed toward the cabin. Some rest would be nice after the taxing road trip, but packing had to be done before check-out tomorrow. As she passed Mueller's Garage, Joan looked over, unable to stop herself this time. Both of the twins were out front, just standing there in the parking lot in their work clothes. Dub lifted an arm and waved at her. They knew her vehicle, of course. Joan smiled and waved back. Her smile then faded. They'd lost a sweet, loving mother. They were left with a harsh, gruff father. The Mueller boys' future seemed awfully bleak.

Four hours later, curled up on the bed under a lightweight quilt, Joan opened her eyes from a sound nap. None of her things were packed. Rousing herself and moving about in a draggy, post-nap fog, she made coffee as if it were morning instead of late afternoon. She carried her cup outside and eased into one of the wide, varnished wood rockers on the front porch. Smiling at the tin can "vase" of wisteria twigs, she reached over and touched the blossoms very lightly. Under other circumstances, this moment could have felt like a new day with morning coffee, blissful quiet, and all cares tucked away in other parts of the world. Instead, Joan was a restless spectator alongside a noisy parade of names and faces that hadn't existed five days ago. That haunting photograph of Larry Newman, the man whose fate remained unknown. His poor mother, dying without answers! Dub and Luke Mueller, little more than youths, deserving to be released from the chains their father kept tight on them. How could one reach out to them? Jesse's control of his boys and the effect it was having on others, like Bonnie Jarvis, was vexing. Smart, kind, hardworking Bonnie. A nineteen-year-old in love and with her whole adult life in front of her. Kind Sherry, not-so-kind Marilyn, and little Laynie Key. None of these were the mere and faceless population statistics Lee had found online with such nonchalance. They were people whose ups and downs had pricked the heart of a short-term visitor to their tiny corner of the world. They were people who deserved a future of limitless opportunity. Not to mention Dove Sechrist herself. Friendly, capable, patient, devoted. She deserved to find the answers she was seeking on another's behalf. She deserved the freedom to leave Crook Mountain if she wanted to, or to stay here by choice, out from under such a heavy personal burden.

Joan drained the coffee cup and looked at her phone again. Still nothing from Lee. She sighed. Oh, well. It couldn't be helped. When working, he could go hours at a time without being able to entertain distractions. She went inside and brushed her teeth. By the time she had patted her lips with the hand towel, her immediate plans had been made: sign the cabin's guest book, grab an early supper at the Diner, take a last walk around town, and return here to pack. Summarizing her stay in a few words wasn't easy. She held the guest book pen in her right hand. *"Most memorable mountain vacation ever"*? *"Met some interesting people"*? *"Try to visit at Easter and enjoy the church potluck"*? Finally, she wrote her name, city, and "Lovely cabin in a place that makes you think." Maybe the next tenants would read that and be prompted to do their own serious thinking.

——◆——

"You again!" Dove grinned.

"Can't get rid of me, I guess." Joan smiled back and complimented Dove's mint green uniform. Jeans and solid-color tees were acceptable for the other employees, but Dove obviously had her own dress code. And there were Gerald and Edith Givens. Joan lifted a hand and smiled. First time she'd seen the Mrs. here. Before Joan had a chance to decide where to sit, Gerald Givens came over and invited her to join him and Edith. Joan accepted and soon had a glass of water and a set of silverware in front of her. She asked the Givenses what they had ordered, then decided on the same: the special of pork curry, green beans, and purple hull peas.

Gerald Givens sported his usual business look. It was high time Joan asked what this man did for a living, and she did so, saying she couldn't leave town tomorrow without having her curiosity satisfied on that point. The answer, that he was a tax accountant, fell right in line with her predictions. "This is his busy season." Edith's wifely pride showed plainly.

The gentleman tempered his wife's statement by assuring Joan that he had learned years ago not to let himself become overwhelmed. "At this stage of my career, I can be selective in whose business I take on."

He is so thoughtful. He doesn't want me to feel bad about his having taken time to change my tire during his "busy season." Joan told the couple she and Lee were relieved of that stress for another year, having had their tax returns done in February. Edith remarked how nice it was of her to visit Laynie and her parents at the hospital. *Yes, word does get around.* "I'll be sure to leave my e-mail address with Dove so I can stay updated on Laynie." Edith asked if Laynie had received the CD, proudly letting Joan know it was Gerald who had arranged for someone from Blueberry Creek Band to visit Laynie and deliver the gift.

Peals of delighted laughter caused all three to turn and observe the merriment at a table where Dove was refilling beverages for a family of four. "If you're not aware of it, Mrs. Ryan, having been in town only a short time, this place has become like a whole new restaurant since Miss Dove has been here. The food *and* the service have improved dramatically."

"Mercy, yes! Why, Gerald wouldn't have *dreamed* of takin' me out to a meal here before that time! It never used to be this clean, this good of quality, or this *happy*." Gerald added that, knowing of Dove's unsettled childhood, in terms of moving often, he believed the slow pace of life in their town agreed with her. Might that be wishful thinking? The couple's high regard for Dove made Joan turn and look again at the woman whose faithfulness to Harriet Newman was having a trickle-down effect, benefiting other people, including all who patronized Crook Mountain Diner. How would the Givenses and Cora Haskew take it when Dove, of whom they were so fond, finally solved her problem and moved on? Clearly, the pretty brunette with the radiant smile and uplifting attitude would be missed when that time came.

The three ate their dinner specials. It was interesting that Gerald should call Joan's time in Crook Mountain "short." How much longer than a week it felt! The older couple prepared to excuse themselves not long after their plates were empty, saying that Edith had baked a blueberry pie that day for their dessert.

They invited Joan. "That's very sweet of you, but I'd like to stay right here and gather my thoughts. And I need to check in with my husband." She reached into her purse and brought her phone out.

"Well," Gerald said in parting, "We're glad you came our way, and we wish your friend's sister-in-law the best."

Joan stood and shook hands with the couple, thanking them for their hospitality "above and beyond." She complimented their home and even hinted that she might return for another visit sometime. "We tend to migrate to the Smokies now and again when we're not renting a place at the lake. I hope my husband and children will have the privilege of meeting you both."

As the Givenses left, Bonnie Jarvis came in, straight brown hair swinging as she stepped to the Take-Out end of the counter. Her brief conversation with Dove seemed to indicate a standing order on Wednesdays for food taken to a Bible study for "tween"-aged girls, led by Bonnie and her next-younger sister. "Let the younger women learn from the older," Dove said, handing over a large, brown bag. "Those girls are lucky to have you and Jenny as their teachers." Bonnie smiled and hurried out.

Joan spent the next twenty minutes indulging in low-fat hot fudge cake with coffee that was black because the cake was sugary enough, and decaffeinated because what she'd just brewed at the cabin wasn't. She barely lifted her eyes from her phone all the while, working the keyboard whenever she wasn't taking a sip or a bite.

At the cash register, she held a twenty-dollar bill out to Dove. "My compliments to the chef!" The money was discreetly declined. Gerald Givens had covered Joan's meal. "The town's 'quiet money,'" Joan said softly. "That was so sweet of him!" She lowered her voice another notch and asked to speak with Dove privately. Moments later, they stood in the narrow corridor leading to the restrooms. "I've just notified my husband and my neighbor that I'm going to be away one day longer than planned. Now, how soon can we talk about what I can possibly do in an extra twenty-four hours to help you fulfill this promise and get on with your life?"

Chapter 11

For the first time since Joan had gotten all tangled up in this business, things were actually moving quickly. It had to be that way if her offer of one day's help was to be of any value. The Diner happened to close early, by rule, on Wednesdays, so people could get to their church activities. Still, it was after eight when the three women pulled their chairs up close to Cora's kitchen table for their serious conference. Emily the cat watched and purred as if to encourage Cora, Dove, and Joan to hatch a good plan. Anyone who might inquire why Dove and Cora were absent from church could be told that the hospital visit followed by a shift at the Diner had tired Dove excessively, that Cora had chosen to stay at home with her, and that both women wanted to visit with their new friend Joan, who would be leaving town soon—none of which was untrue.

Getting it all down on paper, with an actual pen in hand, was helping to make some sense out of the chaos. "What really needs to happen is for someone to get into the back lot of Mueller's and take a thorough look at that car. That won't be easy, but let's put it on the list." Joan wrote a few words, then set the pen down. "Here's what we have: Cora will call tomorrow morning to find out if the TV station will air the same anniversary story about Newman's disappearance that they ran before, now that it has been another whole year since the incident. If they don't seem interested, she will try to persuade them, by her viewpoint as a local historian, that they ought not to want the case to stay a loose end, an unsolved mystery." Surely after her long and faithful service in the community, Cora would command some sway with the local press. "If the story is scheduled, and if the station will tell us when it's going to air, we—or *you*, I should say—will do whatever it takes to have the key people present. At any rate, Cora can point out that it shouldn't have to involve much more work for the station than pulling their archive footage and introducing it."

Joan forged on. "If we get past that first hurdle, we'll need a plot for the next step. Getting the Mueller men into a room with other witnesses to watch their reaction will be tricky. Maybe a surprise party or a town hall meeting on some political or social issue."

"Maybe the personalities of Gavin or Marilyn or even Mayor Dyle can help us if we dangle the right bait. Cora and I will put our heads together and see what sort of 'party' we can concoct. If there's some way to make Marilyn the guest of honor, maybe we can recruit Bonnie's help in seeing that the twins and Jesse attend."

"Good thoughts, Dove. It's even possible that tying an event to the Key family might work. But I don't like to think of using them that way." Cora and Dove murmured that that approach wouldn't be their first choice, either. "Meanwhile, I'll be taking this picture of the man in question to Cluny's Ridge tomorrow to see what I can stir up." Joan tapped the top end of her pen gently on the border of the picture Dove had shown to her in the car. "You never know. Assuming the authorities did the same thing two years ago and got nowhere, it might be a long shot. But, if Dove's feeling about the man at Addison's is legitimate, maybe I can unearth something." Unknown in Cluny's Ridge, Joan might pass herself off as an old school friend of Larry Newman's who had just learned of his disappearance and knew that with his family being deceased no one else might be trying very hard to solve the case. She hadn't worked out exactly what approach she would take. "Dove, your job is to stay behind the scenes and not blow your cover while you figure out if there's any possible way to recruit help from Gerald Givens or Serena Stillman, even without their knowing why you're asking them to do whatever they might do."

"Serena may have more contacts and more reason to want the Muellers' guilt exposed if it exists, assuming we get to the point of telling her everything, but Gerald Givens might be better in the area of keeping confidences and not asking too many questions."

Perfect. Dove had taken on an assignment that would allow her to stay in character, thinking for as long as possible before acting. "My first step is to find out if I can spend tomorrow night in the cabin, or if I have to check out as originally planned." On the off chance that someone might answer one of the office phone numbers listed on the business card Serena had given her, Joan dug for the card and dialed. She got a recording and hung up. "I'll try again in the morning. It says they open at nine." Dove promptly suggested that Joan might spend Thursday night right there at Cora's, on the day bed, or even at the Givenses'. Joan declined. If the three of them did manage to stir anything up, it could be better for people not to see herself appearing to be as thick as thieves with the other two. "If I can't add on one more night at the cabin, I should be able to find a hotel in Cluny's Ridge." Picking up the loose sheets of note paper with both hands and tapping the lower edges on the table to neaten the stack, she aimed a brief smile at the other two. Maybe the energy generated by her efforts would ignite the solution Dove had been seeking for so long.

"I hate to think of your going, Joan. I've gotten used to having you here." Dove rose as she spoke, patting the shoulder of Cora, who was starting to droop. "You know, you might try Serena's personal number tomorrow. She might could pull strings that a regular booking agent wouldn't know about."

Joan promised she'd keep that in mind. Before stepping out the door, she bent down and stroked Emily's soft, gray fur. Driving back to the cabin, she tried bolstering her own spirits. *This can work!* A little voice taunted her in return, casting doubt, telling her she was just being silly. Oh, well. Even if it *didn't* work, it was better than doing nothing. Involving herself to this extent in a situation so outside her own, comfortable world wasn't exactly out of pattern, else she probably wouldn't be doing it. Her humanitarian approach to life was nothing new. It was how genuinely meaningful she was finding the situation that was surprising.

Before retiring, Joan checked to be sure Cluny's Ridge had a basic office supply store with copy services. One of tomorrow's first tasks was to make a quality copy of Dove's photograph of Larry Newman. That copy was going to be autographed, in Joan's best imitation of a man's handwriting, with a message to *her.* She read over several web pages about pipes and pipe tobacco, picking up terms like *porous briar* and *Burley* and *Cavendish,* and learning that some tobaccos were fire-cured while others were flue-cured. She'd bought Jerry's sampler pack half by educated guess and half by the memory of her friend's preferences. But, tomorrow, she planned to know a little more about the products for sale in Addison's, while *appearing* to know almost nothing at all.

———❖———

Joan blew her breath out of pursed lips, then chugged the last third of her water. Invigorated by her twenty minutes of stretches and cardio exercises, she stood in place, continuing to move her leg muscles by swaying. The morning fog reached right up to the cabin. It appeared to shut off all civilization, but civilization was out there, making requirements of her. Today's schedule was tight. She showered, dressed, and started packing, all without having had breakfast. Finally, over instant oatmeal with added-in raisins, dried mango, and coconut, she reviewed the departure checklist. Even if she got the green light to stay here one more night, she must be ready for the alternative. And if a cleaning crew happened to arrive on the early side of check-out time, she'd rather not be in their way. There were still plans to make for Cluny's Ridge, too. She could go in Addison's Pipe & Tobacco and return or exchange the sampler pack, saying she'd changed her mind. Browsing for something to replace what she'd bought on Saturday would give her time to check the place out, knowing what she knew now about the shop's role in the Newman case. That part of the story, at least, was a matter of record and not just something Dove had a feeling about. Or, instead of making a return or an exchange, she might mention casually that she had thought of someone else to buy for. That someone else could be named Mueller. She could drop the name *Marilyn* Mueller (pretending to be friends with her, which would be pretense, indeed), and then watch for any special reaction by anyone in the shop. Hopefully, by someone named Neal Coffey. Maybe she would produce the photo right off the bat, saying the man pictured was her brother, who lived in California—*or Cincinnati*. "Study the picture," she could urge. "I know very little about pipes and tobacco, but I've heard you're a real *expert*, Mr. Coffey. What do you think this man would like as a gift?"

Joan loaded her Honda with all she had brought to town, plus all she had acquired, then tucked the cabin's door key into its little, stiff paper envelope and secured the envelope in a zippered pocket on the inside of her purse. By the time an office of Stillman-Breck Realty was open for business at nine to take her phone call, she planned on being in Cluny's Ridge, her car parked safely in a public lot centrally located, the picture copy and a fine-tip Sharpie in hand, and samples of men's handwriting in view on her tablet. Next to the tablet would be a tall cup of café mocha. Just over an hour later, in a quiet corner of Stofer's Coffee, Joan sipped her steaming beverage and licked the flavors of chocolate and coffee off her lips. Her scheme was underway.

Besides calling on Addison's in a few minutes, she was going to look for anyone in the area who would say with confidence that Larry Newman had been in town on the day he had gone missing. She would start that process right here in the coffee shop just as soon as she had inscribed the back of the photo, "From your loving brother, Larry." "To Joan" would not precede that. For now, at least, she was going to keep *her* name out of it.

But brandishing Newman's photo in the coffee shop produced nothing at all, unless you counted it as rehearsal for her center-ring performance upcoming. The curtain would be going up on that very soon. Joan left Stofer's and, on impulse, stepped into a drugstore for cash back on the purchase of the kind of puzzle magazine she'd been wanting. The cash would be helpful at Addison's, in case of another transaction there. Little good it would do to keep her name off the back of Newman's photo if it was plainly visible on her debit card and on the merchant's copy of her cash register receipt.

Gradually building up her nerve, she ventured into the establishments either side of Addison's to learn how well the man Coffey was known or esteemed. One of those was a clothier. The other carried local preserves, honeys, and baked goods. *Blinders on! Now's not the time to get interested in other shopping!* She had one goal, and that was to ask about Neal Coffey. When she did ask, no one said they recognized that name, and this told Joan one thing: Neal Coffey—assuming he still kept shop next door—didn't go out of his way to be neighborly. This wasn't particularly helpful information. These days, it seemed to be more common, and even more acceptable, for people to keep to themselves. Being neighborly had become almost synonymous with being creepy. Very, very sad.

Addison's Pipe & Tobacco appeared empty of employees when Joan pulled the door open. But a man she decided instantly was what Neal Coffey should look like materialized right away, even though there was no bell on the door that should have alerted him. Probably a surveillance camera or a motion sensor was the signal. Yes, this man looked like someone who would prefer something other than a happy-sounding jingle bell to tell him a customer had entered his shop. He wasn't quite middle-aged. He was medium-tall and had a light brown crew cut. He definitely was *not* the shorter, tattooed twenty-somethinger who'd sold her the tobacco sampler. *Okay. Here goes nothing!* "I'm looking for Mr. Coffey. I've heard he's the best person to answer my questions."

Narrowed eyes with blond or no lashes on them peered at Joan. A smoker's gravelly voice asked, "What questions?" The man had neither confirmed nor denied that he was Neal Coffey, but logic suggested that he was. Anyone other than Coffey probably would have said "He isn't here" or "I'll go get him."

Awkward in the extreme! But, really, how else was an errand like this going to feel? Joan had never put herself in such a position before. She wasn't at all practiced at ruses, acting, or subterfuge. *I guess that means I'm basically honest.* She plastered on the professional smile she used during nutrition consultations with patients who might or might not care to listen. "I found a great gift in here several days ago for a friend back home, but I realized later that there's someone else I should have shopped for at the same time."

"Well?" The tone was impatient. "Look around." The words amounted to an invitation, but the face wasn't inviting. It was stony.

Joan pushed ahead. She was way too nervous. *Relax!* "I need something for my brother. He's quite the pipe smoker. I don't see him often—he lives up north—and I want to surprise him with some tobacco he'll really like."

"Best brands 're right along there." This information was half mumbled and half growled as the man gestured toward the shelves behind Joan.

She turned and spent several moments looking over the stock. In spite of the brief research she'd done last night, it was still pretty much "all Greek." She might as well be illiterate, trying to choose a good tea, coffee, or chocolate bar by colors and pictures. "Well, it's all very *pretty.*" She reached into her purse and fingered the critical envelope. She pulled it out. "I know this may sound *silly*, but..." She opened the flap. *Ugh. Sweaty palms. Probably because I'm not used to lying.* "This is a picture of my brother holding his favorite pipe." She removed the photo. Could the man hear her heart racing? "Would you mind taking a look?" She extended the photograph, breath catching in her throat. "Does the picture suggest anything?" She watched the man's face. "Does the kind of pipe, and my brother's 'style'—*you* know, his face, his *look*, his *clothing*—make you think of any particular type or flavor of tobacco?" The request seemed about as ridiculous as asking an accountant to figure a tax return based on the colors of fish in a client's aquarium.

If his glare was any indication, the man who had taken the picture from her hand, but hadn't said yet whether he was Neal Coffey, agreed that her request sounded foolish. "Pipe's a Meerschaum. High quality. If ya want ta-bacca that'll impress, Dunhill, Hearth & Home, er McConnell. Take yer pick."

"Okay..." Joan turned one-eighty and stayed with using prettiest packaging as her guideline, quickly taking two varieties of the Dunhill off the shelf. She set them on the sales counter and paid cash, placing the bills on the counter instead of aiming them toward the man's large, stubby fingers. She was being frowned at all the while. If this hadn't been reconnaissance, and if it had been any other employee, any other place, she'd have been very tempted to pull out of the transaction solely on principle. Nobody who dealt with customers in such a surly manner deserved to make sales. The picture of Larry Newman lay on the counter, facing her. The Addison's man clearly was done with it.

Joan hesitated, then slowly stowed her photo without looking at the ill-tempered man. The sight of her phone down in her purse sparked an idea. Heart beating faster, she pulled the device out, threw caution to the wind, and slid her finger across the bottom of the screen in the pretense of answering a call. "Hello?" A second or two to hear the pretend response. "Yes." *Think!* "Fine." As if asked how she was. "Yes. Yes, it was Mueller. Mueller's Garage in Crook Mountain." She pretended to listen to her caller, at the same time giving the shopkeeper a look she hoped seemed both apologetic (for taking a call while transacting business—as if her "rudeness" in doing so could possibly compete with *his* bad manners!) and innocent (about saying the name "Mueller" clearly and repeatedly). "Yes, the boys are twins," she added for good measure, "and Marilyn is their sister. I had my flat fixed there. It's out of town a little way. Okay. Good luck!" The unfriendly shopkeeper had been fiddling with some impulse-buy merchandise on the counter. Now, he was opening a new box of cigars with fancy-looking red and gold seals on them. If he had taken any particular notice of the face in the photo, or of Joan's having dropped the name "Mueller," he wasn't letting on.

"Sorry." Joan dropped her phone into a pocket. "Friend with a minor car emergency." No reaction. Her glance fell on the cigars again. *"Cigar smoking is a form of thumb sucking." There I go again with the movie quotes!* Mitzi Gaynor had zinged Kirk Douglas with that line, playing sophisticated Kate Brasher to his conniving attorney Deke Gentry.

"What's funny?" Coffey was looking at her disdainfully.

So, he can *still talk.* Joan threw her plastic smile back on and hoped Marilyn Mueller Walker would have been proud of her. "Thanks for helping me with this. Men can be so difficult to buy for." Joan gathered the bag containing her purchase, ignoring the man's question and his horrible manners. She pushed her way out the door of Addison's, thankful to be leaving a place that wouldn't make the top fifty in a Cluny's Ridge Most Friendly Business competition. If she didn't find a good use for the tobacco she was carrying, Jerry was going to be overwhelmed by her generosity, come Christmas, when she presented him with these tins of Dunhill as well as the sampler box.

———◆———

He watched the tall blonde leave, then bolted from behind the counter and looked out the door to see which way she had gone. Reaching with one hand to grab his baseball cap off the counter, he used the other to throw the Open/Closed sign around the other way. From a front pants pocket he yanked out a crowded key ring. Slowly, he pushed the shop's door open and leaned out, looking this way and that. Slow. Not getting any notice from anybody on the sidewalk. As if it was the most natural thing in the world to lock up in the middle of business hours, that's what he did.

———◆———

Pausing once or twice to make notes in her phone, Joan headed for her car, where she could sit for a few minutes and regroup. She needed to get her umbrella. Her weather app showed the rain coming on in as predicted. There was her trusty, rainproof Honda, a far cry from that sad, old Datsun she'd started to college in. Lee used to make fun of it.

"What're ya playin' at, lady?" The voice behind her startled Joan so badly that she jerked one-eighty and dropped her phone, which landed noisily on the pavement. Although half of the man's face was hidden by the ball cap, Joan recognized him immediately by the clothing, the raspy voice, and the not-very-white teeth. *Breathe. You're in control of this.* She willed her pounding pulse to settle down, but it was matter over mind. Hoping the man would see that she cared more about her dropped phone than about being afraid of *him,* she stared him down for a moment before deliberately retrieving the smartphone in its pretty turquoise case that was a recent Christmas gift from her children. It had better not be broken. The case, or the phone.

"What are you talking about? And why did you sneak up on me?" She glanced in several directions to see if other people were about. Sure, he would see what she was doing, and he would take it as a sign that she was on the defensive. But, it couldn't be helped. *Pepper spray.* It was always with her. She reached into a front pocket of her relaxed-fit cargo pants and felt the dispenser in there with her car keys. She wrapped her fingers around the vial. Right now was the closest she'd ever been to thinking she'd actually be using it. At such close range, though, the enemy would have a good chance of wresting it from her before she could aim and shoot. It was highly unlikely he'd just stand there and watch her aim and dispense!

"That man in the picture ya showed me. He ain't yer brother.

What reason ya got to lie? You a female detective or somethin'? Tryin' t' make a name fer y'se'f by solvin' a cold case?"

Joan forced a short laugh. "What makes you ask that?" *Answer questions with questions. Admit nothing.*

"Ya seem t' think I know somethin'. Ya know I'm the one the police questioned when that guy went missin'. I 'member hearin' it said then that 'e was a *only child.*" He sneered the last two words and accented them by bobbing his head twice, as a nine-year-old might do while saying, *"So there!"*

The man had a point. During the investigation, anyone could have learned that Newman was an only child. Right now, the only person who appeared guilty of pretense was herself. But she would not be intimidated, nor admit to having lied. This man had just owned up to being Coffey, the one the police had questioned. If Dove was right and Jesse Mueller had done something to hush Coffey up, possibly paid him some of the money the town gave for his wife's funeral (and she wouldn't put that past Mueller), maybe Coffey had followed her now with the hope of using against her the deception she had just tried. Maybe he thought a well-dressed stranger with nice jewelry on her fingers would like to pay him something not to blow her cover. Could she trip him up? "So you do recognize the man in the photo."

"Sure I do. But it ain't cuz I seen 'im in person. It's cuz I seen 'is picture on the news an' in the fat, pink hand o' some cop back when."

"Oh! Then you *didn't* see Larry Newman in your shop two years ago. You know for certain that some *other* man bought tobacco from you using Newman's credit card. What did *that* man look like?" Coffey frowned. *Paydirt!* Joan wasn't going to press the point just now, though. Not without backup. She relaxed the hand that was still gripping her pepper spray and went for her keys instead, pressing the red alarm button. Her car horn beeped loudly at short intervals. The lights flashed on and off. Coffey cursed, glanced about nervously, and quickly put strides between himself and Joan before slowing his gait to a casual swagger.

That the noise had sent Coffey on his way, Joan was thankful. She pressed the red button again so the alarm would stop. Her act at Addison's hadn't exposed any connection between Coffey and the Muellers, but the man's behavior certainly didn't seem above board. It wasn't a great leap to think such a man capable of lying to the police. Joan pressed her unlock button and got in, locking the door again and resting her phone beside the cup holders. The case had several dings from the pavement. Grimacing, she gripped the safety belt to fasten it. Her hands were shaking. She sighed and watched them tremble. *Bother! I must not be cut out for this line of work.* She took slow, calming breaths, letting her hands rest open on her lap until the shaking stopped.

———◆———

Hat still pulled way down to conceal as much of his face as possible, Neal Coffey unlocked the tobacco shop and stepped inside. Leaving the sign reading "Closed," he locked the deadbolt and dialed a number. He told some of what had just happened, all the while standing a few feet back from the front glass of the shop and watching. Would the nosy broad come back to snoop some more? She was a good-looking female, but he wasn't telling that right now. No, he wasn't showing all his cards. Not till he knew what was in it for *him.* "Think about it. Ya got my number." He shoved the phone into a back pocket. Then, he took a Punch cigar off the counter and removed the wrapper. He looked at it and turned it a couple of times. The stogie felt good in his fingers. He ran it slowly under his nose, inhaling deeply and closing his eyes. Leaving the cellophane trash lying on the counter, he flipped the sign to "Open," undid the deadbolt, and carried the cigar into the back room.

———◆———

It might have been the sight of impending rain, or maybe it was the need for comfort after her run-in with Coffey. Something reminded Joan she had no shelter lined up for the night. It was a quarter of eleven. Still in her car, she pulled Serena's business card out. Instead of dialing right away, she started the motor. She wasn't going to stay here any longer where Neal Coffey could be watching her. She pressed a button. "Directions to Cluny's Ridge Police Department." The phone did its thing and showed the destination to be two miles away. Joan put the CRV in gear and set out, taking wrong turns on purpose in case she were being followed. The navigation guided her back on course each time in its comforting Australian accent. Finally parking in one of the diagonal spaces out front of the municipal building, she undid her seatbelt and dialed Stillman-Breck Realty.

"We have another party arriving at that property today." The booking agent said what Joan had been hoping not to hear. "May I suggest another option for you, Mrs. Ryan? How many bedrooms were you needing?"

Joan hesitated. Most rental houses would have a minimum stay of two or three nights. *Wait.* What about Serena's house, the one with the view of Mueller's Garage? It was still vacant, as far as Joan knew. To the agent she described the house and its location, but she hadn't made any record of the address. She wasn't even certain it was one of their listings. "It's not far from the place I was staying. I could check Google Earth and try to figure out the house number."

"That won't be necessary. Give me just a moment, please. I should be able to… Ah, yes. I have it up now. Let me take a look." Staying in that brick house might let her spy further on Mueller's, assuming that she would be back before dark and that the rain wouldn't hinder her. "Unfortunately, I must tell you that that property is not one of our public listings. Reservations are restricted to personal acquaintances of the owner."

Joan smiled at her windshield. "How fortunate, then. I *am* a personal acquaintance. What if I give Serena Stillman a call, and she approves me as a guest?"

"In that case, she can give you an access code, and you will provide that to us when you call back."

Thankful for the great convenience of mobile phones—a blessing her children couldn't imagine having grown up without—Joan dialed Serena's direct number and explained that she was enjoying her stay and wanted to extend it, but that the cabin was booked. Serena immediately offered the house, and Joan thanked her. "When I call back, are they going to say there is a minimum stay? The thing is, I don't know that I'll need to be there but the one night. My plans are a little uncertain."

"Not a problem. For a friend of Dove's, I can let you have it by the day. Just let the office know when you're vacatin'. I'll call after we hang up and tell them they'll be hearin' back from you. It's a second step of security in case the access code was to get leaked out—you know, to friends of friends of folks in our office. It's happened, and I don't intend it to happen any more. And be sure they give you the code for the number pad to raise the garage door. It's comin' up a rain later today, I hear. And you'll need a key for the gate, along with the house key."

Joan thanked Serena again for her kindness. Silently, she thanked her for not asking nosy questions. *That's settled.* She dialed another number. The call went to voice mail, but she received a call back within a few minutes. Joan explained her new housing arrangement and told Dove she'd had a tense time with Neal

Coffey. "It's too much to tell over the phone, but we should meet and talk after I get back." She suggested that Dove casually say enough to certain people to get word around that Joan had left town. Maybe, if it appeared to everyone else that she was gone, she could come right back into Crook Mountain and do more spying during the remaining daylight. She would park her car inside the garage to make it appear that the house was still vacant. "This reminds me of a TV western," she told Dove. "The bad guys all saw Victoria Barkley leave on the stagecoach, but then she sneaked right back into town to keep looking for her missing daughter." Joan's last words hung in the air, too close to reality to be laughed at.

"That's ironic," Dove said softly and paused before continuing. "Spreading the word that you've left town shouldn't be hard. It could be as simple as complimenting Mayor Dyle on how our fair town enchanted a recent visitor who has gone home to tell all her friends that this is *the* place for true Smoky Mountains hospitality. The minute I turn my back, he'll be writing notes on a paper napkin so he can quote you in his next speech. And I could always tell Marilyn Mueller Walker that you've left and that the cabin is going to have new guests for her to 'welcome.'"

"In her sincere and warmhearted way. But she'll stop listening after you tell her I've left. That'll make her day!"

"Oh, goodness, I almost forgot! We have a development on this end, too! Cora found out that the story on Larry was actually up for broadcast in February and it got bumped when they had a severe weather outbreak to cover. It's still in queue. They've agreed to let Cora know when it will air."

"That's *great*, Dove!" Joan's spirits, still flagging a little after her close encounter of the scary kind, rose a notch. Maybe the TV news angle would be a real help, in essence recreating what Dove had witnessed a year ago. *Too bad I won't be here to see it.* Watching the clouds grow still darker, she stayed in the police parking lot, thinking and idly fingering the new nicks in her phone case. She hadn't anticipated that Neal Coffey would know she couldn't be Newman's sister. But, her fib about that had drawn the unsavory shopkeeper out. What could have been a problem had actually worked for good. Was there a chance the separate parts of this crazy plan were going to converge at just the right time and result in success? Wasn't that what she should be expecting to happen? With her husband spouting project management terminology all the time, and herself a seasoned planner who was always highly organized, it shouldn't surprise her that an idea that had her handprints on it should be moving forward. It was just that *this* idea and the situation requiring it were so drastically different from any she'd ever had her handprints on before.

Chapter 12

The rough-running Mercury Sable crunched over the gravel in front of the McCain cabin and slowed to a stop. "Whew! That climb seems t' get steeper all the time."

"Look!"

There was a man up there on the porch, in one of the two wood rockers. He looked to be tall, broad-shouldered, and dead asleep. Or maybe just *dead!* His head was leant back against the chair, and his eyes were shut. His blue jeans, yellow shirt and black jacket looked to be expensive. "I don't think he jus' wandered up here from the woods, like one o' those backpacker hikin' types. Hey! Maybe he's the *bank robber* that's on the loose! It was on the news!"

"Could be! Look at that black bag by 'is feet. That's prob'ly where the money is. Least, it's always like that on TV. An' I've heard that criminals fall asleep afterwards cuz of all the stress they been under, plannin' an' executin' the crime! I know *one* thing. I'm not budgin' an *inch* with him on that porch, even if we *are* s'posed ta get this cabin clean fer new folks. Call 9-1-1."

Her little sister might be just bein' dramatic. But, even if he wa'n' a bank robber, that man *was* a stranger, and he wa'n' s'posed ta be here. And *she* wa'n' goin' up there and past 'im, neither. He'd prob'ly wake up while she was unlockin' the door. "Ya think I should?"

"Yeah."

She giggled. "It'll be somethin' t' see what th' sheriff does!" She made the call, first time ever reportin' an emergency.

"But should we *leave* now, in case 'e wakes up an' comes after us?"

"No. If I crank up this loud-runnin' motor, that might wake 'im up fer sure. We'll sit right here an' watch 'im. But make sure all the doors're locked."

———◆———

"Wake up, mister, an' don't try nothin' funny."

A pudgy face came into focus. It was on the body of a uniformed officer. Was this a nightmare? Make that a *day*mare? No, it wasn't. The bad end of a firearm was closer to him than one had ever been before. The next thing he knew, he was in handcuffs, his common-sense protests being completely ignored. He was prodded down the cabin's front steps and "encouraged" to climb into the back seat of a patrol car. Who was in that other car he had no idea—unless they lived here and he'd gotten the address wrong. The officer, who gave his name as Deputy Sheriff Darryl King, put the black bag in the front seat beside him. He turned a deaf ear to explanations and turned country radio on.

———◆———

Joan finished her breakfast-food lunch. This pancake house was fine, but it was no Crook Mountain Diner! She smiled and pushed the plate away from her so she could work one of the puzzles in her new magazine. The server refilled her coffee cup. There was time to kill, while word was spread around town that she had left. She used her phone to look at afternoon movie showings, not sure she ought to get quite that involved in passing

time. The theater was several miles away. An incoming call
overwrote the screen. Unknown caller, but the same area code
as Dove's. Instinct said to let the call roll to voicemail. She did.
Wrong numbers happened. *But, wait.* Her pulse quickened. Could
Neal Coffey have tracked her down somehow? Had he seen her
Georgia license plate? The back of her car was out of view when
Coffey had followed her to it. But he could have lurked and
watched her drive away. Or maybe he had found her name in
his log of sales transactions from Saturday, when she had used
her debit card. He would have to have talked to the young man
who had waited on her then, and that guy would have had to
remember her, and what day she'd been in the shop. Why had
she chattered so much, letting on that she had shopped there
another time in recent days? That hadn't been necessary. The
fellow who had rung up the sale on Saturday had been marginally
engaged in her customer experience. He'd been more interested
in his phone. So, he might not even remember what she looked
like. And, besides, Coffey hadn't given the impression of being
terribly resourceful. On the other hand, first impressions could
be deceiving.

The phone changed again, showing notification of one new
voicemail. Heart pounding, Joan retrieved the message. It was
Lee's voice! What a relief! But, wait. Lee? Calling from a Tennessee
number?

—————◆————

It was unbelievable. Lee's message had said little more than
for her to call back, but what a ridiculous ordeal he was telling
her now. "I'll be there as fast as I can, honey. Hang in there." Joan
threw some cash down on the table and hoped the server would
enjoy the extra-large tip. It seemed forever before she finally
reached the county sheriff's office a full fifteen miles away.

"You think we'll laugh about this when we're older?"

Joan squeezed Lee's hand. "I hope so, honey. I am *so sorry!*" She hoped the deputy was hearing and was picking up on their mood.

"They've been making calls to confirm that I live in Duluth, that I'm with the bridge project, that our crew has been given some days off, and that I landed at the regional airport this morning and took a taxi to a certain cabin in Crook Mountain... *where* I had expected to find and to surprise my wife." Joan's face contorted. She felt terrible. "Furthermore, my black bag *doesn't* contain bank holdup money, but a shaving kit, one change of clothes, a spare pair of shoes, and one small box, attractively wrapped, which is a bottle of perfume for said wife." The items in question were strewn across the deputy's desk. Joan felt *really* terrible.

She promptly explained to both husband (more important) and deputy (less important) that she hadn't been at the cabin because her rental agreement was up and she was in the process of moving to different lodgings for the additional night she had decided to stay. "I left my husband a message that I was going to be staying *'in the mountains'* an extra night," she told King, "and he naturally assumed I would be at the place where I had started out. I didn't bother to say I was moving, because of course I was never expecting him to show up! If you knew how busy he stays, then you would understand my not bothering him with the minor detail that my original reservation was up."

Her saying "my original reservation" was going to prove problematic in a moment if the deputy decided to check *her* story as he had done Lee's. The name on the reservation wasn't Joan Ryan. It was Melinda Clark. Joan didn't want Melinda bothered with this, especially with all she had on her plate, and she didn't want anyone at the realty office to happen to mention to anyone else that she had reserved another property through them. The way gossip spread around here, that little detail was sure to make its way right back to Crook Mountain. Joan's heart sank a notch, then, when the deputy did in fact ask an assistant to find him the number for Stillman-Breck Realty. However, after King had dialed the number and was holding for a representative, a report came in that the bank robbery suspect for whom Lee had been mistaken had been apprehended in a teller's car. The teller, of course, had described the vehicle very accurately to police, right down to its license number. After hearing this, Deputy King quietly placed his phone's handset back in its cradle.

"World's dumbest criminals." Thank goodness she wasn't going to have to explain why she had been staying in a cabin that had been rented to someone else.

"And they're in good company," Lee muttered. Before the insulted party, scowling at that, could say anything, Lee held up a hand. "Look. I get like this when I'm sleep-deprived. Let's just wrap this up, shall we?" He stood and started repacking his duffel bag without obtaining permission to do so. Joan hid a smile. Lee stood a good head taller than the deputy, who seemed to be drawing his stomach in and straightening his shoulders. This wasn't the first time she'd seen her husband have that effect on another man. "And be very sure of one thing, Deputy—. *There will be no arrest on my record.*" Joan looked at her feet and tried not to laugh. Lee had wanted to say "Deputy Fife." He'd wanted to *badly!*

"Oh, fer sure, Mr. Ryan. It's all just a little misunderstandin'." The deputy looked sheepish. "No harm done."

You don't know how much my husband would like to do harm—to you!

<hr>

"By the way, sweetie, I don't imagine you want any more surprises today, but I do have one *little* one." Joan and Lee sat close together in a corner booth at the Grand Fork restaurant in Cluny's Ridge. Joan had driven them there, in the rain, after things had been straightened out at the sheriff's office. "I know I told the county's finest that we were going to be getting a hotel room here in Cluny's Ridge for the night and returning to Atlanta tomorrow, but..."

"What part of that are you about to tell me we aren't doing? And how long have you been in the habit of giving false information to law enforcement officers?"

"How many times have I even *talked* to law enforcement officers?" Joan grinned and took another bite of her New York strip. This wasn't the intimate, home-cooked dinner Joan had visualized for the evening of their reunion, but it sure was wonderful to have Lee here. After their week apart, she wouldn't have cared if they'd been eating burgers at Sonic.

"Mountain lion got your tongue?"

Joan had to laugh. "I've really missed you."

Lee reached across the table and squeezed her hand. "That's good to know. Why do you think I'm here? I've missed you, too."

Joan's insides did a flip. "But you weren't missing me enough to answer my last few messages. If you've been so busy that you're sleep deprived, how is it that you managed to sneak away for a rendezvous with your girl?"

"Dreaming of this rendezvous has been my motivation, honey. We kept on the job to get just a little ahead of schedule, and that's what made it possible for the whole crew to have two days of R and R."

"Good planning."

"Which brings us to *your* little secrets. Where were *you* this morning when, after I flew for four hours and spent another in a cab, my big surprise turned into so colossal a fail that we'll probably tell our grandchildren about it someday? Thanks to the locals who watch too many *Andy Griffith* reruns."

"I was being a good 'girl scout,' helping a friend in need, as you encouraged me to do." The account of her adventures should stay light, at least for now. If she gave Lee an orderly run-down of every detail, he would worry. Besides that, he might strongly discourage any further involvement in Dove's problem. And then she would have a dilemma. Because, the thing was, this was no longer just *Dove's* problem to Joan. It was Bonnie Jarvis's problem, and Cora Haskew's. And Dub's, and Luke's. It was Harriet Newman's problem, posthumously, and certainly it was *Larry* Newman's problem, too, the poor man! Because of all that, the problem had become Joan Ryan's problem.

They shared one dessert, a frothy lemon concoction with a graham cracker crumb crust. Probably there was some cream cheese in the top layer. Joan swallowed a delicious bite of it, then explained about Serena Stillman's house, where, because she had met Serena on Wednesday, she had been welcomed to stay without a set checkout date. "At a 'friends and family' rate, too. The place is nice and it has a great view." She didn't add, "Unless you're looking south." She *did* add, "Assuming you're here long enough to see it in the daylight, that is. I hate that your first impression of Crook Mountain has been marred by Deputy King's handcuffs earlier, and now by bad weather." Even though it was barely 5:00, their view through the restaurant's large windows was of pitch dark except where streetlamps shone through the torrents of rain. That steep grade leading up to the house might be a challenge tonight. To take her mind off that, Joan told Lee about some of the people she had met. "I want you to meet them, too. Some, because they would amuse you, and others, because you would like them."

"Salt of the earth?"

"Something like that, yes."

They paid the check and started for Crook Mountain. The

rain seemed to slacken. Joan set her navigation for Serena's house, now that she knew the address. The dark and the rain wouldn't help her to see that red mailbox post easily. They rode mostly in silence. This wasn't the time to start in about the whole Addison's ordeal, the TV news story scheme, or even the sad plight of Laynie Key. But Joan did bring up the bluegrass concert. "You guys would have loved it. Especially Sam." Lee's gutteral reply from the reclined passenger seat told Joan he was already fading. The interior lights went on and off while Joan climbed out, then in, then out, then in, with umbrella going up and back down, as she unlocked, passed, and relocked the security gate. Lee slept through it all.

With any luck, this "Victoria Barkley" ploy was going to work, although what she hoped to do about the Newman case while nobody realized she was still in town, Joan had no idea at all. *Speaking of luck*... She gripped the wheel tighter and willed her faithful Honda up the driveway. Then she saw what she'd forgotten after her time here on Monday. The steepest part of the drive wasn't gravel. It was paved! Hallelujah! And how would one get concrete to set on such an incline? Wouldn't it all slide to the bottom? She'd have to ask the engineer that one. But the point to be appreciated was that Serena had the means for paving, for garage door openers, and for motion-sensor security lights.

With the vehicle safely inside and the garage door lowered again, Joan gently nudged Lee awake. "We're here." He groaned and climbed out slowly with his leather tote. By now quite weary herself, Joan rummaged among her things in the back and pulled out as little as would keep her until morning. In the house she located and set the burglar alarm as instructed. Lee asked drily why the salt of the earth needed burglar alarms.

I think I know why Serena wanted this *one.* "Obviously, to keep out dangerous tourists like you and me."

They found clean sheets and made the bed together as Joan briefly pitched the idea of contacting Dove in the morning to see if she and Cora could come up for a visit. "Fine by me." Lee yawned and stretched his long, tired limbs. "Now, before I fall asleep again, how about...?"

"Oh!" Joan intercepted a wandering hand and pushed it away teasingly. "You mean you didn't travel all this way just for a steak dinner, good conversation, and a bashful kiss on the doorstep?"

"Not on your life!"

⬥

Friday morning was wet from the rain, but comfortable, with light traces of fog predicted to clear up early. From provisions on hand, Joan set yogurt, granola, fruit, and cinnamon rolls on the table and picked up where she'd left off on the happenings connected to Dove and the whole improbable missing-person investigation. About Addison's, she said merely that she had shown Newman's picture around in that shop and adjacent ones, learning nothing. *What about that natural inclination to honesty you were congratulating yourself on?* Joan stirred her yogurt unnecessarily. It wasn't as if she didn't have a good reason for not telling Lee absolutely everything. He had gone to considerable effort to get here for some carefree time with his wife. Now wasn't the time to worry him with something that was over already and hadn't hurt her. It was presumptuous enough to attempt to involve him directly in the Newman mystery, assuming that he would take part in the conversation about that once Cora and Dove arrived. He didn't know yet that that topic was the sole reason she'd invited the two women to come over.

Refilling Lee's coffee mug, Joan smiled to herself. She could be Dove right now. Just add a flattering uniform and a long, dark wig! "Dove is convinced that Jesse Mueller paid Coffey to change his story, to try to steer the investigation out of this area. We are just baffled what the motive could be. But, if looks and unsavory personality make a bad guy, I'll put my money on Coffey to be one of them."

Lee said the whole thing sounded like a tempest in a pot of tea. "Or would that be in a jug of moonshine?"

Joan reminded him that he'd said earlier that the problem was a good one for her to put her mind to. And then she gave him a sweet kiss in advance of informing him that she and the other ladies were going to pick his brain.

By prior arrangement through text messages with Joan, the guests arrived and knocked on the front door around 10:15. Dove looked her usual, glowing self. It didn't appear she had worked the early breakfast shift. And Cora looked the same as always. Strong, sharp-eyed, conservatively dressed, and quietly capable. "I *thought* we might find you with a companion this morning, Joan," Dove said after introductions were made. "All the talk in the Diner last night was about the bank robbery suspect apprehended right here in our midst. And how he turned out to be not a bank robber at *all*, but our sophisticated visitor Joan Ryan's *handsome, romantic husband* come to surprise her!"

"What? How did *that* get out?" Really, she should know by now that virtually *everything* eventually "got out" around here. However it had happened, it definitely ruled out any ideas she had toyed with about persuading Lee to play a role, pretending to be a random tourist unconnected with herself. He could have been a private investigator hired by Harriet Newman's attorney to look into the disposition of her estate, to find out what had happened to her heir, so Florida law could be carried out with respect to any other relations who might be entitled to Mrs. Newman's assets. Maybe it was just as well the town all seemed to know about Lee and who he was. It would keep Joan from asking him to do something so absurd. And it would explain why she'd "turned around and come back" to Crook Mountain after supposedly starting for home on Thursday.

Dove looked at Lee. "Yes, the young ladies who ratted you out are none other than two sisters earning extra money as domestics. Bonnie and Jenny Jarvis." Joan's surprise was audible as Dove continued, "Even though the deputy made them stay in their car, they managed to crack the windows enough to hear you trying to explain who you are and what you were doing there. Mr. Ryan, after all the buzz you have set off, I expected you to be nine feet tall, wearing armor, and riding a white horse!"

"You're not far off, sweetie." Virtually the first words Cora had spoken were so unexpected, Dove and Joan broke up, and Lee actually looked faintly embarrassed. Joan loved it. "And knights on white horses are always *trustworthy.*" Both Joan and Lee assured Cora they would keep the situation completely confidential.

"It's truly kind of you to indulge us this way while you're here," Dove told him. "I'm not surprised, though, after knowing your wife. I'm really grateful to you both." She launched right into good news. Cora had learned that station WTSE was scheduled to air the story about Newman's disappearance on the 6:00 news that very night, in place of another story that had had to be killed.

"Well, there's your first break. From what my wife has told me, Miss Sechrist—and I certainly admire your forbearance—I think you need to be more aggressive. Unless you begin to show some of your cards, nothing much is likely to happen. The more questions you ask, the more likely something will give." *That's Lee, my partner in overachieving. Birds of a feather!* Neither of them liked to see a started project go into hibernation. Backing off the proverbial gas pedal felt like downtime. Not that big projects didn't require some breaks for rest. Lee's very presence in Crook Mountain right now was testimony to that. But, if the Ryans were to figure into the keeping of Dove's promise, something major needed to happen in a major hurry. Lee had to be back at the airport the next evening, and Joan could feel her own opportunity for helping Dove beginning to slip away.

Lee kept the floor. "If you think that covered car needs to be examined, then you have to find a way to get in there and see it. Can someone get this Mueller out of the way and go to work on the sons? Ask them to show the car? If they act afraid or unwilling to, that's a sure sign they're hiding something."

"Well, let me ask a question." Joan wanted to hear her husband's opinion. "Would a car in the general vicinity of a person's last-known whereabouts, a car that stays covered, be reason enough for authorities to get a search warrant and examine the car? After all, it *is* the job of law enforcement, and not of private citizens, to solve cases like this. Right? And wouldn't someone on the force in Ohio or Florida be eager to crack this case? I should think the idea would appeal."

"Police or F.B.I. picking up the trail you think is here? Tough to say. Unless you have some kind of proof that the Mueller family had a motive or a connection to the case, well...I know *I'd* be skeptical." Dove's shoulders fell a notch. "However, I do suggest you try that as the next line of attack if whatever you can manage on your own—manage *safely* on your own—fails to satisfy your goal." That was directed at Dove. "I can't say I'm willing for my wife to invest in this to the degree that *you* have." *That* was directed at Joan, even though Lee was still speaking to Dove. Lee *was* skeptical of the whole business. That was obvious. He was being a sweet husband, going with the flow, supporting her. It was awfully good of him. "I have an idea that should help you evaluate people's reactions to this news story," he offered, "assuming you can actually get your persons of interest in the same room with you when it airs. And, to that end, where is the closest shopping district around here?" Joan suddenly felt better than she had in days. Her clever, nine-foot-tall husband had something up his sleeve!

The next half hour was spent discussing and discarding various ideas. It was a stimulating process. Not often did Joan and Lee get to apply their separate intellects to a challenge this unusual. Ultimately, and with the help of paper and pen again, a plan with intricate timing emerged. The essence of it was a small dinner gathering to be staged at the Diner that night, assuming the invited parties were free and would accept the invitation. Dove would request a favor of Gerald Givens in that regard, telling him little more than that there was a need for his help. To involve Gerald could encourage Jesse Mueller's attendance. Joan pointed out that if Edith Givens would tell *her* that Gerald had given the lion's share of money toward Mrs. Mueller's burial, then others in town, including Mueller himself, probably knew it, too. If there were anyone in Crook Mountain that a man like Jesse Mueller actually respected, or, at least, had a reason to stay on the good side of, Gerald Givens should be that one.

"Barring that, Jesse may agree simply for the sake of a free meal, and of course because he just generally feels he has to keep a close eye on Dub. Especially if the things I suspect are true, Jesse won't allow Dub into a situation among outsiders without being there himself. Don't forget the way he reacted when he saw you out there near the car, Joan."

"True. Then, too, it may strike Jesse as a whole new world, the idea of someone *honoring* his boys, when he himself appears to consider them nuisances. And that may intrigue him enough to attend our little soirée without a great deal of persuasion."

Dove would not eat the meal with the rest of them, but would be on hand, serving in her expected role as the Diner's chief cook. "I'll fix 'Fancy Meatloaf' as our entrée. It's a *New York Times* recipe and one of Jesse's favorites. I'll get Mr. Givens to mention that detail when he issues the invitation. We'll use the dining area that's partitioned off, and I'll get at least one more worker in tonight than we usually have on Fridays, so none of our regulars will be neglected."

A wall-mounted television, in the nook where they would set up the private party, would be tuned to the proper station. Just before the Newman story was to begin, Dove planned to make an "accidental" crash of dishes behind the counter, a noise that would startle the entire place into silence, getting the Muellers on edge along with everyone else. Then, maybe the broadcast really would catch them off guard. Dish-crashing? Sure, it was a bit unimaginative, a bit ridiculous. But it had worked once on *Gomer Pyle,* to cover up an explosion set off by crooks so they could get into a bank building from the basement of a café. So much for not asking Lee to get involved in anything absurd!

Dove sincerely expressed her gratitude again for what Joan and Lee were doing, and she and Cora went on their way. That left the Ryans to make *their* preparations. Joan wanted to take Lee out and show him the view of Mueller's Garage, but there was only time right now for her to point toward the spot. They would check it out on Saturday.

With Lee at the wheel this time, they headed north to a shopping district. Joan looked out the window. Watching the green foliage, including mimosa trees with their silky, peach-colored flowers, she thought of Bonnie. "By the way, I hope you won't be too cross over Bonnie Jarvis and her sister reporting you as a suspicious character. Bonnie is a sweet girl, and smart. If *I* saw you asleep on a front porch, *I* wouldn't try to walk past you. You're *imposing.*" Lee uttered a sound that was neither agreement nor disagreement. But Joan had never met a man who wouldn't take "imposing" as a compliment.

Her phone pinged, and she read aloud a text message from Dove, saying that Gerald Givens was very glad to join them in a small dinner gathering at the Diner at 5:30 that evening and was looking forward to meeting Joan's husband. "That's one spoke of our wheel in place!" No doubt Dove had come up with some tactful way of making the request so that omitting Edith from the invitation had made perfect sense.

They continued toward the retail complex that was in the general direction of the regional airport. Joan pulled up the Shopping List note in her phone to make some adds. Besides whatever Lee had on *his* list that he was still keeping a secret, they were after a pair of binoculars and "twin" items of some sort that would do for thank-you gifts, one of them in a shade of green. Joan brainstormed possibilities as they drove.

Chapter 13

"No. Definitely go with the stripe." It was fun giving Lee shopping advice. He hadn't counted on co-hosting a dinner party at Crook Mountain Diner, so they were supplementing his wardrobe for the occasion. They settled on the shirt, and Lee took time to confirm his flight reservation while Joan looked for the twin gifts and for a "thinking of you" card for Melinda's brother and sister-in-law.

Ping! Dove had more good news. "Success!" Joan waved her phone at Lee. "Gerald Givens has persuaded the Mueller men to be there tonight!"

"Brilliant." Joan laughed out loud at the dry tone. Lee *was* being a great sport about all this. She slid her fingers into his.

At 5:15, the schemers climbed out of the CRV in the Diner's parking lot. In his new casual slacks, open-necked shirt, and lightweight jacket, Lee looked very attractive. Sweet Gerald Givens could hope for runner-up, at best, in that department tonight. He'd undoubtedly show up in a sport coat; Joan had never seen him in anything less businesslike. As for herself, she had chosen the shorter, colorful dress from Easter, extra-confident in it since Lee had seen it and had said she looked well in it. "I hope we're not grossly overdressed in the eyes of our special guests."

By 5:30, everyone had arrived. "Awkward" was an understatement for the tension in the air as the group waited to be seated. Joan's social confidence, normally very strong, barely edged out her anxiety over what might transpire within the hour. And the Muellers, not surprisingly, were fish out of water.

Dove greeted the six as she would have done any normal customers on any normal night and showed them to their reserved table. The seating arrangement around two square tables grouped as one rectangle had been carefully devised and was made known by name cards cut from plain office paper in an assortment of spring pastels. Dub Mueller grinningly commented right away on his name card's being green. He and his brother sat on one side, opposite Lee and Gerald, respectively. Jesse was at the end near Gerald Givens and Luke, conceivably at the head of the table if he wanted to see it that way. Joan was at the other end, flanked at the corners by Dub and Lee. If Jesse preferred to keep Dub literally within arm's reach, he was out of luck for the next little while.

Like the rest of the Diner, this nook's walls were decorated with an assortment of antiques: a vintage football jersey, colorful metal signs advertising brands of soft drink now extinct, and a bicycle handlebar. The hope was that none of the unsuspecting guests would notice a small, battery-operated alarm clock resting on top of some 1920s primer textbooks on a corner curio shelf. The clock was a very recent addition, and it wasn't an antique. Directly above it was the wall-mounted, wide-screen television where Larry Newman's image was going to be plastered in high definition in about forty minutes. Assuming the others could interest the Muellers in turning toward the TV at the proper time, they could half watch the story and half watch for any telling reactions to it.

In Joan's purse was the remote control for the television. Lee was going to operate the device, but for now it was out of sight so no one else might happen to become interested in changing the channel or in turning the set off. Whereas the Diner's atmosphere normally was driven by the playing of tasteful music, leaving those interested in television to watch captions or to read lips, tonight, on *this* television, the volume would be up.

By prior arrangement, Gerald Givens stood at precisely 5:35 and said with the public-speaking ease of an executive VP or a deacon of the week (or both), "Welcome, everyone. Thank you for being here. Our guest in town for the past week, Mrs. Ryan, and her husband, our *newest* guest in town, have graciously asked some of us to break bread together tonight, before they leave tomorrow. Seems these boys of yours, Jesse, have been of service to Mrs. Ryan during her stay, and she wants to say thank-you." Gerald then offered a short prayer of thanks for the meal and the occasion, adding on a petition for safe return travel.

The meal was served. In her pale violet uniform dress and white apron, her long hair smoothed back into a low ponytail, Dove looked polished and professional. And too good for this line of work. Too good for this town. Joan instantly countered her own prejudice, though. *She'd* come to appreciate Crook Mountain—both its beauty and a number of its citizens. That was all well and good, and unchanged by the fact that that young woman setting meatloaf, vegetables, and hot rolls around the table ought to be freed from her present burden so she could follow her heart's desires anywhere in the world she chose.

Elsewhere in the restaurant, the Friday night crowd was sporadic. It would probably pick up about the time this dinner should conclude, and that was one fortunate by-product of the news beginning at six. With any luck, this private party of strange table-fellows would be over quickly and wouldn't give rise to any more local curiosity than ultimately could be explained away. As for all of the Muellers being invited except for one, Dove had predicted that if Marilyn were privy to what was going on, she would be miffed on principle at being excluded, but ultimately relieved to have all of the men out of the house, given that Jesse had been demanding of her the traditional female housekeeping in return for her room and board.

Jesse Mueller pretty much stuck to his meat and potatoes, washing large mouthfuls down with sweet tea and having almost nothing to say even though Gerald, Joan and Lee each directed some comments his way. Topics included the weather (obvious), cars (same—and Joan wished she could ask outright if his favorite make was Mercedes), and how Laynie Key was faring (much better). Joan wasn't even able to detect in the man any hint of fatherly pride when she stood and presented Dub with a gift box containing a quality dress shirt in a striking clover green as a belated thank-you "for saving my shoes the night of the concert." A bit of laughter answered Joan's explanation of that incident. Next, Luke was given a very similar item in a bold slate blue, "for the help repairing my tire."

The twins were shy about the gifts but gave evidence that both the recognition and the shirts pleased them very much. Joan hoped desperately this night would make a deep impression on both of the young men, showing something of a world that offered more than hard work, unvarying company, and slovenly surroundings. It was a reasonable guess that Dub intended to put his new shirt on right then over his plain, mustard-yellow T-shirt. He was pulling at the pins and the pieces of lightweight cardboard. But his father commanded, "Leave that an' eat yer food."

The news broadcast had started. Joan tried to keep things light, for the sake of her own nerves not least of all. She asked if they all had heard the story of Lee's detainment at the sheriff's office. "Thank goodness being taken in for questioning was all it amounted to!" She laughed. In order to keep the Muellers unaware of any spying opportunity she hoped to have with Lee tomorrow, she was also careful to imply that they would be staying the night in Cluny's Ridge and returning to Atlanta the next day. It was very tempting to pull out all the stops and drop the name "Addison's" as a place they might wander into in Cluny's Ridge, just as she had dropped the name "Mueller" at Addison's.

In the midst of all this pretense and drama, the meal was exceptional, right down to the yeast roll in Joan's hand, which was what good bread—hot, with real butter—always was: a little taste of heaven. The people around here had a gem in Dove Sechrist. How many of them realized that? Were they not going to know what they had until it was gone?

Lee's job was to monitor the newscast, so he called attention to the sports preview right after it aired. Its being the advent of the Major League Baseball season, he said, and himself and Joan being big Braves fans, they would beg their guests' indulgence during the sports segment. A moment later, the remote control mysteriously appeared on the table beside Lee's plate.

Dove brought apple cobbler and vanilla ice cream, drizzled with caramel sauce, in large, white bowls with matching plates underneath. Lee quickly stood and helped to set a dish at every place. Coffee was poured and other beverages refilled. Joan checked the time. It was 6:19. Maybe the Muellers and Gerald would engage their desserts enough not to notice it if she and Lee were too preoccupied to do their own portions justice.

Sports came on, and Lee turned the volume up. Gerald Givens followed his host's lead, giving his full attention to the screen. Luke and Dub also looked toward the television, but their father, whose back was to it, did not turn. If Jesse were interested in preseason baseball hype, he was getting his information strictly by audio as he kept his head bent and used his large fingers to fork generous mouthfuls in. *Does he always gobble? Or is it just that he wants to get this social obligation over as quickly as possible and leave, dragging his sons behind him?* The blond sportscaster wrapped up his spiel, and it was back to the red-clad anchorwoman whose short, raven hair looked carefully tousled with styling gel. "Coming up after the break: a two-year-old police case remains unsolved. Stay with us."

Joan's heartrate spiked at that. She excused herself and started toward the ladies' room. She had to calm these nerves! And where was Dove? Was the dish crashing still on? The woman with the most at stake appeared to be stuck across the room, taking an order from an undecided customer. Couldn't someone else be doing that? This suspense was worse than any in recent years, except maybe for when April was texting by the hour before finally learning she'd been selected for her internship over the other applicants. Ducking inside the empty restroom, Joan snatched a length of paper towel and clenched it first in one moist palm and then in the other. Were things about to get super, *super* awkward? Disastrous? What?

The waiting was over. No dishes crashed, but Lee nudged the sound still louder and sipped some water as Joan slid back into her seat. Their eyes met. It was ludicrous, what they were attempting. Absolutely ludicrous. And thrilling! Had she and her mate ever pulled any antics quite like these? *Where is Dove? She needs to get in position to watch the Muellers!*

"It has now been more than two years since Clarence Dean Newman, known to friends and family as Larry, disappeared while traveling from Cincinnati, Ohio to Vero Beach, Florida, with a planned stop in Cluny's Ridge." Newman's face was in full color across the screen. It was surreal. Joan's eyes were glued to the television.

"Newman did not reach his destination, and the one report of his being seen in Cluny's Ridge on the day of his disappearance has proved unreliable. No traces of Newman or his white 2010

Mercedes CL550 have been found." The camera was on the anchorwoman again. "Persons with information are urged to contact authorities in Cincinnati or Vero Beach or to call this toll-free number." A one-eight-hundred number appeared on the screen, and there was a lull in the audio.

"That is so *sad!*" Joan threw that out with a sweeping glance around the table, trying not to stare at anyone, but hoping some interest or discomfiture might show plainly on at least one Mueller face. "Imagine his family, not knowing what happened to him." No response. Dub fiddled with his new shirt some more, and Jesse didn't prevent him.

But the story wasn't over. "WTSE has more from Ricky Davenport." A slightly unkempt-looking young man in a yellow golf shirt and khaki pants appeared. He was standing in a drab-looking cubicle and clutching a microphone. "This reporter interviewed Miss Cora Haskew, a retired teacher and volunteer church librarian in Crook Mountain, seven miles north of Cluny's Ridge. Miss Haskew is representative of all concerned citizens who would like to see this missing-person case solved. She said, 'For this mystery to remain unsolved reflects on our community. If Mr. Newman fell into bad luck around here, we all will rest easier if we can learn what happened.'" And then the anchor team previewed the weather segment with a bit of banter, and it was on to a noisy ad for an area car dealership.

Automatically, Joan looked at Lee, who bumped the obnoxious commercial down in volume as he would have done at home. Beyond that, Joan was a statue. She managed, eventually, to comprehend the state of her ice cream. It was a melted mess over the cobbler that would now be lukewarm. One hand eventually got working enough to stir the soupy stuff a little. Now, she let go of the spoon and reached for her coffee. As she lifted the cup slowly, she raised her eyes to look across at Lee. His hand was still near the remote.

Joan had been so unprepared for this extra information, this new, local tie-in, that her own reactions during the story had made her useless in trying to study anyone else's. Cora hadn't breathed a word about being interviewed or quoted! Had she deliberately put herself out on a limb to protect Dove, trying to draw any possible negative reaction about the story toward herself instead? Where *was* Dove? Before Joan could locate her, the buzz that was already happening in the restaurant drifted in their direction. Some patrons had seen enough of the subtitles on other televisions to follow the whole thing and were impressed that one of their own had just been mentioned on television. Others had been engrossed in their food and conversation, and had missed it. They were now being put in the know by those who had caught the story firsthand.

Gerald Givens remarked, "Well, isn't that interesting. I didn't know Cora was following that case. I'd forgotten all about it, myself."

For Cora's sake, Joan tried to cover up. "Librarians tend to remember a lot of things other people forget." *That came out wrong!* If anything, Joan's statement would make Cora seem *more* of a threat, not less of one, to the Muellers if they knew something about Newman's disappearance.

Dove showed up at the table, sounding a little more breathless than she should have. "What else can I get for anyone?"

"Dove, did you know Cora was going to be mentioned on TV? I wonder if she knew this was going to be on tonight." Joan's voice sounded a little less natural than she wanted it to.

"I didn't." Dove's head was bent as she gathered empty dishes.

"But what an interesting and unfortunate case!" Joan looked at Gerald Givens. "You say you remember something about it?

Did the investigation come this way, or was it focused in Cluny's Ridge?" *Lee, please be watching the Muellers! I just can't look at them!*

"I don't recall anyone ever asking questions around here. I'm not sure I ever heard of the incident until sometime later, on the news."

Note to self: find out if Gerald was in here the day Dove said the Muellers saw the story and got out fast. If he *had* been here, maybe he would remember some little detail. As for the Muellers' reactions tonight, there hadn't been much that Joan had caught. But, then, she had been all off course at the critical time. Maybe Lee saw something. Or, maybe there had been absolutely nothing *to* see. Maybe, after the last time, Jesse had successfully drilled into the boys how they must behave if Newman's name ever came up again. Or, maybe all three had become so calloused about whatever they'd done that the name Larry Newman no longer made them jumpy. *Or,* maybe they'd had nothing whatever to do with the case and were staying out of the conversation now for the simple reason that they were clueless, besides being socially awkward.

"Boys." Jesse Mueller uttered the one-word command in a clipped voice as he pulled the paper napkin out of the neck of his shirt where it had been serving as a bib. He stood up and said stiffly toward his hosts, "Thank y' fer the meal." Was there actually a vestige of proper upbringing deep inside the gruff man, or was he merely blowing smoke, acting polite to cover up his guilt? Luke and Dub dutifully clambered to their feet, then bent again with the unison of synchronized divers to retrieve their shirt boxes from the floor. Everyone else stood after them. Joan moved toward the twins and extended her hand to each in turn. "I am truly glad to have met each of you. Thank you so much for joining us tonight." The brothers offered shy thanks for the shirts and the supper, and their father ushered them out.

Joan sank right down onto a chair. Any chair. It didn't matter that it wasn't the one she'd used at dinner. This was going to take some debriefing! Had the general awkwardness about the broadcast been sensed by Gerald Givens? Would Dove decide to trust him with her sacred secret now? And what on earth was the deal with Cora Haskew being named and quoted in the news story? For the second time in as many days, someone surnamed Ryan had sprung a surprise on someone else, only to have it backfire.

———⊷◆⊶———

In her living room, from an overstuffed, chintz-covered chair and with Emily the cat purring on her lap, Cora Haskew pressed the power button on her television's remote control, then took a long, slow sip of warm mint tea. Yesterday, that friendly-sounding administrative assistant at WTSE told her the Newman story was in queue, ready to go. But there'd been no hint that her name and some of her telephoned comments would be part of it. Now, she'd best be pondering about what else to say on the matter if asked. The kitchen telephone jangled. Cora set her cup down. Make that *when* asked.

———⊷◆⊶———

Joan beckoned for Dove, who still had normal job duties going on, to come and sit for a minute. The men stood as she approached. "Well!" Dove shone as bright a smile on them as the stress of the evening might allow. "My goodness! Thank you both for your gallantry."

"Thank *you* for the wonderful meal," Gerald Givens answered, and the Ryans echoed the sentiment.

Out of sheer habit, Joan started stacking dirty dishes. Lee

interrupted. "Why don't we men bus the table, and you two ladies can visit." Kind Mr. Givens was up for that immediately and said he should have thought of it himself.

Dove could have asked someone else to come over, but she probably realized the private party ought to stay private just a little longer.

"It's a good thing Cora isn't here," Joan whispered. "How awkward it would be for her to have to answer people's questions."

"But that's unavoidable. I guarantee you her phone is ringing already."

At 6:45, Lee paid the check, reminded by Joan to include an extra-generous tip for Dove, who wasn't going to be able to leave when they did. As he was stowing his wallet, Joan rested a hand on Dove's arm. "Would you like us to run over and check on Cora?"

"You read my mind!" Dove's enthusiasm for the offer was obvious, and Lee's lack thereof was equally obvious. He wasn't interested in this business lasting all night. "Oh, come on," Joan cajoled as they climbed into the car a minute later. "I need to bounce some things off you, and fast."

"Okay, dear. Whatever you need of me."

He was on the verge of impatience. From the passenger seat, Joan directed him to turn right onto Hill Street, then left onto Main, and then right again onto Rocky Road. They passed the church and left the heart of downtown. If Dove's prediction was accurate, that Cora was being questioned even now by curious neighbors and friends, the elderly woman might be very upset. Might she say things that would get back to the Muellers, implicating Dove? Or would she blame the out-of-towners for snooping into things that were none of their business? Plus, having heard Cora's name on the news, might the Muellers have decided to do something about that already, even in the short time since they had shuffled out of the Diner? Joan bounced these questions off Lee and gave him no time to answer. She was on to wondering if that Davenport schmoe had gotten Cora's permission to quote her. "Of course, *I* was the motor-mouth during the broadcast, saying how sad the story is. If Cora says anything that Gerald or the Muellers eventually put together with my actions tonight… And another thing. If further developments actually force Dove to leave Crook Mountain, Cora will be losing a renter, a companion, and, to an extent, a caregiver. Still, Cora is a strong woman." She was a teacher inspired by another great teacher whose life was lived in the service of humanity. She wasn't of weak character, that was for sure. Joan's thoughts were a jumble, all over the map.

The short drive was over, and Lee made light of the one-sided discussion. "Glad to have been bounced off of. Did you resolve anything?" Joan had nothing to reply.

They parked, got out, and approached the house, quickly taking the four stone steps up to the porch. Immediately they saw Cora through a window. Sure enough, she was on the phone. Joan stayed Lee from rapping on the door. She wanted to stay right here and listen for a second. If Cora were talking to a peer, age-wise, and that person had an average degree of hearing loss, that could account for how loud this end of the conversation was. They'd been dispatched here as protectors. Eavesdropping was justified.

"Oh, no, it wasn't a surprise, except that it ran *tonight*," Cora was saying. "I didn't know exactly when it was scheduled to be on. Yes, that reporter fellow called up at the church a week or so ago, trying to drum up information for his report." *Wait. There's not a grain of truth in that!* "Told me he'd drawn a ten-mile radius around Cluny's Ridge and just started making calls, hoping to get some new information on an old story. I get the impression, after seeing him on the TV tonight, that he does a lot of his *legwork* sitting on his *bottom*." Joan grinned from ear to ear. Leave it to the feisty native highlander to be handling the situation like a pro! "Davenport must not 'a' turned up anything much with his phone calling if the best he could do for his story was to quote what *I* said, which was next to nothing, really."

Lee went ahead and knocked firmly on the door. Cora looked out the window, raised an index finger to mean "just a second," and signed off from her phone call. Admitting her visitors, she said she was glad for their timing. That call had been from Edith Givens, fifth in line after the hairdresser, Mrs. Jarvis, Sherry Kirkpatrick, and a former student who lived away, but still in the same viewing area.

Joan pulled her phone out. "Dove is concerned. I need to text her that you're not only *okay,* but thinking faster on your feet than the rest of us were tonight."

The octogenarian's eyes twinkled. "So, you heard. I figured it was my right to fib a little after that Davenport fellow misrepresented my phone call as an interview and gave my name and quoted me, without permission. No need for worry, tell Dove. The calls are getting spaced out a little more now. Now that a few key talkers in town have the *facts*"—she winked at that—"from me, they'll spread the story around and the phone will get quiet." And that was exactly what happened.

"Davenport asked me if I had a special reason for wanting the Newman story to run and if I knew of any developments in the case. And that's when I said what we all heard on the TV."

"Do you really think suspicion of the Muellers is founded, or are you going along with that theory just to be nice to your friend?"

Cora's response to Lee, "I'm not drawing any conclusions just yet," sounded a lot like Dove. She said no more on that, instead asking how the dinner party had gone. "I'm sure you have things to tell me." She had, of course, already asked the guests to sit and to take tea. Lee was making a fast friend of the household pet, his fingers stroking Emily's head, neck, and back. *He's missing Wally.* Joan listened. She was as eager as Cora was to hear Lee's take on the charade.

"Well, either these Muellers are entirely unconnected with the case, or they are cagier than any of you anticipated, never appearing to bat an eyelash when the story was plastered on the TV." Lee paused, then continued, "*Or...*"

"Or, *what?* Don't keep us in suspense!" Joan gripped his arm.

"Or, our 'secret weapon' may reveal something we missed with the naked eye." Lee pulled the small alarm clock from a pocket inside his jacket. "Handy gadget, this."

Joan explained to Cora about the hidden camera they'd placed on the shelf below the television. As soon as they retired to their quarters for the night, they would transfer the footage to Joan's laptop and view it. Cora was duly impressed, but Joan cautioned her not to expect too much. "I certainly didn't see anything special in their reactions. Definitely nothing to send me right to the authorities, as we were hoping. So, I don't know that this video will turn out to be worth anything."

It wasn't easy to convince Dove, once she got there, not to whisk Cora off somewhere for safekeeping against possible retaliation by the Muellers. Ultimately, it was Cora's unworried take on the situation that settled Dove down. That, and what Lee said. "If the Muellers got through dinner and the news with no more show of nervousness or guilt than any of us saw, they would be very foolish indeed to go and do something right afterward that would point the finger of suspicion right back at themselves."

"*I* have the impression that Jesse and his sons don't really talk, I mean, not in the usual sense of a conversation between adults participating equally, with each one's voice heard." Maybe a little off topic, but it was what Joan was picturing. "If our little dinner party gave them something to talk about, I can see Jesse pacing and trying to decide whether the story's being on TV with an audience all around the three of them was coincidence, or whether it was a setup and therefore a threat to them. He might do this *in front of* the boys, but not *with* them." She was tuned in to family communication patterns. Evidence of manipulation and domination always bothered her. This, about Jesse Mueller, was feeding her interest in the situation as much as any other angle was.

Cora persuaded the rest of them that the Mueller *children*, at least, would never harm her, possibly not even if their father demanded they do so. The frequent nails in tires, and other unexpected mishaps, had never happened to *her* car in all these years.

With a look, Lee made it clear that he'd had a long day and was still in need of extra rest. Joan stood and promised to be in touch soon. She glanced around. Was there a security system here that Dove or Cora would be setting before they turned in? Seeing no evidence of one, she asked about it.

"None here, Joan, my dear. My ancestors' security system was to have a firearm handy and to know how to use it! Now, off with you youngsters. We'll be just fine."

Chapter 14

Joan roused herself on Saturday and discovered Lee already up, showered, and dressed. He brought coffee and the laptop to her, his mouth half full of granola cereal. "I suppose I'm as curious to see this as you are."

Joan sat up and positioned a couple of pillows behind her back. Accepting the coffee with a "thanks, sweetie," she sipped and watched Lee use the provided cable to connect the sneaky little gadget to the computer. The video footage downloaded, and both of them watched it through, twice.

"Could there be something obvious here that we aren't seeing because we expected to see something else?"

"Maybe," Joan answered. "*I* think their ignoring the television so pointedly is telling. At least, that goes for Jesse and Luke. Dub I can't vouch for. Now, *my* face is priceless, starting when Cora's name comes up."

"Agreed. Let's hope you can pitch this as a 'funniest home video' someday."

"Nah." This was too sophisticated, and too boring, to compete with fainting bridegrooms and pet dogs going berserk over a water hose. Still, it was too bad Lee's great idea hadn't produced some dramatic evidence. That the Muellers would repeat history had been a pipe dream.

Sunlight poured in through windows and skylights, and it

was a fine morning in spite of the video non-event. Joan pointed out some of the finer amenities of the house to Lee. By the time she had sat on the edge of the bed with her second cup of coffee, though, she was right back to mulling over last night's dinner party. Was Mueller clever enough to suspect that it wasn't by sheer coincidence that the Newman story had aired at just that time? If Neal Coffey figured in somehow, he'd be able to describe her and her car to Mueller. No value in bouncing more of these thoughts off Lee. But she did ask him about Cora. Would she be on the hot seat in spite of her offhand attitude last night?

"She isn't worried, so you ought not to be, either." That there was local interest in solving the case was out in the open now, Lee said. In theory, that could work in Dove's favor. He had a point. Joan resolved to put the whole thing out of her mind. Her phone pinged, and she saw a message that wholly undermined that resolve. "You're not going to believe this," Dove had texted. An image was attached.

"You've got to be kidding me!" Half laughing and half wondering about the implications, she explained the gist of Dove's message to Lee. "It seems a couple of youngsters with time and energy on their hands took it upon themselves to print some flyers last night and post them around town early this morning. Take a look!" She handed her phone over so Lee could view the image. "WANTED" was the top line of text, in all caps, on yellow paper. The page was done with clip-art to resemble an old-fashioned "wanted" poster with ragged edges. Below the title it read, "Information about Larry Newman's Disappearance." Below that, "Help Miss Haskew solve the mystery!" The enterprising and goodwill-minded children had even included the website URLs for the online version of last night's news story and the U.S. Department of Justice site for missing and unidentified persons, plus the e-mail address to use in reporting leads. "This is actually pretty impressive work for eleven-year-olds. They've grown up finding pretty much anything on the internet."

"So... The plot thickens."

"It does, indeed!" Joan sat on the bed. "Wow." It was spring break all last week, so by last night most parents would have been gung-ho about *any* constructive project their children found to occupy themselves. "Dove says one of the younger Jarvis sisters and the preacher's daughter came into the Diner at seven this morning asking permission to put one of these signs up. They were headed to the general store as soon as it opened, and the ice cream parlor and anyplace else that has Saturday hours. They also tacked copies to lamp posts and bulletin boards."

"What do you know? A grassroots movement breaks out in small-town America. It's inspiring, as well as comical." But Joan frowned. "What's the matter?"

"I'm just trying to think of possible fallout. On the one hand, these posters suggest more than ever that *Cora* is the one determined to stir up the dust. And that could make her vulnerable if the Muellers actually are guilty and are going to get very nervous, now that inquiries are happening right here under their noses. On the *other* hand, if the town at large gets interested in this mystery—and, with the benefit concert done, it sounds as though the good citizens may need a new short-term cause—then any guilty parties couldn't very well squelch every voice, young or old, that asks questions, could they?"

"No, not likely. If a guilty person gets nervous and begins to show his hand, that should help to bring the truth out. But, I don't like to think of a guilty Mueller showing his hand by bringing harm to Miss Haskew, Dove, or you. And if *you* don't have a good idea how to be sure nothing like that happens to *any* of you, I'd advise you to stop playing detective right now. Look at this reasonably, Joan. If some in this town are murderers, you ought not to be messing with them. And, if the people you suspect—or that *Dove* suspects—are entirely innocent, then you are merely wasting time and energy."

He made a sound case. Joan had to admit it. "And these little girls, of course, have no idea that some individuals in this town are considered suspects by others. For a respected, retired teacher to have said 'this reflects on our community' would naturally spark some interest. I agree with you that a 'wait and see' approach is best."

"Is that what I said? 'Wait and see'? Or did I say, 'Forget the whole thing'?"

"Well, I don't recall *either* exact statement coming out of your mouth. Umm, why don't we walk outside with those binoculars we bought yesterday, sweetie? I feel a sudden urge to go bird watching to the south."

Lee sighed exaggeratedly and rolled his eyes, but then he smiled his lazy, charming smile and supposed it would be healthy to get a lungful of fresh, mountain air. Outside, from a position that should be hidden to anyone down below, they took turns zeroing in on the covered car on which Dove was pinning so much hope. "Do *you* think it could be a Mercedes, and they've stuck a Ford logo on the grill as a coverup, so anyone who happens to see it will think it's the late Mrs. Mueller's Taurus?"

"With only the wheels to go by, that's tough to say. It's easy enough to change car parts out. You could Google the respective lengths of a CL550 and a Ford Taurus, and see if there's much difference."

"Good thought. And aren't you science types able to calculate the sizes of distant objects?"

"Not without more variables known, dear. And I don't see any infrared reflectors or total stations lying around here labeled 'Use Me.'"

Joan giggled. "An ACME crate from the Road Runner show would be most handy!"

"Yep. I'm neither a land surveyor nor a magician. Sorry to disappoint."

"Big help *you* are!" Joan punched him on the arm and sighed. "I guess that's that." How was anyone ever going to examine that car? Could Marilyn be manipulated into showing it? That seemed unlikely. Marilyn would probably be treated like any other nosy customer or trespasser by her hard-shelled father in matters of the garage. She was a female, and probably "had no place" in a man's realm, in Jesse's opinion. Just an educated guess.

They took an invigorating walk to the foot of the drive and back, visited, flipped through the television channels, and raided the remaining provisions to make lunch. After they'd set the kitchen to rights, Joan went for her camera. "Nature calls me back outside. Plant life!" She puttered around with that, then stuck her head back inside the door and persuaded Lee to come out and pose with her for some "selfies." "We've got to keep up with our kids on social media! Now, let me get some of just you. This light is great on those little glints of gray that you keep saying are blond."

Soon, Joan was downloading the pictures in the attractive kitchen that was done in chrome and black, with a few touches in a shade of red that was between salmon and watermelon. Joan wanted to know what else had been going on with the posters concocted by Tammy Jarvis and Kelley Kirkpatrick, but she resisted the impulse to text Dove, who was bound to be busy at work. And what about Cora? Had the phone started right back up again with calls from those considerate enough to wait until morning?

"You *are* good with the camera." Lee came up from behind and leaned over.

"And you're a terrific subject!" Joan showed him her favorites from the group of images and, from then on, gave him her undivided attention.

At 5:00, they sat close together in a quiet corner of the Carry On lounge in the airport terminal. Lee had saved the bottle of perfume until now. Their farewell tête-à-tête was a much better setting for it than the county sheriff's office was! Joan accepted the gift appreciatively, already feeling the pangs of Lee's imminent departure. "Next time I see you, I'll be wearing this." Joan smiled at her husband, then tucked the pretty box into her purse.

"Let me know when you've come down off the mountaintop." One lingering kiss, and Lee was gone.

What was it about airport goodbyes? They sure could get to you. Joan bought a fruit smoothie to keep her company on the return trip, then trekked back through the terminal toward short-term parking. It was back to Crook Mountain to find some dinner and to pack for leaving tomorrow. Tonight would be the second extension of the original getaway. She shook her head. No, this vacation hadn't been a getaway in the usual sense. It hadn't been especially quiet. It hadn't even been relaxing, except here and there. Crook Mountain faces and names made a slide show as she absently followed the signs toward the parking deck. Dove. Cora. Gerald. Edith. Laynie. Gavin. Marilyn. Luke. Dub. *It's such a failure to leave Dove little or no closer to fulfilling that promise of hers. Maybe I'll try making more inquiries once I'm home.*

Inside the car, she dug for the parking stub and some exit money. With good time, she'd be back in Crook Mountain soon after dark. Just as the bar lifted for her to proceed, her ring tone sounded. She touched the answer button and took the call hands-free.

"Joan, it's Dove. I have something important to tell you!" There was no mistaking the urgency in Dove's voice.

"Is anything wrong? Not Cora?"

"No, nothing like that. Everything's fine. Well, sort of. Cora phoned me at work. Bonnie Jarvis is at the house with her."

"Bonnie? Has something happened? What's the trouble?"

"I'm not really sure if it's trouble, but, if it is, I hope it's also a chink in someone's armor."

Joan's pulse quickened. Bonnie was Luke Mueller's secret sweetheart. Had Luke come to Bonnie and said something about the dinner they'd staged last night? Was it something important enough, or disturbing enough, that Bonnie must tell it to a mentor figure like Cora? "Do you want to tell me about it now, or when I get back? I'll be another forty-five minutes, at least."

They left it that Joan would call as soon as she got back. Dove definitely had implied that whatever was going on with Bonnie was related to all the rest. There wasn't any sense in spending the whole drive back speculating what it might be, though. She'd find out soon enough. She punched a couple of buttons and started a good driving playlist for dusk on unfamiliar roads. Songs with energy and a good beat. Her body just might decide that the preceding days, very out of the ordinary, warranted some well-earned drowsiness. Being sleepy behind the wheel was absolutely miserable. She sipped the smoothie and tapped the steering wheel with her fingers to the beat of a classic big band tune.

Twelve miles before the next turn. Traffic was almost nil, and the road's surface was in good shape, even if it was getting narrower and curvier. *Narrower and curvier. Sounds like what a lot of women wish their bodies were!* Joan glanced in the mirror. How long had that car been back there? It was too close. And it was staying too close. *Bother! Is this the tailgating capital of the world?* She glanced in the rearview mirror again, and still again, frowning.

A week ago, Dub Mueller had dogged her bumper in that green pickup. Another glance, this time in the side-view mirror.

This definitely wasn't a truck. She'd never seen any of the Muellers in any vehicle *but* their truck, but that didn't mean anything. Mechanics might restore any number of junk cars. Still, why would Dub, or any other Mueller, be tailgating her way over here?

"Back off, you idiot!" Why were some people so stupid? There wasn't a slow lane to move to, and there wasn't a well-lit parking lot to dive into. This stretch of road wasn't just lacking in shopping centers and doctors' offices. It was desolate. Of *course* it was! Just her luck. Did the tailgater know that, too?

A broken yellow line for passing came up. No oncoming traffic. *Let's hope.* Joan let up on the accelerator, but the car made no move to pass. Her slowing had only brought it closer. She couldn't even see its headlights in her mirrors. Saxophone improv was blaring, making an irritation out of a song she usually liked. She killed the music and gritted her teeth as the road curved again. *Stay cool. Eyes front! Nothing's going to happen.* The pursuing vehicle bumped her. Just slightly, but the sensation was terrifying. *"God in heaven!"* Who *was* this, and why were they after her? Desperately, she set the emergency flashers on. But what good would *that* do? If any oncoming drivers paid any attention, which they probably wouldn't, they'd assume her engine was running hot or that she was hauling fine china poorly packed or plants that might spill their dirt. Or, was *towing the car behind her!* Any other time, the irony of that would have been funny. Joan kept the flashers on, anyhow, even though using them must look like an admission of fear to the menacing driver.

On they went. Civilization had to show up soon! This was maddening, like an endless table tennis volley between even opponents. Who would crack first? Her right wheels left the pavement, and, if possible, her heart thundered still more violently. Instinct kicked in and she got the tires safely back on the road. *Hold it together, Joan. Focus!* The other car hadn't rammed her again, so far. And it hadn't tried to come alongside and force her over. *Drive your game.* She always told Lee and the kids that: Just drive your game. Keep your speed, and let the other guy be stupid if he must be.

"In eight miles..." The navigation voice scared Joan out of her skin. She didn't hear the rest of what it said. She jerked one hand through her bangs and clamped it right back onto the steering wheel as she panted and tried not to keep looking in the mirror or at her speedometer.

Jesse Mueller was rumored to have killed the doctor who hadn't cured Sarah of cancer—killed him in just this way, running him off the road. *If I die here tonight, I could be another unsolved disappearance with my car deep in a ravine and never found!* That earlier worry, about possibly getting drowsy behind the wheel, was laughable now. Before that, contemplating a change from ash blonde to golden blonde next visit to the stylist—*that* was *scornable* now. Later, she was going to cry about the shallowness of that. If she lived long enough.

She was glancing in the mirror too often. Maybe that doctor went off the road because he let someone scare him into driving badly, not because he got bumped from behind. Last night at dinner, the Muellers had heard Gerald Givens say she and Lee were leaving Crook Mountain, but the implication was that they would be driving to Atlanta. For the Muellers to have found her out here meant they'd followed her car the whole way, finding her alone and easy prey after Lee was gone. But, it wasn't just the Muellers who knew her car. Neal Coffey did, too. Still, maybe this was just a Saturday night drunk driver, or a person high or on the wrong kind of meds for driving. *Steady does it! You're going to get through this.*

Joan flashed her high beams at an oncoming car. Would the driver realize what was happening and call for help? *"Oh!"*

Call for help?! Joan's nearest defense wasn't that pathetic canister of pepper spray, or better driving, or the alertness of a passing driver. It was her phone. Why hadn't she thought of it sooner? She engaged voice command. "Call 9-1-1." While the eternity passed between dialing and getting through, she held on for dear life and heard herself calling for a greater help, in strange cries and awkward whispers.

The one in chase had taken to flashing his high beams on and off, on and off. Maybe he'd seen by now that she wasn't going to flee fast, lose control, and go hurtling off a cliff of her own free will. Seriously, this could be just an absolute low-life idiot, amusing himself at her expense. One of *those:* big ego, loud car, low I.Q. Even that tap could have been unintended, because it hadn't happened again. And if it was a Mueller twin, put up to this by Jesse, he *could* be trying to obey orders, yet willing only to scare her, not hurt her.

She must have sounded crazy to the emergency operator. She'd given her location as best she could, but she had no idea, now, what she'd said. Could a patrol car really find her? "Please! *Please!*"

An oncoming car looked vaguely familiar, shape-wise. Wasn't that a row of police lights across the top? *Please!* The lights went on just before the car met her, and Joan saw with spare glances in her mirrors that it was stopping short. At the same time, the car chasing her backed off and seemed to disappear. The driver must have found a handy side road. Stupid enough to pull this stunt on her, but crafty enough to see cops in time and get away. Who lived like that by choice?

But it didn't matter. Both cars were gone, and she was safe. Safe, but barely in control. Too shaken even to be shaking. She tried to ease her grip on the steering wheel, but couldn't.

She wasn't going to the house. That decision seemed to have

made itself. Yes, the house had a security system, and no, she wasn't going to stay there alone. The Muellers might have found out that she had moved there. She went straight to the Diner, stopped next to Dove's car because it felt safe there, and tried to move the gear shift. She got it into Park on the second try, then shut the engine off. She was a mess, clothes damp through. She sat.

Had it really happened, or was it a bad dream that she hadn't woken up from yet? She shut her eyes and leaned her head against the steering wheel. Tears might help, but tears had been scared away. *Inhale, hold, count to five, exhale.* She did it a second time. *I will never leave you nor forsake you.* Was that a voice? Where had that come from?

⋙◆⋘

Almost as soon as Joan slid weakly into a booth, Dove was over with a fresh glass of iced water, her face concerned. "Are you all right?" In as few words as would cover it, Joan explained what had happened. "That's *dreadful!*" Dove's voice was hushed, but aghast. "I'm so sorry! Look, let me fix it so I can get away, and we'll go. I'll get one of the others to close up." Joan nodded and lifted the water to her lips, sloshing some of it over the rim of the glass. When Dove was free, she walked Joan to her Elantra and they left the Honda behind. Life mattered more than cars. Let them sabotage hers now, if they wanted to.

Around the kitchen table at Cora's, hot tea and purring cat were offered, and Joan availed herself of both comforts. This time, Dove lifted Emily and set her on Joan's lap. Dove repeated to Cora what Joan had told her, and Joan followed with a fuller account. Both of her listeners indicated familiarity with that stretch of road, known for its sharp curves and steep drop-offs. It wasn't where anyone with good sense would turn the keys over to an inexperienced driver. Both women were lavish with words and touches, expressing great relief that Joan was safe.

"This was done by someone who is worried about being found out! If there was nothing to hide, they would let whoever wanted to investigate Larry's disappearance investigate it to their heart's content."

Joan looked at Dove. "Unless what happened to me just now was completely unrelated. There *are* a lot of crazy people in the world. It could have been a drunk driver or just someone playing dangerous road games for kicks."

"Well, no matter *who* did it, or why, it was just as horrible for you, I know!"

Cora chimed in, changing the subject to something she said was about facts more than speculation—the children's campaign to help her solve the disappearance.

Dove called it bizarre. "I couldn't have predicted that in a million years!"

"You need to find a way to use it to your advantage." Joan's voice had settled to a monotone. She stared at the steam rising from her citrus-flavored tea. *You. Not "we."*

"That may be happening on its own," Cora put in, and Dove explained. Bonnie had come to Cora that afternoon, concerned about something Luke did after the posters went up around town. "But let's not get into that tonight. You'll still be here tomorrow?"

Joan looked up. "I need to figure that out. Starting with the fact that I don't want to spend tonight up there at that house all alone."

"Just stay right here." Dove looked at Cora. Cora nodded.

Joan hesitated. If all of Dove's suspicions were right, then Cora was as much a potential target as Joan was. And last night Cora had laughed off the idea of a security system. Nothing bad had happened to Cora since the news story ran, but that didn't mean it couldn't still. Should all three of them stay together right here under one roof, like sitting ducks? She definitely wouldn't sleep if they did. She expressed her reservations.

"What if I call up Gerald and Edith Givens about their spare room?"

"No, Dove. Please don't. That would feel really awkward and imposing."

The next idea, to call the Kirkpatricks, had more appeal. "Gene and Sherry have the gift of hospitality, and they love unexpected company," Dove said. "That's the absolute truth, and it's the perfect solution." Standing to go and place the call, she paused long enough to place a hand on Joan's shoulder.

It was arranged. Joan and Dove would retrieve the CRV, and Joan would follow Dove to the pastor's home. Setting Emily gently on the floor, Joan addressed Cora. "Do you use your ancestors' form of home security?" There weren't any gun racks mounted on the living room walls. Maybe in Cora's bedroom.

"I'll never tell! But don't you worry."

In the car with Dove, Joan remembered what she'd heard earlier. *I will never leave you nor forsake you.*

Chapter 15

"I was pretty vague with Sherry. I said just enough for her to get that you don't need to be alone tonight. I didn't mention your ordeal. She won't ask questions. She's very tactful and sympathetic."

Great. They probably think I'm a mental case or in a troubled marriage or something.

Joan switched cars and followed the Elantra from the Diner to the two-story Kirkpatrick home on Mountain View, which roughly paralleled Hill Street. They weren't far from the Givenses' if her sense of direction were true. It certainly was quick to get around, around here. As a guest in the preacher's home, she might get a firsthand account of what had led Kelley Kirkpatrick and Tammy Jarvis to make their posters about helping Miss Haskew solve the mystery. *I must be getting over my scare.*

Turning Joan over to a group of very friendly Kirkpatricks, Dove stayed only long enough to hand over a fabric tote bag. Joan discovered in it matching pajamas and robe, a pair of purple slipper socks, and a couple of toiletry basics. She stepped outside to thank Dove privately, saying that she hadn't even thought about so much as a toothbrush. Dove nodded sympathetically. "Listen. I do want to hear about Bonnie and Luke. Do you want to talk tomorrow?"

"Absolutely. Now get some rest." Dove hesitated, then moved forward and gave Joan a hug.

It was already coming on bedtime for two preteen children and for parents who were bound to need Sunday mornings to go as smoothly as possible. Joan had barely greeted Kelley and met seven-year-old Ian before good-nights were being said. Sherry led Joan to the guest bedroom upstairs, pointing out the bathroom and talking about the family's Sunday schedule.

"I appreciate this so much, Sherry, and I hope you won't think ill of me, but I'm not up to church tomorrow." She couldn't explain her wish to avoid the Muellers. "I just need to rest, and to think." *Yep. I'm playing the part of an emotional wreck well.* Sherry said she understood completely and left the room.

A Shaker night table next to the bed held the essentials: lamp, box of tissues, electric alarm clock. An unopened bottle of spring water, cold from the refrigerator, stood on a stone coaster with a couple of paper napkins beside it. "The gift of hospitality," Dove had said.

Twisting the plastic cap off the bottle, Joan took a drink and surveyed the room. It had the classic, homey guest room touches. Patchwork quilt. Braided rug. Soft blue walls. On the writing desk a clear plastic cube held note paper that looked familiar. Where had she seen that design with its colorful border of small flowers? Where? She frowned and concentrated. *Ah.* When Sherry had flagged them down in the Diner's parking lot on Wednesday, the foil covering her plate of brownies had had a piece of this paper taped to it. The note had been a message of encouragement to the Laynie Key family, and it had consisted of the exact words Joan had "heard" earlier tonight in her hour of distress.

⊰◆⊱

When a couple of light taps sounded on the bedroom door at seven on Sunday, Joan was already awake. She invited Sherry in. The lady of the house was carrying more hospitality: a generous-sized mug of coffee. "I have cinnamon rolls downstairs. Will you come down and join me, or would you rather have your coffee in bed? I carve out personal time early on Sundays before Gene and the kids get up. It helps me gather myself for the day."

"I'll come down." Joan put the borrowed robe on over the borrowed pajamas. She'd slept in the slipper socks and now reached to pull them a little more snugly on. Down the stairs she followed Sherry, past framed photos of the children at different ages. Some were the typical sports and dance portraits. "What is your son's name again?"

"Ian."

The kitchen windows showed the promise of another pretty day. Across the table from one another, the women ate a little, drank their coffee, and made quiet small talk. *Would I have looked as calm and as relaxed as Sherry does, to the eyes of an unexpected overnight guest, when Sam and April were as young as Kelley and Ian?* The house wouldn't make *Better Homes and Gardens,* nor was it especially tidy, but Sherry hadn't said the standard, "Please forgive the mess." She did tell Joan, now, that in spite of her parents' misgivings about their grandchildren being raised without some of the advantages a larger city could offer, she and Gene were more concerned about teaching Kelley and Ian to know and to want *good* things, not just *nice* things.

There was that flower-bordered note paper again. This piece was held by a magnet to the refrigerator door and had a couple of grocery items listed on it. Joan looked at Sherry. If that comfort from heaven, or whatever it was, last night, had been God's answer in her moment of great fear, then that was a tremendously personal thing. What one had been praying about and how God seemed to be answering or working was not often discussed in her family or circle of contacts. But here was a pastor's wife. Sherry Kirkpatrick ought to have some wisdom to impart. Not only that, but it seemed the nice thing to do, to tell Sherry that the note she wrote to the Key family had served an additional purpose. So Joan explained, as well as memory served her, how the words had entered her mind "at a moment of great need" on Saturday night. She'd almost said "after I was chased," remembering just in time that the road scare and the possible reason for it were still a secret. "I didn't realize until I got here and saw your note paper again that those words had been taped to your plate of brownies. I confess I haven't had a lot of 'answered prayer' experiences like this one."

Sherry smiled and wiped her mouth with a napkin. "Thank you for telling me, Joan. It's always sweet to hear how the small seeds we plant yield results we never imagined. God often works that way. I suspect He has often spoken to you, but this time you maybe were *listening* in a very different way." Sherry smiled again, then took a short sip of her coffee. "As for 'hearing' Him speak to you in a time of crisis, well… don't be surprised if it's the first of similar experiences. Not similar *crises,* I hope!" Another warm smile. "But, similar evidences of His love for you. Most of us tend to think God's love is expressed exclusively in the obvious kinds of blessings: health, a happy family, a steady job. But His love includes taking a very personal interest in each of us, to help us grow or change for the better. Sometimes that process isn't all sweet and happy-feeling. I'm sure you know growth can be painful. We learn by mistakes, we have to correct our children, we fall down while learning to walk. When it comes to God, though, suddenly people don't see the parallel. They really have trouble seeing God's presence and care during times of huge challenge or sorrowful loss."

Joan had never had coffee or a one-on-one conversation with any minister's wife before. Had she been shortchanging herself?

Joan had stayed out of the way, hearing through the closed bedroom door the sounds of Sherry getting everyone dressed, combed, fed, and off to church on time. Now, she ventured out of the guest room and downstairs to the empty kitchen. Her hostess—busy wife, mom, and welcomer of unexpected company on the night before what might be the most demanding day of her week—had also managed to get something going in a slow cooker. That hadn't been there during the women's early breakfast chat. Of course, it could have been Gene who'd done food duty. *My traditional-gender-role prejudice is deeply rooted. That, or I just naturally attribute the best and brightest gifts of multitasking to my fellow womenfolk!* No recipe card or cookbook was lurking nearby. Was the recipe memorized, or had it been printed right on the packaging of one of the ingredients? Whatever the dish was, it was already smelling good. The Kirkpatricks seemed to have things very together. *I've always thought I did, too.*

A couple of baskets of unfolded laundry by the living room sofa were labeled "clean" with more note paper bordered in flowers. Inspired, Joan set about a thank-you task, folding the clothes and placing a "clean" label on the topmost bath towel in one basket and on the topmost T-shirt in the other. Next, she washed and dried the dishes, wrote her own "clean" note, added "Thank You!", and stood the note between two juice glasses upturned on a kitchen towel. The housework felt good. Therapeutic. She glanced over the kitchen, wet a paper towel, and wiped over several places on the linoleum floor. Back at home, a trusted friend was keeping watch over *her* house. There was something about the integrity it took to manage another's belongings as you would want your own cared for. Accountability mattered. Joan put the borrowed things back into Dove's tote bag, gathered purse and keys, pulled the Kirkpatricks' front door closed behind her, and drove away.

Arriving at the rental house, she stopped outside the gate, glancing in every direction from safely inside her CRV. All seemed quiet. It was 11:30. Maybe the whole town was at church. She climbed out, unlocked the gate, drove past it, and left her vehicle again to close the gate and lock it. This took her close to the rear bumper, and last night's ordeal came rushing back. Her eyes flew to the car to inspect it for damage. She bent, looked, and touched. Just a few small scratches. Barely anything that mightn't have happened in a grocery store parking lot if another driver had grazed the back end and never owned up to it. Last night, her car and the other one were moving in the same direction. A tap under those conditions wouldn't do what other collisions would. Joan sighed and straightened up. It was a wonder she hadn't had bad dreams last night at the Kirkpatricks'. On the other hand, in that particular house, maybe it *wasn't* a wonder.

Up at the house, she scanned the area for signs of threat in any form. Again, all seemed quiet and safe. Instead of pulling her CRV into the garage, she turned it around, nose toward the driveway. Then, with great stealth and caution at every step, she unlocked the door, opened it, looked in, listened, and finally entered. The binoculars were still there, as well as her laptop, her luggage, her shopping purchases, and everything else. She locked the door, set the alarm, and cautiously toured the house in search of any place someone might be likely to hide.

A very quick shower and change of clothes later, she straightened things up and went out to a chair on the sun deck. Phone, pepper spray, and binoculars all were in hand or within reach. Completely peaceful it was, full of the quiet sounds of nature. But the calm setting was only masking the fright of last night. *Justice*. Well…sure. There was *that*. But more than whatever punishment ought to happen to the person who'd done it, there needed to be something positive made out of it. Determination was the easier approach to take right now. Because, aside from that angle, the experience needed to go as far away as she could push it, even though she knew better than anybody did that burying a bad experience wasn't a healthy way to cope with it. Pretending something didn't happen never helped a victim push through to a better place. She'd deal with all of that later. For right now, she was going to stay the course. It was the right thing to do.

She raised up and looked all around again. People who tried to scare curious inquirers or hired investigators off a case didn't deserve the upper hand. She couldn't let herself be the victim of scare tactics. She didn't want to waste the peril, so to speak. In her childhood reading, detectives like Trixie Belden and the Hardy boys would insist, once on the other side of their many and improbable brushes with mortal danger, "I'm okay now! Don't make me give up on the case!" And it wasn't just the missing-person case. The bare truth was that, for a combination of reasons, Joan wasn't ready to leave Crook Mountain yet.

She lifted her phone. Lee had to be told her decision, and she had to word the message so it wouldn't concern him. She'd gone this long without telling him about her run-in with Neal Coffey in Cluny's Ridge. Now that he was back at work, it wouldn't do to worry him with the greater scare of last night. She sent a short message.

Now, what was the deal with Bonnie? Joan messaged Dove about that, then held onto the phone with a finger poised over the last 1 of 9-1-1. Her other hand gripped the pepper spray. Not exactly the most relaxed pose for a Sunday afternoon rest, but it was the pose she opted for.

⟫◆⟪

Once again, the threesome of Joan, Dove, and Cora was convened around a kitchen table. "On Tuesday morning, I am bidding Crook Mountain farewell, more answers or *no* more answers." Joan was the hostess, but she wasn't wasting any time on hot tea and small talk. Coffee, yes. And bottled water. "What's going on with Bonnie?" She didn't know if she were addressing Dove or Cora. *Whoever answers first, I guess.*

Dove led off, as she always seemed to do, as if Cora, in her eighties, didn't get her mouth in gear as quickly, or just chose to conserve her strength. *Or,* had learned the prudence of holding her tongue. "First, did you ask Kelley about the poster campaign?"

"I meant to try to learn whether she and Tammy Jarvis had taken posters to Mueller's Garage, but I didn't have a chance."

"It doesn't matter. We know from Bonnie that they did. She drove them there."

"And how did that go?"

"Well, some side news first. Laynie Key went with them. Cast and all!"

"She's home?"

"Yes! Isn't that great? Not only was she released from the hospital yesterday afternoon, but the doctors have said her last surgery should be the end of it."

"That *is* wonderful news. What a relief for them all." It really *was* wonderful news, but there wasn't time to revel in it. "So, it was three bubbly young girls with Bonnie at Mueller's, asking to put posters up." That intrusion would have annoyed at least *one* of the Muellers greatly, no matter what the posters had been advertising. "Wouldn't you like to have been a fly on the wall?"

"Well, only figuratively speaking, of course." Cora put her unexpected two cents' worth in.

Joan grinned at her. *True. No person in his right mind would want to be a fly literally. Not even for five minutes.*

"It boils down to this." Dove had the get-down-to-business tone Joan had set from the start. "Bonnie got upset because Luke was very rude, and she's never seen him that way in all the time they've been going together. He's had to be shy and reserved with her when his father is around. She's used to that. But this was different enough to bother her enough to come to Cora for advice about it. Bonnie saw that the little girls' request bothered Luke. A lot. And, when she asked him about it, not only would he not say why, but he shut her off and wadded the poster up. Bonnie says he seemed like his father, and that has upset her considerably."

Cora spoke up. "Bonnie took the girls home and then came to me. I talked with her at length about herself and Luke, and the future."

"Back up a second. Was Jesse at the garage at the time?"

"Bonnie didn't see Jesse, but Dub was there with his brother. According to Bonnie, Dub was very interested in the poster. He started to say something, and Luke stopped him."

Interesting. "It certainly does seem that something touched a nerve, doesn't it? If Luke has known something about Newman and has been keeping it suppressed for two years, I'm not surprised that something like this could set off anger in him, especially if he's been forced by his father to keep quiet. Unconfessed guilt will really eat at you." Joan turned a bottle of water up to her mouth and took several swallows. "Are you prepared to talk to Bonnie again, maybe tell her everything you suspect and ask her to help you get through to Luke?"

"I believe that is the best option left to us." For once, Dove didn't say she wanted to think the idea over.

"I do want to talk with the youngster again, myself, now that she seems to be 'all ears' in a moment of crisis. I try to be an extra mother figure to her in the time we spend together in the library, her own mama so busy with all those younger children. I left Bonnie with the expectation that we would talk again today, as a matter of fact. I'm going to impress upon her that she must encourage her young man to get on with his life if she wants any chance at all to have him in *her* life for the long haul."

Cora's desire to support Bonnie's relationship with Luke was worth a quick rabbit-chase of scrutiny. The woman had never married. Maybe she'd had a young love of her own that for some reason hadn't worked out. Had *she* decided to "get on with life" many decades ago? To go for her romantic dreams, only to have things go sour?

The three decided to ride down into town after picking up Bonnie at her house. Cora and Bonnie would go to the amphitheater and talk, and Dove and Joan would take a casual stroll nearby. "I'll take my camera along. The afternoon light calls to me. And while we take our nature walk, Dove, you and I are going to dream up a way to turn the town's growing interest in Larry Newman into a well-orchestrated distraction. Some kind of brouhaha that the Muellers can't wad up and throw away."

<hr />

"Were you a Girl Scout?" Joan watched Dove pull a cushion out of a large, plastic shopping bag in the trunk of her car. It was for Cora to use while she and Bonnie sat to talk on the hard seating of the outdoor amphitheater.

"No, but being prepared with things like this becomes second nature after you've cared for an older person day in and day out. You catch onto little things. Like the fact that although *baby* bibs can be found in baby stores, drug stores, convenience stores, general stores, grocery stores, and craft markets, bibs to protect the clothes of shaky-handed *senior adults* pretty much have to be ordered online if you want any selection at all."

Noted. And of course she's talking about Harriet Newman. Cora Haskew wasn't shaky-handed in the least.

The patch of wildflowers was picturesque, and it would put

some distance between them and the other pair. Bonnie mustn't feel inhibited or embarrassed while Cora counseled her. Joan and Dove walked. "I haven't any supper plans, by the way." The light snack she'd called lunch had done about all it was going to do for her. "If the Diner wasn't closed on Sundays, I'd make you let me get behind the counter and do some of the cooking."

"I guess you're looking forward to being back in your own kitchen. May I stop right now and tell you once more how grateful I am that you're making all of this effort for me, and staying in town even longer now?"

"You may. It's been *almost* entirely a good experience. And you can repay me by letting me take some pictures of you in this great light. You have no idea how often I see a great photo op in public and can't do anything about it. You can't exactly ask strangers to freeze so you can take a good picture of them in perfect lighting or against an amazing background. Well, maybe I could if I went into doing photography at a carnival, one of the many industries that capitalize on customer vanity." She laughed. "Lee would just go for that in a big way. *Not!*" On the other hand, after what she'd been up to in Crook Mountain, maybe he'd drive her to the carnival himself and carry her tripod around. Dove agreed to the scheme, and the two vented steam by getting a bit silly with the camera. The pretty thirty-somethinger probably didn't often "let her hair down" in such a way. At least, not during the past two years. "I can alter these with a photo editor and make you look like a movie star. Not that you don't already look that way naturally!" With her phone, Joan took a "selfie" of the two of them and texted it to Melinda, saying "hello" and that they would have a lot to talk about soon.

<hr />

Cora liked what she saw across the way, the blossoming friendship between Dove and Joan. It sparked a perfect point to make with young Bonnie, now that she'd told Bonnie all about Dove and why she'd come to Crook Mountain. "'We've all got to pull together in order for any of us to move in the right direction.' That's what Miss Mildred Cantrell would say about our situation, Bonnie. Take a look at those two ladies over there. Mrs. Ryan was a complete stranger to Dove until a week ago, but she has taken her vacation time and even put herself at risk to help Dove try to solve this thing. And Dove has already spent *two years*—a young woman in the prime of her life—to help Harriet Newman. You and I aren't going to stand by and not support that kind of commitment, are we?"

"But what should I *do?*"

"You know Luke is worried and not acting like himself. You want to help him. I know you do."

"I know somethin's been troublin' 'im a long while now."

"Then the best thing you can do is to go and talk to him. It seems that his trouble might be connected to what Dove is trying to do. At least, it's time for Luke to be asked about that straight out. You can help a lot of people, Bonnie, if you will gather your courage and do the right thing. You tell Luke how much Dove and Joan Ryan and Mr. Ryan have sacrificed for the benefit of people they aren't obligated to help. Except, of course, that *love* does obligate us to look out for the well-being of other people. To lay down our lives for a friend."

———◆———

The photography was proving a welcome outlet after the stress of recent days. Joan handed the camera over and prepared to play subject for a change. "I'll pick one to edit and frame for Lee and put it with his place setting for the reunion dinner we're planning." She checked her face with a powder compact, then applied lipstick. Dove started shooting. A couple of minutes into their banter, both women were startled by a voice from close range. "Do my eyes deceive me? Or is it the two loveliest ladies in Crook Mountain?" The women exchanged a short glance. Both sighed, but Joan was actually more relieved than irritated. Gavin Kidd probably wasn't such a bad guy. His approach right now seemed like a blessing, in fact, after encounters with the likes of Neal Coffey and Jesse Mueller. And an unidentified menacing driver. Kidd was honest about his likes and his plans, at least. No still waters running deep.

"Mr. Kidd. How are you enjoying this fine day?"

"Great! Just great." He nodded greetings first to Joan and then to Dove. "I didn't realize we still had the pleasure of your company, *Mrs.* Ryan. Seems I heard you left yesterd'y, with your better half."

"Yes, our plans changed once or twice. I'm sorry you missed Lee. He would have enjoyed meeting you, I'm sure." Not necessarily true, but *she* would have enjoyed watching the two of them size each other up!

"Soooo...the old man had to go on without ya?"

"Yes, he did. And that means there's no reason you and I can't get that banana split together now, if the invitation is still open." Apparently, the offer surprised Gavin speechless. "Dove? What do you think? Should we throw dietary caution to the wind and have ice cream for supper? You're included in this deal. I'll even buy."

"Well, *yeah,* in that case!" Gavin had recovered his voice.

The Lickety-Split ice cream parlor, Dove remarked, tended to get extra business on Sundays since the Diner was closed. And those clinging to the very last vestige of spring vacation were supplying plenty of that extra business just now. Dove asked Gavin if he had seen the posters (there was one right over there on the wall), and Joan said it was quite a tribute to Miss Haskew that the town's children wanted to help her make the community look better in the public eye. Gavin Kidd's response suggested he neither suspected anyone in town of involvement in the case nor had any opinion on the subject that would be helpful. Joan and Dove didn't linger over the refreshing treat. They apologized to their blissfully ignorant companion and hurried back to the amphitheater, where Cora and Bonnie seemed to be watching for them. Walking alongside Joan, Dove said she'd thought of someone who might draw Jesse Mueller away from the garage so Luke and Dub could be questioned. She had a more conspiratorial look than Joan had seen on her face during their brief and strange acquaintance.

"Who would that be?" Was Dove thinking of calling on Gerald Givens again? Or the mayor, maybe?

"Serena Stillman. Jesse fell for her in a big way, don't forget. I've been hearing about that drama from different people for a long time now. If Serena turned up somewhere with car trouble, or told Jesse of some made-up business proposition, or said just about anything in the right tone of voice, I think he would go and meet her."

"Even though she's married now?"

"Well, of course, it doesn't have to be anything suggestive. But, he might hear it that way. That's why she'll need someone with her, or really close by."

"It's worth a try. Do you really think she would agree to something like that?"

"I think I can persuade her. We just need to stress having backup. At this stage, nobody needs to be putting themselves in obvious danger."

Chapter 16

Joan still had her copy of Larry Newman's picture. On the phone with Dove a little while after they'd left the amphitheater, she asked for the printout of the news story. "And do you happen to have a picture of Harriet Newman, too? If not, when you come over let's look online for some kind of family history page. I want to put both Newman faces in front of Dub and Luke tomorrow. In fact, let's round up a picture of Sarah Mueller's doctor, too. I want my pockets full of ammunition. Yours, too. Can you come up with a food offering to get the boys' stomachs on our side before we start working on their consciences?"

Dove arrived after dark, and Joan walked down with a flashlight to meet her at the gate. As they climbed up the driveway, Dove pulled a manila folder out of her handbag. "I won't have to get into too many particulars with Serena. If she's willing to help, she'll come up with her own interesting idea of how to draw Jesse away. She's known him a lot longer than you or I have."

Inside, Dove placed the call to Serena. Joan stayed there in the large, open kitchen-living area so she could listen. At the same time, she browsed online for some of the items they were after. Dove's folder already held the news article. Joan added to it the photograph of Larry Newman. Also, one of the "wanted" posters, lifted off a light post downtown. She smiled about the posters. Dove was right. Nobody could have predicted that development in a million years. *I wish the children were out of school again tomorrow. I'd practically pay them to go door to door, holding clipboards and canvassing the town: "We're working to find out what happened to a missing man and his car. May we please see all the cars on your property?"*

Dove made a thumbs-up gesture from across the room. Good! Serena Stillman was on board. Dove thanked her friend and signed off. "Serena is going to contact Jesse at ten tomorrow morning. And we will go pay a visit to the younger Muellers once she texts that he is with her."

"What reason did you give her?"

"I just said we need Jesse out of there so Bonnie can talk to Luke about their relationship. You know. All the world loves young love! And it doesn't hurt that this is a chance for Serena to give a little payback to the man who basically drove her out of town."

"Brilliant. I'm banking on Jesse Mueller having a 'hashtag Monday morning' he won't soon forget."

Dove laughed. "I hope you're right. And I have a surprise for *you*. Cora is making a phone call of her own as we speak, lining up an extra measure of security for you, me, and her. You're spending the night with us at her house tonight." Joan started to shake her head, but Dove held up a hand. "No argument. We aren't taking any chances."

———◆———

Sherry joined Gene at the top of the stairs. "Whew!" Kelley and Ian had wanted to stretch out the nightly talk-and-pray time, naming off school friends to pray for, and being unusually inquisitive about what would be in their lunchboxes tomorrow. It sure was hard to settle back into the regular routine after spring break!

"They'll be dead to the world in five minutes."

Downstairs, they silently took seats at the kitchen table for their Sunday night ritual. The strong smell of ground coffee was a comforting element, as always. Gene had set up Monday morning's brew, by timer. "It's your week to go first."

Sherry got started, taking a blue card off the top of a stack in the center of the table. They took turns reading the current week's prayer concerns turned in by members of the congregation. The last card in the pile was Gene's to read. "From Dove Sechrist, asking for guidance, open doors, and courage." As they'd done after each of the other cards, the two joined hands and prayed.

<hr />

Joan was having a bad night. It wasn't that the day bed at Cora's was uncomfortable. It was nerves. Why didn't dawn just go ahead and get here? But, no. It was only 2:25. She swung her feet to the floor and padded as quietly as possible to the bathroom and back for the second time since retiring at eleven. Plumping the pillow, she tried sleeping with her face toward the window this time. Her phone, charging in the wall outlet, was in reach. She texted Lee. "Restless night. Must be missing you! See you soon." She added heart and kissing-face emoticons and pressed *Send*, then set the device away and stared into the darkness until sleep finally came.

<hr />

Foot on the brake, he stopped the pickup next to a vacant lot. He killed the motor and stepped down onto weeds. Best leave the door open in case he'd be returnin' at a run. He grabbed his supplies from the bed of the truck and set out. These dark pants an' shirt oughtta hide 'im good, if anyone was lookin' outside this time o' night, what with plenty o' street lights blazin'.

There it was, the house where some meddlers needed t' be taught not t' meddle. He gripped the gasoline can's handle tighter.

The dirty rags wadded up in this other hand felt rough, but that weren't nothin' new. Soft things hadn't been around much. Not in a long time.

He stepped onto the grass to go right for the cars. "What the-?" Curses near flew from his mouth, loud, in the customary way. Up there on the porch. Wha-? He blinked a couple of times, clenching the stuff in his hands till he had to let up on his grip. *Cain't b'lieve it!* Two armed men. Now, how'd Cora Haskew done that? She hadn't even been one t' lock doors at night, right along, and that was a fact, from what folks said. Them two dark shapes were steppin' here an' there. Watchin' the yard. Holdin' them firearms like they meant bizness. Tall. Like Army. What was t' be *done?*

He swore in a whisper and ducked his head down hard. He'd be stampin' 'is foot but fer the noise it'd make. Look at them nice, shiny automobiles parked there on the driveway. They were goin' t' get t' *stay* nice an' shiny, he reckoned. Least fer right now. He had t' give it up. Had t' get out o' there 'fore them men spotted 'im. No need fer runnin' back t' the truck, after all. He gritted his teeth and started back, angry. This gas can here was s'posed t' have been lighter on the return. He kicked at every clump of weeds and every stone he could make out.

———◆◆◆———

Cora appeared to be enjoying the role of hostess as she placed a plate of scrambled eggs, grits, and biscuits in front of Joan and then Dove, before serving herself. Joan ate lightly, though. It wouldn't do to be weighed down during whatever the next hours might bring. "In the words of Mildred Cantrell, 'If a man wants a chair to sit on, he builds it himself.'" Cora said her teacher's literal description of life in the 1940s could also mean taking a dilemma by the horns. Joan smiled. That sounded like a variation on *God helps them that help themselves.* And that probably was Cora's philosophy, to a degree. "You ladies have my greatest respect. I know that what you go to do this morning will come to good."

The Diner's parking lot was fairly deserted when Dove pulled in and parked. "People are recovering from spring break. It's hard to let a week-long break end. People tend to stay up late on the very last night of vacation."

"We were the same way when Sam and April were in school." They sat, watching for Bonnie to show up. What would they do if she chickened out?

The aroma from the pan of warm cinnamon rolls on the back seat gave the familiar feeling of "comfort food." If only the setting were Christmas Eve morning, or something equally festive! Dove turned some soothing music on, but, before the first song was over, Bonnie Jarvis pushed the front door of the Diner open and trudged toward the car. She looked worried. "I helped mama get the kids off t' school an' told 'er I'm helpin' you fer a spell," she said to Dove as she climbed into the back seat. She sounded as nervous as Joan felt.

Dove's phone beeped. "This is it. Jesse took the bait. He's pulling up in the truck to where Serena asked him to meet her, to discuss something about landscaping along the property line between his house and her cabin." *The cabin.* It had been days since Joan had even thought about the attractive rental where she had started her vacation.

Dove moved the gear shift, and they were off. They got from Hill Street to Main in a matter of seconds and were crunching over the gravel out front of Mueller's Garage before they knew it. There was no telling how long Serena would be able to occupy Jesse, so the three didn't sit there trying to gather nerve. This was the point of no return. They climbed out.

The plan was for them to wander in, greet the boys, and offer the food, hoping Dub and Luke's breakfast had been long ago enough that the cinnamon rolls would appeal right away. Then, Dove and Joan would ease away from Luke and Bonnie, asking Dub an innocent question or two. How was he liking his new shirt? Did they have many cars in for service right now? What were he and Luke expecting to eat later in the day? Maybe just one or *two* cinnamon rolls wouldn't spoil their lunch.

Both boys' faces brightened when the ladies trooped in. Luke's was the first to change, however. He appeared glad to see Bonnie, but it was also clear he was ill at ease. Joan let Dove guide the initial small talk, since she was the one holding the food. The all-important folder of papers was in Joan's handbag. Bonnie knew enough of the lay of the land to gather a handful of paper cups so there would be water to drink. Both of the twins eagerly accepted the food gift, pulling off a large cinnamon roll apiece. They started eating and kept not speaking.

After a few awkward minutes of that, Bonnie maneuvered Luke aside with her body language, eye contact, and quiet words. This was Joan's cue. Immediately, she pulled the folder out. Using Dove's printer earlier that morning, she'd added to the arsenal a few papers with which to blow smoke—everything from a couple of the shots she had taken of Dove in the park to several pictures of cars, including a convertible Mercedes and some Land Rover models. "I'll be leaving town soon. I wanted to stop in and say goodbye, and to ask what you think of some of these cars." She opened the folder and laid it flat on the counter. "My husband wants us to trade my Honda soon." His attention captured, Dub bent his head over the first picture. This was *Dove's* cue. She eased out of sight.

Joan let Dub look at the car pictures for as long as they seemed to keep his attention. Meanwhile, she listened as Bonnie gently tried to persuade Luke to open up about his troubles. She told him that unless he talked about them, they would never get better. She took his hand and continued to speak softly. "Imagine life bein' different for us than it is. I want ya t' be happier than ya are now."

Dub touched the hood area of a pictured car and was naming off his favorite parts of an engine when Luke's voice rose from over where Bonnie had him cornered. If Bonnie were asking him to admit to something criminal, even if he had been only an accessory after the fact, she was asking a lot of him! Either way, Luke's agitation meant only one thing to Joan. She'd better hit the deep water. Right now. She flipped a page in the folder, trying to ignore the tightness in her stomach. There lay the picture of Larry Newman. Joan watched Dub's face, but it didn't seem to tell much. "Nice-looking man, isn't he? Did you ever see this man?"

Dub replied without hesitation. "Yeah. I seen 'im."

Joan's middle clenched tighter. "Where did you see him?" She tried to keep her voice calm and steady. *Please don't say "on TV the other night."*

"In 'is car." A pause. "*My* car now."

The car! Joan bit her lips as if that would keep her churning insides down. Her voice shook in spite of all her efforts. "Do you know where this man is now?"

Dub nodded. "We buried 'im."

Joan's heart skipped a beat. *Did I hear him right?*

"Shut up, Dub!" Luke bolted over as he yelled. *"Shut up, y' hear?"* He grabbed his brother by both arms. And then something happened between the twins. Joan understood it instinctively. The hurt on Dub's face crushed Luke, who had just become their father, taking a role with his brother that was the direct opposite of the loving, protecting buffer he'd probably always tried to be between Dub and the tyrannical parent who considered him an imbecile, an embarrassment, and a burden.

Joan finally found her voice after the shocking admission.

"Did one of you kill this man?" She held the picture up to add force to her question. *Jesse, please stay away!*

"No!" He'd backed off a second ago, but now Luke moved close to his brother again. "That ain't how it was!" Joan believed him. She even managed to relax a very little, warmed by the sight of Luke defending Dub instead of scolding him.

"It wa'n' no killin'. That man was dead when I found 'im. All we done was t' get 'is car." Dub actually smiled a little. Yes, he loved his beautiful Mercedes, once white, now green. "Pa took most o' th' engine out, but 'e give *me* th' outside."

"That's all true, ever' bit of it." Luke shifted his weight from one foot to the other, and back again. His fists clenched and unclenched. "The guy was slumped over, an' the car was in Park. He musta been feelin' bad an' pulled over. Had a heart attack or somethin'. The car wa'n' wrecked. It was perfic'." The younger twin, who bore responsibility as if he were the older, looked ashamed and fell silent.

From where she had been glued to the wall, Bonnie hurried to stand close to Luke. "It's gonna be okay." She looked from one brother to the other. "It'll be okay."

The front door swung open with a squeak and Jesse Mueller stopped short, his blank expression instantly going stormy. "What're y' doin', turnin' this place inta a *social hall?* Why ain't ya boys *workin'?* Cain't take mah leave of ya! Cain't turn mah *back* on ya! You an' that contrary sister o' yorn, bringin' me woe!"

He hates everyone and everything, including his own existence. "Why don't you calm yourself?" Joan tried working on Mueller as if he were a frustrated hospital patient dissatisfied with his dietary restrictions and upset about being confined and helpless. The man's eyes were darting around as if he were trying to make sense of the odd situation. The shy, browbeaten twins weren't likely to be comfortable enough in female company for this scenario to be something their father was used to walking in on. Maybe the confusion would keep him disconcerted long enough for things to turn out well. Yet, Joan stood there helplessly as Mueller's eyes landed on the "wanted" poster on the counter. It had been below Newman's photo, and now it was on top. He looked angrily from one person to the next, finally catching sight of the photo of Larry Newman in Joan's hand. His mouth changed.

Joan quickly went on the offensive. "We know what you've been hiding these two years. Luke and Dub are not going to go on living in the fear of being found out."

"Yeh done *told it?*" Mueller looked incredulously at his sons. Luke stared at his feet. Dub seemed unabashed. "Fools!" He looked at Joan. "They're outta their heads, both of 'em! An' you nosy *females*"—he spat the word—"interferin'. Meddlin'. A-comin' here on my propitty where ya got no bizness!"

"It's no good, Mr. Mueller. Your sons are much smarter than you give them credit for. It only remains to learn what *you* are guilty of, besides being a miserable tyrant." Joan had been here long enough, had invested herself in this saga enough, to figure she had the right to speak her mind. She moved toward the doorway that led to the garage area, where Dove had gone earlier. She said over her shoulder, "Shall we go have a look at Larry Newman's car? Is his body buried back here as well?" And she kept right on walking.

Outside, Dove stood beside the uncovered green car, holding the Mercedes CL550 owner's manual up like a giant gold nugget unearthed. Joan thrilled at the sight of the long-awaited victory, but quickly looked back as Dub led Luke, Bonnie, and the angry Jesse into the junkyard. "It's his car, all right. There's even a note they must have found and stowed in the glove compartment. Larry wrote that he was afraid of not making it to the nearest hospital in time, and—" Dove's voice broke. "And wanted his mother to know, just in case he didn't. He must have counted her *need to know* even more important than getting help for himself." Joan went to her. Dove had found the car, but she hadn't heard the boys' confession. "They say they found him in the car, Dove, already dead. They buried him so they could keep the car." Joan put a hand on Dove's arm.

Dove lifted her head, straightened her shoulders, and looked toward the Muellers. "I cared for a woman named Harriet Newman. She died with a broken heart because she never knew what became of her son." Her grief-torn face went more stoic. "I don't know if *any* of you understand what you have done." She didn't seem to be making eye contact with anyone, though. She had a faraway look. Poor Dove! She was probably reeling not only from the shock of learning what had happened two years ago, but also from the growing realization that her elusive goal had finally been met. Her promise was satisfied. It was a victory, to be sure, but it was also a letdown. Her world had just changed very importantly.

Jesse Mueller suddenly lunged low and brandished the first thing he could get his hands on: a rusty tire jack lying in the grass. "Listen t' me, yeh *ingrates* an'… an' yeh…" He apparently didn't have the vocabulary to describe how violently he resented the three women, so he unleashed a storm of profanity.

The twins hung their heads—probably their standard reaction when their father flew into a rage. But this was no time to be musing about family dynamics again. What were they going to do next? Mueller stood between the rest of them and the only way out, back through the building. *And my pepper spray is in that building, inside my purse, along with my phone.* Joan never left her purse unattended! Why had she done it now? Could they all pile into the Mercedes and lock Jesse out, then call for help on Dove's phone or Bonnie's? No idea was too crazy if it ended up working. But why not have Dove call right now? If Jesse tried to stop her, the rest of them would just have to overtake him. Only…would the twins really help do that? Defy their father that way? Physically wrestle him down? *Talk. Distract him.* "Was Serena Stillman's landscaping idea to your liking?"

Mueller jerked his head in Joan's direction and curled his lip. "*That* one. She was just a-wastin' my time. Her an' 'er rich husband. He come rollin' up later in 'is fancy car like—" Then he seemed to realize that Joan shouldn't have known about that. He nodded, glaring at her. "So. Y' cooked it up between yeh? A *conspiracy!*"

"Why don't you tell us about that night? It's out in the open now. Did you think Dub had done something to Larry Newman? Were both boys together when they found the car pulled over?" A few minutes ago, Dub had said, "when *I* found him." Try to get him talking; that was the thing to do. Get him into rewind mode. Take him out of his present fury! "What kept you from just calling the police if you saw that Newman was dead?"

Instead of answering Joan, Jesse Mueller directed a furious tongue-lashing at Dub, who cowered under it. Luke stood bravely in between. The gist was that this was all Dub's fault for ever having gone to that strange car on the side of the road. "An' *you!*" Now he started in on Luke. "Yer brother's keeper. *Yer brother's keeper!*"

"How *dare* you lay guilt on Luke that way?" Now, Joan was angry, too. Mueller swiped in her direction with the jack. A warning. How far would he go against so many? But, how many was it, actually, "against" him? Was it likely that anyone but herself, and possibly Dove, would try to resist this man right here, right now?

Dub moved. In a few graceful steps he came to stand beside Joan. Dub Mueller, who had brought flowers to her, who had recovered her shoes for her, who had received a nice shirt in his favorite color from her, who had had gentle, considerate attention from her on a consistent basis over the past week, spoke his allegiance without uttering a word. And what he said sent Jesse over the edge.

Raising the jack, he swung back with both arms. Who did he mean to strike? Not knowing what she was doing, Joan propelled herself toward the man. But not with an air of authority that she hoped would change the balance of power. "*Jesse.* No," she said quietly, shaking her head. She dropped her volume. "Please, if you must do this, aim for the car! Please!" He longed for an outlet; that was so obvious. "Hit *it.* Do it." Joan acted out what she hoped the man would imitate. She raised one foot, praying she wouldn't injure herself, and kicked the rear fender of the Mercedes. Okay, she hadn't broken her foot. She kicked again, then looked back at Jesse Mueller and saw his face change, even though he was still holding the jack as a ready weapon. "Don't harm your flesh and blood, Jesse. Or any of us women. This *car* is what started the whole thing, isn't it? If only this car hadn't caught Dub's eye that night!"

Mueller looked at the dark green automobile. His mouth trembled. Joan prayed, *Please! Please! This is exactly the right scapegoat, and Dove will get that. The Mercedes represents this whole, sordid situation. It represents the huge mistake in judgment the Muellers somehow made. It represents wealth, education, and opportunities Larry Newman had that this family has missed out on. And there's no value in this piece of metal even though it* is *a strong connection to the Newman family. Its use to them is long gone!* Joan stole a glance at the twins while all else seemed frozen in time. Dub's reaction to her sudden scapegoat idea she couldn't predict, but surely he could be made to understand that any trauma he might feel over damage to "his" beloved possession was preferable to having his father inflict injury on him, on Luke, or on anyone else. Adrenaline high, Joan forged on. She'd come this far. If Mueller tried to hurt her now, she was sure the others would overtake him! Could her resemblance to Sarah Mueller reach this man? She gripped his arm and tried to lead him. And, miraculously, he let her! Jesse Mueller dealt blow after blow with the tire jack, denting the green-painted body and shattering window glass. While he vented his fury, uniformed officers quietly moved in unnoticed by him, coming through the building and into the back.

By plan, Dove had made the call to 9-1-1 the minute she'd come out here. And it was Dove who intercepted the officers and quickly explained. When Mueller let up from sheer exhaustion, he made no resistance nor uttered a word as the jack was taken from him and handcuffs fitted on.

Luke and Bonnie rallied around Dub, ever the object of their gentle love and concern. Luke was saying something to his brother in a low voice. And Bonnie, bolder than Joan had ever heard her, said to both, "It's better this way. It's much better to have it come to light."

"Havin' th' car made Dub happy," Jesse muttered as he was being led away, as if the man who had him by the arm needed to know that. "It's little anuff 'e's ever had t' be happy about." It was the first time Joan had heard him use Dub's nickname instead of saying *yeh* or *boy*. She couldn't agree with him about his son, though. Dub probably had had plenty to be happy about, and would have had much more if his callous, disagreeable parent could have met him halfway.

Another of the dispatched officers talked with the rest of them by turns, but more statements would have to be given at the sheriff's office. If Deputy Darryl King still felt disappointed that Lee had turned out to be a law-abiding citizen instead of a bank robber, he soon would find out that "good things come to those who wait." The humor in that wasn't as satisfying as it would have been if observed about somebody else's situation.

Joan watched the twins. Normally, children whose one surviving parent had just been whisked away to a fate unknown would be asking how soon they could go to be by that parent's side. Luke and Dub Mueller were lost lambs. There was more at stake for them than what their father was going to be charged with. How might a defense be built for each of *them*? A good attorney would spin each Mueller's role and his resulting accountability to best advantage. Was it a crime not to report finding a dead body? It was morally and ethically wrong, of course. And to have *buried* the body! That made it so much worse. *Poor Dove!* Joan sighed and suddenly found it necessary to draw several deep breaths. She gazed into space and shook her head. Dove came to her.

"Joan!" She looked happy, sad, and incredulous all at the same time. "You were brilliant! How did you ever find the nerve? You are really a pro. I just don't know what else to say!"

"Not me, Dove. I never felt more unsure. I guess I was going on sheer instinct. *You* are the hero here, nosing out the truth long ago and convincing me you were right. But also for keeping your cool and getting the critical phone call made. I don't know if we could have managed Jesse beyond a point. What a relief to have backup arrive at the right time!"

"'Up' is right, Joan. Our greatest backup is the help that comes from above." Dove smiled, but she shook her head sadly right after. "Look. I ought to call Gene." She dialed the Kirkpatricks' house with fingers Joan noticed weren't exactly steady. "Gene," was all Dove managed to say before having to stop for a couple of deep breaths herself. She finally got across to the pastor that there was a crisis situation at Mueller's Garage. "Please don't talk to anyone about this. Just come over here as fast as you can. And ask Sherry to pray! Oh, and if you can, swing by the church and bring Cora with you. I'll call her next."

Chapter 17

After that extended session sorting things out at the sheriff's office, the open road was going to be a comfort, with home beckoning from a few short hours away. Finally, Joan was leaving Crook Mountain and, with any luck, leaving without ceremony. Emotions were too raw and nerves stretched too thin for fond words, hugs, handshakes, and tears. Even the notion of stirring up dust especially for Marilyn had lost its cuteness. No, now that the worse and the better had happened, it was time for the catalyst to disappear. She had helped a needed reaction take place, and now it was over. The others must remain to deal with their shock, devastation, and gossip, but Joan was going home.

She headed straight for the rental house, loaded her car, and left by way of dropping the house and gate keys by the church. She would ask Dove to go pick them up and return them to the realty office. One final stop now, by the C.M.G.M. for a snack to take on the road. Joan made small talk with the party standing behind her in line as they waited to pay Mr. Oden. They turned out to be the ones who'd taken the McCain cabin after her. Joan told them she was the previous occupant and had found the place very nice. From the store's exit, she couldn't resist calling back, "Watch out for flat tires. The rocks around here can be sharp!" And then, Crook Mountain, Tennessee, was in her rearview mirror. By some miracle, the news about the Muellers hadn't come up at the General Store.

At her first rest stop she phoned Lee. It was probably good that she got his voicemail, since there was too much to tell in the little time he would have to spare for a phone call. "Honey, it's me. Call me when you can. I have a lot to tell you! Call me! I miss you and love you."

Joan rolled into her driveway around eight on Monday evening and relived recent history, too tired to pull anything from the car but what would suffice until morning.

—————◆—————

The perfume from Lee rested on their bureau, unopened in its box, where it would stay until their reunion dinner on Friday. Three days, still, to be ready for that. Joan made herself get up and go over there to turn the little box to a more pleasing angle. Then, she plopped her pajama-ed self right back onto the unmade bed. The next three days *might* be long enough to "come down off the mountain," as Lee had put it during their last moments together at the airport. Right now, it was tough to count on that. Moving slowly since crawling out of bed late in the morning, she still hadn't finished unpacking. And she hadn't finished thinking about Crook Mountain. Not after spending ten days there. Not after having driven away only twenty-four hours ago.

Near the bedroom door sat the tobacco products, next to other Christmas purchases she would carry when she felt like it, to a spare bedroom closet where the clearance-priced gift wrap bought after *last* Christmas was safely stored. On the bed, she zipped open an outer pocket of the larger tote-on-wheels. With any luck, she'd be entirely done with unpacking before the day was over. Out came the flip flops for the pedicure she never got, and, after those, the book she'd never opened. She looked at the title and laughed out loud. Maybe she would look up a "contact me" page for Mr. Conway, the author, and tell him he'd inspired her to find her *own* things of interest "not far off the beaten track." Writers always loved getting positive feedback out of the blue.

Downstairs, there was sign after sign that Mary hadn't cut any corners in watching after the house. The mail was in, neatly stacked, and even bundled and labeled according to the day it had arrived. Now, *that* was going above and beyond! *"Ah. Bien!"* She and Lee had dispensed with most print subscriptions, but here was the latest issue of a magazine worth getting in hard copy, *Cuisine Aujourd'hui*. Joan clutched the resource and walked through the rest of the downstairs. Bless their sweet neighbor! The plants looked healthy. The fish was alive and seemed well. Joan tapped on its bowl to say hello. There was even a loaf of home-baked bread and a "welcome home" note that included mention of some opportunities Mary thought might be of interest: a parish dietitian opening, a paid position, part-time; and a call for volunteers in health professions to go on short-term assignments in Africa.

Ping! Dove was texting. "Are you awake? Just checking on you." Joan would respond later. Dove had phoned at about seven last night, during Joan's last hour on the road, not especially to talk about everything that had happened, but mostly just to touch base and make sure Joan was all right. The conversation had helped at a time of oncoming drowsiness. Now, she was trying not to think about the misery of driving while sleepy. Or while being chased! Trying not to think about *anything* that had happened in the past ten days, Joan kept unpacking and getting the house just so. Here, she felt in control. Carrying the bundle of new yarn to a large storage basket on the sun porch, where it would be a pretty focal point until time to wrap it for Christmas, she let her fingers linger over the colorful fibers.

Order in this house…beauty in these soft strands…but chaos in Crook Mountain. She shook her head. It was impossible *not* to think about it.

Far away from the Muellers' stomping grounds, both Harriet Newman and her son Larry could now rest in peace. Surely, the son's remains would be recovered and returned to Florida for a proper burial beside the mother. The most important thing Dove *had* mentioned about the matter during her phone call last night was that Luke and Dub and Jesse, interviewed separately at the sheriff's office, each had described a certain place in the woods near their house where the authorities should look.

⋙◆⋘

Of all people, Melinda, whose invitation had started the whole thing, needed to be caught up! Joan brewed some late-afternoon coffee and, during an hour-long FaceTime visit, lost count of the number of disbelieving exclamations Melinda made, also of how many times *she* replied, "I know!" Finally, they got around to Melinda's latest happenings, all the way down to a cameo appearance on camera of the adorable bunny rabbit that had come home with her children from their grandparents'. "We'll see how this goes!" Melinda laughed. "We don't have a name for him yet. Text me your ideas. The kids always love hearing from you." They set up a lunch date and signed off.

⋙◆⋘

Joan slowed the treadmill to a stop, chuckling, not for the first time since she'd been home, over how nice it was that the machine's jogging surface wasn't *gravel*. She showered, got breakfast, and tidied up, and it still wasn't nine yet. Sometimes, semi-retirement didn't offer enough structure. The whole day loomed with opportunity. But…opportunity for what? The answer would have to wait a little longer. She reached into her purse to answer her ringing phone.

"I'm glad you called, Dove. Lee's still away, and the house is too quiet. I did finally start the research I thought I was going to do while I was holed up in my boring, little cabin in your slow, little town." The start of her research was only about twenty words scribbled on a legal pad last night when she couldn't sleep, but it was a start, just the same.

"This *is* a slow town—or it used to be, and will be again, I trust. But, since you left, things have been happening quickly." Dove backed up long enough to apologize for the intrusion, even though Joan had just said she was glad for the call. Then, she launched into the news she said she knew Joan would want to hear, especially about the twins' visit from the sheriff who had heard Jesse's full confession. Bonnie, it was no surprise to hear, had been with Luke at the time. Consequently, Cora knew of it, and Cora had related it all to Dove. "Jesse talked freely. Your instincts about his needing catharsis were right on target, Joan. He said the incident happened on a Friday night. Jesse was out stalking Serena McCain, for lack of a better word, and Luke had gone over to see Bonnie. You know, his less-than-ideal home life has always made Bonnie's house with its big, warmhearted family very inviting. But that left Dub all alone. He got the truck out and drove to Cluny's Ridge, then came across the Mercedes on the side of the road. Larry was slumped over when Dub found him in the car with the doors unlocked. Dub went and got Luke then. When they were certain the man they'd found was dead, Dub got very fixated on the car, as if it was meant to be his reward for stopping to see if there was engine trouble he could fix."

Joan pictured it, shaking her head. "I can imagine that both Jesse and Luke felt guilty for having left Dub alone, and for having a 'normal' life. That could explain why they went so clearly against common sense and decency."

"Jesse admitted almost that very thing, according to reports. Still in a state over his wife's death, and not feeling up to the job of being a single parent, he went a little crazy once he had caught up with the boys that night. And then, what happened happened. The three of them buried the body in the woods near their house and took the car to their garage, where they soon removed some of the identifying marks, changed the hubcaps, and repainted the body. Bonnie's story, now that she's putting the events of that night together, is that when Dub came looking for Luke at her house, he said enough in front of her for her to know something strange was up, but that was all she ever knew. It was actually Jesse who decided they could just bury the body and keep the car. At least, he may be hoping that confessing it that way will protect the boys in terms of the law. Anyway, two years ago he ordered the boys to keep quiet about it, and they took enough vital parts out of the car to make sure Dub wouldn't drive it around, raising questions about where it had come from."

A virtuous action by the one who seemed the darkest villain in the story? Maybe Jesse realized now that to claim all of the blame, whether it was properly his or not, was the most helpful thing he could do as provider for his sons. It felt redemptive to be able to credit him with that. "But what about Neal Coffey? How did *he* figure in? Have you learned anything on that?" Joan still didn't know if she had been chased that night by Coffey, by Mueller, or by some random fool. Monday at the sheriff's office— had it really already been three days since then?—she'd been so caught up in the confessions, confusion, and commotion about the Muellers and Larry Newman that it had never occurred to her to ask about the patrol dispatched on her behalf on Saturday night. She'd have to inquire about that. Eventually.

"Luke and Dub both say their father paid Coffey to say he wasn't sure he had seen Newman, after it was all in the news that he had. Jesse used some of the money the town donated for Sarah's funeral expenses. Coffey came snooping around in Crook Mountain before meeting with Jesse. He ended up with a flat tire, and had to come to the garage anyway, to have it fixed. How funny is that? The twins heard the transaction. Jesse didn't try to keep any of it from the boys. For Dub to be able to keep the car, the three of them were in it together. Gerald Givens specifically told Jesse that any extra money given by the town ought to go to the three children for their education and whatever care Dub will eventually need when he has no other support, but Jesse used the surplus his own way. Gerald regrets that not all of the gifts collected were given directly to the funeral home, or to the Muellers in gift cards, or simply put in the bank and managed by himself or Ron McCain, in trust for the boys and Marilyn. Or for any other funeral in the family that there wouldn't be any money for." Dove paused for breath and then kept right on. "And I guess it's okay to tell you this now, since nothing happened on Sunday night when you stayed over at Cora's. I told you before you came over that Cora had lined up some protection for us."

"Yes, you did. I assume it had something to do with Gerald Givens. Am I right? He comes to mind as the protective type." *Since the first time I saw him.*

"Excellent guess."

"Don't tell me that dear man slept on Cora's front porch that night."

Dove giggled. "Oh, no, of course not. I can just imagine Edith allowing that! No. What he did was arrange for someone *else* to come and guard the place all night, only Cora told me today that Gerald came and apologized profusely to her. He found out on Monday that the man never got there. He had a family emergency."

"I guess we were fortunate, then. But what did Cora tell Gerald to begin with, that would make him hire a security guard for her house that night, but not make him burn with curiosity?"

Silence. Then, "Well...I guess it's okay to tell you *this* now, too."

"What, for heaven's sake?"

"Forgive me, Joan, but to Cora and me it was the most convenient excuse to give, your being a stranger to all of us in town."

"Let me guess. You told him I have a *second* husband, besides Lee, or a deranged *ex*-husband, and I'm on the run from him."

"Yikes! Another excellent guess. Kudos."

"Good grief. Wait until I tell that to Lee. He's due home tomorrow."

"Oh, do you have to tell him? I don't want him to think the worse of me and Cora. Anyway, whatever we hinted, about your having some serious issues, it's all been set straight now, and you're just about a saint in Gerald's eyes, if that brings you comfort...and a forgiving spirit!"

If Gerald Givens thought that, it would have been Dove, with her tales about Joan's help, who had led him to that conclusion. But Dove was the greater saint here, no question. How much of the "story behind the story" would ever become known? The news of the Muellers' strange and disturbing crime was going to get out there, but would Dove receive the recognition she deserved for her personal sacrifice in staying the course until she'd kept her promise? Thoughts of praise and recognition brought someone else to mind. "What have you seen or heard of Marilyn since Monday?"

"She doesn't seem to be so 'in your face,' which is understandable. Maybe she'll take an interest in the family business now, assuming Jesse will serve time. She could answer the phone and a lot more. Jesse didn't pay his sons any wages, but with their experience they certainly could still work there. Maybe someone like Stillman or McCain will buy the place, hire a manager, and make a real business plan, employing Luke and Dub legitimately. If they're lucky enough not to be in prison themselves, that is. They're going to need a good lawyer. I fully expect Gerald Givens and Gene Kirkpatrick to take an active role in all of that."

"Wouldn't it be great if the extenuating circumstances meant they'd only have to do community service to pay their debt to society?" But Dove might not have the same take on that. She might want—need—all of the Muellers to be prosecuted to the full extent of the law. *Hurt* and *inconvenienced* were vast understatements for what she and Harriet Newman had gone through because of what those three men did.

"Yes, that *would* be great." Dove didn't sound interested in being avenged. "Luke could actually join up with Bonnie in that summer camp thing she's doing. Both of the boys could teach auto mechanics. Not just to children, but to teens and adults. Also, Gene says they ought to repay the value of the car to the estate of Larry Newman."

Dub, at any rate, wouldn't stand trial as a competent adult, surely. Edith Givens had said that all of the Mueller children had unrealized potential. "If her brothers become less reclusive now, distanced from their father's control, even Marilyn may relate to them better. And maybe, if there are attorneys buzzing around her brothers, she'll find that next meal ticket she's been wanting." Poor Gavin Kidd might be outmatched! What *did* that guy do for a living? She'd never found out. And actually didn't care.

"I'll keep you posted on her progress. If she sticks around, that is."

"Does that mean *you* are sticking around?"

"For right now, yes. I mean…well, for one thing, Gerald Givens wants to introduce me to a new work associate of his. A tall, broad-shouldered bachelor."

Joan injected a teasing lilt into her reply. *"Oh?"*

"Well, *you* know. He's been such a sweet friend and a comfort. How could I refuse?"

Nice. "Well, I hope this tall bachelor and you hit it off grandly. You deserve some special things you've been depriving yourself of for the past two years. You might just have Gerald cue this guy to be rehearsing his most impressive life stories if he hopes to compete with what *you've* been up to lately! And, you need to set one of those great photos I took of you in view when he comes to pick you up. Unless it's one of those casual meet-ups. 'It's just lunch'? But go somewhere besides the Diner, lovely as it is."

Dove laughed. "I'll let you know how it goes." She paused. "You know, I guess, now that Harriet Newman's will can't be carried out as written, I mean, I'm assuming, here…leaving everything to Larry, maybe some of her other relatives will benefit. She had nieces and nephews. It will be nice if they get one of those letters everybody dreams of: 'This is to inform you that you have just inherited…'"

"Was Harriet wealthy?"

"I couldn't say. But her house should bring a good price. And that doesn't take into account *Larry's* estate. I don't know if *he* had a will."

It was funny how things often came full circle. Here they were talking about wills and inheritances, the very topic Joan had once wondered about, regarding Dove's motivation. That earlier suspicion was absolutely irrelevant now. If either Harriet or Larry happened to have left anything to Dove, Dove deserved every penny of it.

"How was the rest of your drive home on Monday, after we talked?"

"After you kept me from falling asleep? Smooth as silk. Speaking of which, I'll probably think of Bonnie Jarvis every time I pass a mimosa tree, or silk tree, now."

"Good thoughts?"

"Oh, I think so. At any rate, her 'silk trees' are a reminder of a very unexpected bend in the road." *For a lot of people.* "I can safely say I'll never forget Crook Mountain. Unless I get so old I'm wearing those bibs you have to order online."

"I hope you'll come back again," Dove said over a chuckle. "And long before you're in *that* shape!"

"Dove, I haven't said this yet, and I need to. Please accept my condolences. I am so sorry for your loss of Mr. Newman. I know you've probably suspected and feared the worst all along, but..." Joan stopped. There would be a period of grief for Dove.

"I appreciate that. Thank you. You are truly kind and sensitive. I picked up on that pretty early."

After the lengthy conversation, during which there'd been time for moving about the house to reposition a book here and straighten a pillow there, Joan used the blender to concoct a fruity pick-me-up beverage. Then, duly picked up, and at least temporarily over her Crook Mountain aftermath, she started into serious prep for the special dinner. Eggs out of the fridge. They needed to be at room temperature so she could do the red velvet cake tonight. Honey out of the pantry—and why was the soy sauce hiding behind that box of pasta? Lee may have been rummaging in here before he left for Texas. What else went into the marinade for the grilled salmon? She riffled through the pretty recipe box Lee's mom gave them on their tenth anniversary.

Later in the evening, after admiring the finished cake one more time and licking the last of the spare cream cheese frosting off one of the beaters, she checked e-mail and found a message from Dove. "It looks as though Neal Coffey can be charged with reckless endangerment by vehicle, based on what you reported, and for obstructing justice in the Newman case. He admits he took a bribe from Jesse Mueller and lied to the authorities. Your friend Deputy King was able to give enough of a description of the car he lost in chase to match it up to Coffey." So, it *had* been Coffey chasing her! That sick, miserable…lowlife! *Anger. Fear. Justice.* And… *forgiveness?* No, no. She backed away from the computer screen and took a calming breath. It was still too soon to hash through all of that regarding herself. Much easier to step away and look at this thing from Dove's point of view. *Her* attitude, toward the Muellers, seemed to be in the area of forgiveness. In fact, except for those tense moments out by the Mercedes, she'd seemed little interested in placing blame or in asking about justice.

Some little detail was nagging at Joan. She looked back at the e-mail. That was it. She grinned. Lee needed to be told that Darryl King had made Coffey's apprehension possible! Then, the officer could be exonerated a little. Judged more fairly and not thought of as "Deputy Fife."

And how had Dove learned all of this, anyway? Was it the pretty brunette's effect on men that had gained her such quick access to what Neal Coffey had told the authorities? No, more likely it was that she was given information because she was the primary person pushing for a resolution of the cold case. Joan read more of the e-mail. "It seems Coffey sang quite a song once he decided it was the best way to reduce the charges against him, even though what he says about Jesse Mueller may never result in criminal charges in that doctor's death. Coffey's statement says Jesse claimed to have chased the doctor off the road. But maybe that was just a bluff. Jesse could have said so only as a warning to

Coffey that he'd better not cross him. I guess he is the only one who knows for sure."

Joan leaned back from the computer again. If Jesse Mueller had bragged to Coffey about running someone off the road to his death, whether he had really done so or not, that could be a reason Coffey had tried to do the same to her! Just pure masculine competitiveness, one wanting to prove himself as tough as the other. Like cowboys or frontiersmen trying to outdo one another by shooting the farthest or felling a tree the fastest. Jesse Mueller had needed to ward off anyone and everyone who might try to gain an upper hand. He definitely hadn't counted on its being some smart, persistent women who would discover the truth!

The e-mail continued. "Coffey admitted to calling Jesse on the day you went to his shop and telling him that someone had been nosing around, asking questions about Larry Newman and seeming to know the name Mueller pretty well. He told Jesse, in essence, 'If you want to know what this snoop looks like and in what kind of car, you need to come up with some cash.' And so he did, and then he made a second payment (well, a third one if you count the bribe for lying to begin with), to have him follow you and try to scare you off the trail."

While Joan was still reading Dove's long message, a new one arrived. Sender name, Cora Haskew. Joan grinned, opened the e-mail, and skimmed its content. "Bonnie has been teaching me a thing or two about the computer." Farther down, "Our dear own Mayor Dyle is already trying to spin the news into something quite different from a shocking scandal. Our town's webpage may show up with a new heading soon: 'Crook Mountain—Where Exciting Things Happen' or some such. But, there is at least one thing to tell that truly is exciting. Bonnie and Luke are engaged to be married. I know you are happy to hear it." *Dove warned me that things were happening fast. So, Cora has entered the computer age. She'll probably organize skills classes for other senior adults. Once a teacher, always a teacher. Hey. I don't see any quotes from Mildred Cantrell here. Recent events have got a lot of people out of sorts, and Cora is probably no exception.*

And here came yet another message from a new Crook Mountain sender. This one was from Sherry Kirkpatrick. *Tammy Jarvis and Kelley Kirkpatrick must have posted my e-mail address on the bulletin board outside the town hall! Or else, Edith Givens got it and spent a day with it in one hand and her telephone in the other.* The pastor's wife had written a few well-chosen words of greeting and encouragement. She indicated knowledge of the whole Newman story and of Dove's role in it, as well as Joan's. "I am very thankful for what you have done. I'm not sure I've ever met someone who would do so much toward fulfilling a stranger's promise. I hope your time spent here was more good than bad. I'm constantly having to remind my children (and myself) at times like this—we are really just beginning to sort through the Mueller situation—that there is still more good than bad in the world. By the way, the kids and Gene are asking when you can come back and stay with us again."

Joan marked the message Unread. When she did take time to answer it, soon, she would urge Sherry to commend her daughter on the poster campaign which had proved so important in resolving the case. The unexpected posters had resulted from the unforeseen action of that reporter Ricky Davenport. It was strange how those random incidents had worked together to make success possible. And, if Bonnie hadn't seen Luke's reaction to the poster… That was the spoke that really got the wheel turning.

Joan searched for Sherry's name on social media and sent a connection request. Later, she'd send Sherry some of the better photos of Crook Mountain Church in the Wildwood, or else just tag her in a Facebook album. Maybe they'd even put some of her photos on their church's web page at some point.

Not quite ready to crawl into the big, empty bed upstairs, Joan stretched out on the chaise in the sunroom. A yawn soon escaped her. Dove had said Joan was "sent" to Crook Mountain at just the right time, to help in a way that only she could do. Maybe Dove was right. *If God cared to "speak" to me in such a personal way, through the recall of Sherry's note, then maybe He* did *lead me to help Dove with my curious nature, my desire to help others, and my drive to solve problems. And all by way of a change of circumstance in* Melinda's *life!* What would Melinda say to all of that? And what would Lee make of it? Dinner conversation tomorrow might go some interesting places.

She ran her fingers over the nicks in her phone case. No way was she going to let the drawbacks of her trip, like this damage to her case, overshadow the positive outcomes. As much as she appreciated the gift from her children and wouldn't have chosen to let it get damaged, it was as if these scratches were trophies. Markers. Yes, Coffey had made her drop the phone, but he had come out the loser. Maybe Addison's would get a more friendly clerk in place of him, if he actually did end up in jail. *Not that I plan to go rushing back in there to find out, next time I'm in Cluny's Ridge. No. Next time* we *are in Cluny's Ridge.* Her next vacation to the Smokies was going to be a vacation for two. When *they* went back, she would send Lee into Addison's to check the place out. A mischievous smile played over Joan's lips. She touched the phone, searching out a website for real estate in the Great Smoky Mountains. Choosing the first search result that came up, she copied the link to it. Then, she opened a new text message. "Hurry home, honey. I miss you! Arrive hungry." Adding the link to the site that showed every kind of dwelling from dark brown log cabin to white stucco garden home, she pictured the two of them sipping Sumatran Sizzle, side by side in hand-hewn pine rockers on a front porch that had a great view to either east or west. Sunrise or sunset, every day. Either would do. She wasn't picky. "P.S., are you sure that second home we've been talking about needs to be at the lake?" *Send.*

Book Club Discussion Questions

1. Who is your favorite character? Why?
2. Have you known of a situation that compares to Dove's, regarding the solemn promise she has made or the unselfishness she exhibits? Who is the most altruistic person you can name, whose service to others compares to Dove's?
3. How are Joan and Dove alike? How are they different?
4. How have you observed intergenerational dynamics at work in a positive way that resembles the concerted efforts of Cora, Joan, Dove, and Bonnie (in their 80s, 50s, 30s, and late teens, respectively)?
5. What did you find most comical in the book? Most poignant?
6. What do you think will, or should, happen to each Mueller boy after this book ends?
7. Where does family loyalty end and one's responsibility to report a crime begin?
8. Have you ever "heard" an answer to prayer in the manner that Joan does in Chapter 14?
9. Through Joan, the author states that a mother's heart may be the most vulnerable thing on earth. Discuss.
10. Who approaches Cora Haskew's house in the middle of the night? What does he see, and why does he change his

plans? How is this part of the book explained in the final chapter, and what do you make of that? Have you had, or heard of, similar experiences? Read 2 Kings 6:8-17 in the Bible, where a similar situation is described.

11. Did you catch Joan poking a little fun at what she sees as hypocrisy when Edith Givens brags about her husband's financial generosity but also quotes a paraphrase of Matthew 6:3-4? Those verses read, "But when you give to the needy, do not let your left hand know what your right hand is doing, so that your giving may be in secret." *(NIV)* Discuss.

12. Joan wonders what Dove's take might be on the severity of punishment for what was done. Does Dove's apparent view on that aspect seem consistent with her character? The Bible passage including Deuteronomy 32:35 *(NKJV)* indicates that "vengeance" belongs to God. Does either Joan or Dove seem angry or vengeful? The last time someone cut in front of you on the highway or at a busy intersection, was your reaction "Godspeed, fellow driver. I hope whatever stress you're under, from what you have going on today, turns out fine."? Or, in those cases are you more likely to say, "You idiot! I hope you get delayed farther up the road."? Apply this concept of well-wishing another human being versus wanting retribution and satisfaction to Joan's final thoughts about Neal Coffey in chapter 17. How would you feel about that man if you were Joan? In spite of all that Christ has done for us, and in spite of sayings like "the ground at the foot of the cross is level," are we often guilty of wanting grace and mercy for ourselves and for those we love, but justice and punishment for "random" other people? Read Matthew 6:14–15 and discuss.

13. In a moment of dire distress, Joan regards other recent concerns as very trivial by comparison. Can you think of a similar time in your life, when something you thought mattered a lot suddenly became very unimportant?

14. In chapter 17 Joan appears to make a dig against men in general when she compares two of her Tennessee adversaries to "frontiersmen" trying to outperform one another in tasks requiring brawn and skill. However, elsewhere in the book Joan thinks on competitive situations in which she proudly considers *her* man superior. So, she is viewing the issue of male competitiveness from two angles. Discuss. Is there a real-life example of this competitiveness you would like to share with the group? Are women any different from men in this regard? Please read the sequel to *A Stranger's Promise*. You will find in that book (*No Doubt It's Love*) the theme of self-image in the context of rating one's appearance, talents, and circumstances against other people's.

About The Author

A unique and fresh voice is what reviewers said of Betsy Lowery's first book *Pause: Everyday Prayers for Everyday Women* (2004). Now, readers of her novels are talking about her gift for fiction. In *A Stranger's Promise* and in its sequel *No Doubt It's Love*, Lowery uses vivid description, "real" characters, lively events, snappy dialogue, chuckle-out-loud humor and gems of life meaning to entertain and to go a step further than that. Lowery's personal experience (raised in a Southern Baptist preacher's family, called into ministry at age 20, now married with two grown daughters) enables her to speak through both of these novels and through their characters. What's the message to be spoken? It is a Christ-centered message above all, demonstrated through characters some of whom are just beginning to really value faith, prayer, and scripture!

A North Carolina native, Lowery has called Alabama "home" since her mid-twenties.

Made in the USA
Middletown, DE
15 March 2020